Helen Scarlett is a writer and English teacher based in the north east of England. Her debut historical novel, *The Deception of Harriet Fleet*, is a chilling take on nineteenth-century classics such as *Jane Eyre* seen through modern eyes. It is set in County Durham, close to where Helen lives with her husband and two daughters.

The
DECEPTION
of
HARRIET
FLEET

Helen Scarlett

QUERCUS

First published in Great Britain in 2020 by Quercus
This paperback edition published in 2022 by

QUERCUS

Quercus Editions Ltd
Carmelite House
50 Victoria Embankment
London EC4Y 0DZ

An Hachette UK company

A CIP catalogue record for this book is available
from the British Library

PB ISBN 978 1 52940 758 7
EB ISBN 978 1 52940 756 3

10 9 8 7 6 5 4 3 2 1

Typeset by Jouve (UK), Milton Keynes.

Printed and bound in Great Britain by Clays Ltd, Elcograf S.p.A.

MIX
Paper from
responsible sources
FSC® C104740
www.fsc.org

Papers used by Quercus are from well-managed forests and other responsible sources.

To Mark, Izzy, Maddie and Mary, with all my love.

And to Zoë, who was the bravest person I know
and who believed in always following your dreams.

11 August 1849

Samuel would keep the secrets of their game. He could be allowed to live. Returned carefully to the sanctuary of his crib, so no one would ever know that he had gone. And those who did know would be too afraid to say anything. The future could be stopped and redrawn. All possibilities quivered in equal balance on that August morning. But in the summer, dawn comes early this far north and the household would already be stirring. Each streak of pink and gold across the sky demanded that a decision be made. Soon it would be light and then there would no longer be a choice. They would know his absence.

His soft, chubby fist held up a gift of daisies and grass carelessly wrenched from the damp early-morning ground. His eyes were the blue of distant skies.

He would live.

But the voices spoke again, louder this time. 'Kill him, kill him!' It was impossible to stop them — refusal only made them angry and more insistent. They clamoured with memories of injustices and suffering that could not be ignored. Only vengeance would quieten the voices. He must not live. Yet even the cruel knife hesitated as it was pulled from a deep pocket and raised above Samuel. He glanced upwards, a startled half-scream as he finally understood the game they were playing. At the first clumsy cut, crushed daisies and grass fell and scattered around him. Then it became easier as the keen blade hacked away. The precipice had been crossed and time started again.

CHAPTER ONE

The dark events I recount on these pages happened many years ago, but such was their sinister nature, they are imprinted on my mind as vividly as if it had been yesterday. My story may seem sensationalist in places, yet I can assure you it is an honest account – as far as the passage of time will allow – of that harrowing period in my life, and I have not sought to embellish it in any way.

And now, as Henry lies dying, I am to be left the only living witness. It is for this reason, and this reason alone, that I have decided to set down a final and true account of the occurrences at Teesbank Hall, thus ending the morbid speculation that has arisen over the years.

I was just twenty-one when I arrived at Eaglescliffe, a small village in the county of Durham, which was quite as remote as I had hoped. It was then 1871 and already more than two decades after the main events of the narrative. Eaglescliffe was in the process of reinventing itself and grey factories had sprouted up in once green fields. This was the heart of George Stephenson country and railway tracks cut across the landscape, linking together even the smallest of hamlets. It was completely unlike the golden-lit meadows of my childhood home in Norfolk, and for that I thanked God. This would be my hiding-place.

The railway station was a frenzy of slamming doors, whistles and the hiss of the steam engine as it strained to depart. A uniformed porter stood to attention at the far end of the platform, but I was neither pretty enough nor rich enough to catch his notice and instead struggled to lift my battered trunk down from the locomotive's carriage. Still, I had a little stolen money left and intended hiring a cart to take me the last few miles. I felt in my purse once more to reassure myself that the folded and refolded letter from Mrs Jenson was there.

I hadn't told a soul where I was going, not even Cousin Lucy, my dearest friend. When the outcry had died down, I would try to get word to her but I didn't know how many months or even years it might be before I would dare to contact her, perhaps never. Uncle Thomas Stepford would watch her like a hawk and use her as a way to get to me. She would think I had betrayed her, but I couldn't let myself dwell on that.

Over by the booking office, two men were idling and smoking pipes beside a horse and cart. When I approached and asked whether they were available for hire, the bolder of the two stepped forward and replied, 'Aye, miss. Where is it you wish to go?'

'Teesbank Hall, if you please, sir. Just off Jackson's Lane.' The address was burned onto my memory.

A silence came upon the two men and I was convinced I saw them glance at each other, but it was so fleeting I couldn't be sure.

The man gestured with his hand, 'Teesbank Hall is that way and not far. Close by the river. You'll easy be able to walk it before nightfall.'

'I'm prepared to pay you to convey me there. I have this trunk to carry.'

He shook his head. 'No, miss, it's not for me. I'm too busy and you must find another to take you.' He turned on his heel and walked back to his empty cart, much to my bemusement.

His friend lingered a moment longer. ''Tis a bad place that, miss, a bad place. You don't want to go there.' He paused. 'Is there anywhere else I can take you?'

In my confusion, I wasn't as careful with my response as I should have been and answered honestly, 'There is nowhere else, sir.' It was the plain, unvarnished truth – there was no other place on earth for me to run to – and my desperation, not my personal inclination, must dictate my destiny.

And then he did the most bizarre thing. With his eyes upon me all the time, he took his forefinger and made a sign of the cross into the thin air and said, 'God and all his saints have mercy on ye.' He reached across and tried to grasp my hand, but I instinctively shrank from his touch. His melodramatic behaviour had made me question his sanity. The

Wainwrights had seemed a most respectable family in my correspondence with them, rich with mining from the coal-fields of north Durham. I was unsettled at the strangeness of the man's reaction, but as nobody else was in sight, I was forced to ask him, 'How am I to get to there, sir, if you will not take me?'

'No one will take ye there, miss, but if you're set on going, 'tis only two mile or so away. You must follow the road from Stockton to Yarm and then turn down to the river.'

I thanked him for his directions and began the difficult business of half dragging, half carrying my trunk along the orange clay of the freshly made road, which was mercifully dry. Several substantial villas were being built along this main route, so the sound of hammering and sawing hummed through the air. To my left lay the river Tees but it was hidden behind the dense foliage of woodland and not visible from the road. My progress was slow because of the heavy trunk and I felt a line of sweat form along the top of my lip – several passers-by glanced at me curiously. Stopping to catch my breath, I cursed the two reluctant carters and their refusal to take me.

As I moved further away from the station, the setting became more rural and I found a signpost for Jackson's Lane, which pointed to a dirt path that led to the river. Although I was now less than half a mile from the bustling Yarm Road, I might as well have been in the middle of the deepest countryside for I was surrounded by tall oak and ash trees. It was a clear March day and the deep silence was broken only by the plaintive cry of a curlew. I breathed in the sharp, intoxicating air of freedom and felt invigorated and alive. A wave of optimism swept over me. I had survived.

The walk took longer than I had expected and the shadows of dusk were already starting to lengthen as I approached the house, which stood starkly alone, forming a solid block of darkness against the deepening sky. It was set back behind high, wrought-iron gates that were stiff to the touch but finally opened with a loud metallic clang. The house was imposing, having a kind of austere grace. At the front, it was covered with thick green ivy, and had row upon row of off-white, shuttered windows, a number of which had a curved balcony around them so that the house had something of the appearance of a French château.

I had been on edge these last few days and had struggled to eat even the smallest bowl of soup, so my thoughts might not have been altogether rational, yet I could not shake off the feeling that there was something grim and sinister about this hidden place. I was gripped by the curious sensation that each of the windows was a half-open eye spying upon me, a conviction that grew when I caught sight of someone dressed in red peering down from a window at the very top of the house, seemingly straight at me. I shaded my eyes to see more clearly and raised a hand in acknowledgement but in an instant the figure had disappeared so I dismissed it as a trick of the fast-diminishing light or my over-stimulated imagination. Shrugging, I told myself to think no more of it, that food and a good night's rest would rid me of the cold sensation in the centre of my stomach.

The gravel drive brought me directly to the great oak door at the front of the house and now I hesitated before it, unsure of what I should do next. Would the Wainwrights expect me to arrive at the front or use the servants' entrance? There was no sound or sight of human activity to give me a clue. In many ways I might be considered the social equal of the Wainwrights, and my own governess had always been treated as part of the family, but I knew that was unusual and largely due to Father's peculiarities and notions of fair play. In any case, Teesbank Hall was far grander than our home had been.

There was an ornate knocker, in the shape of a lion's head, which I carefully raised and allowed to drop heavily so that it echoed loudly through the stillness of the early evening. It was several moments before this brought a response and I had almost given up and resigned myself to finding an entrance at the rear when the door opened and a small, bird-like woman stood before me. She was dressed in the black crêpe of mourning and had a ramrod stiff back, with an air of cold efficiency.

'You must be Miss Harriet Caldwell. I am the house-keeper, Mrs Jenson,' she said.

Harriet Caldwell. It was the first time I had been addressed aloud by that other woman's name and I felt the thrill of deception. 'Yes, ma'am. I believe we have corresponded.'

Her sharp dark eyes quickly appraised me, making me

conscious of the slight smudges on my face, the creases of my dress and my dusty, patched boots. In response to her questioning stare, I said flatly, 'I had to walk the final two miles from Eaglescliffe station, ma'am. No cart would take me.'

A slight narrowing of her eyes indicated her disapproval of my dishevelled state. She nodded and continued, 'In future you'll be expected to use the servants' entrance at the back of the house. The Wainwrights are most particular.'

Suitably chastised, I responded, 'Yes, I will—' but was cut short as Mrs Jenson continued, 'It will be more amenable for us to speak in my sitting room, which is below stairs. Please follow me. You may leave your luggage in the hallway. I will ask one of the gardeners to take it up.'

She walked away swiftly and I had to hurry to keep up with her hastily departing back. Finally, I found myself in her quarters, where a small fire was lit against the chill of the evening air. It was a fussy room, crammed with ornaments, samplers of Biblical proverbs and pictures of desolate landscapes. A well-fed spaniel eyed me disapprovingly from his prime position on the old-fashioned red damask sofa. One side of the room was given over to shelf upon shelf of leather-bound books, where the novels of Dickens collided with *The Collected Sermons of John Wesley* and, at the centre of the mantelpiece, an ornate gold clock counted out the minutes. It was the very picture of respectability and each loud tick reassured me as to how foolish and melodramatic the carter's words had been.

She gestured towards a small table, which was covered with neatly stacked papers and receipts. Once we were seated, she took a number of sheets from one of the piles – these were the letters that related to my employment. 'You have travelled from Norfolk, I see.'

'Yes, ma'am. I have been travelling for the last two days.' I was more nervous than I had realized and my words came out in short breaths and pauses. I tried to compose myself but it was difficult being in this strange place, with no familiar faces or points of reference.

Perhaps she felt some degree of sympathy for me because she asked whether I'd like some tea, which she served from a stout blue and white china teapot. I grasped the warm cup and listened carefully while she outlined the terms of my service at Teesbank Hall.

'You will, of course, have tonight to eat and rest before your duties commence in the morning.'

'Thank you.' It was now several hours since I had eaten and I was very hungry.

'However, Mr and Mrs Wainwright have asked that I speak to you first. There are some matters you will need to understand about your role. The Wainwrights don't like to be troubled with household issues.'

I looked at her expectantly.

Mrs Jenson read from the document she held in her hand, 'Your previous employer's letter of recommendation says you are able to teach French, globe work, drawing and the piano. Is French the only language you have?'

'I'm fluent in French – my mother was from Provence and I was brought up speaking the language.'

'That will be of no use to you in this position as Miss Eleanor has learned German and the classical languages. Do you have knowledge of those?'

I was forced to admit my ignorance of anything apart from English and French. Mrs Jenson crossed out something on the document, before continuing, 'Your letter of recommendation also says that you are a good, God-fearing young lady. I presume you are of the Anglican faith?' She paused here and looked at me. 'I hope you have no views of a radical persuasion.'

Although it was not altogether true, I assured her this was the case.

'Good. And you were employed by your previous family for four years?' She glanced at me quizzically.

I had only just turned twenty-one and feared this was the part of my deception that was most likely to lead to my discovery. I didn't answer directly. 'Father died and I was forced to seek a position at a young age, ma'am.' I had decided I would keep my lies as close to the truth as possible so that it was easier to maintain the fiction.

For a split second I suspected she knew the character was forged and I felt my heart freeze within me, but then she continued, 'As agreed in your terms of service, your salary will be fifty pounds per annum, which you will receive six months in arrears, as well as board and lodgings.'

'It is as you said in your letter,' I agreed.

She carried on, 'You will have one Sunday afternoon a month for yourself, when you may visit family or friends.'

'I have none,' I said, and she nodded, as if this was the reply she had expected.

'You will have use of the schoolroom in the evenings, when Miss Eleanor is otherwise engaged, where you may read or sew, and you may walk in the grounds if you have no other duties. The path by the river is very pleasant. On certain evenings you may be requested to join the family for meals and suchlike. It's a quiet household and you will not be allowed visitors.'

'I understand, Mrs Jenson.'

She now looked at me carefully, giving weight to the next words: 'It is also important that you know something of Miss Eleanor, who is to be your pupil. There are matters I did not think it fitting to include in our written correspondence. It is better that we speak of them now.' She stopped briefly. 'She is of a very infirm disposition and as such needs the most careful of watching.'

My first thought was that she suffered from some physical ailment so I asked, 'Is she an invalid?'

Mrs Jenson waved her hand to dismiss my suggestion. 'No, no. Physically she's quite sturdy. Her difficulties are of a different nature altogether. She has a weakness of the mind that makes her a danger to herself and others. Mrs Anderson is her nurse and will be with her during the hours of darkness, from seven in the evening until seven in the morning. At all other times she is to be your sole responsibility. You must not allow her out of your sight and . . .' she stopped here for emphasis '. . . the master and mistress expect to be kept fully informed of all her activities.'

'But why is that, ma'am?' I couldn't help myself from blurting out.

She viewed me critically with her shrewd dark eyes. 'Miss Eleanor can display some qualities that must be . . .' she searched for a word '. . . suppressed. It's your responsibility to observe and report upon her so that Mr and Mrs Wainwright are able to act if necessary.'

I felt a deep unease. 'What are these qualities?'

Mrs Jenson replied, with an air of finality, 'It is better that I say no more. Should an issue arise, and God willing it does not, you will understand the need for vigilance. However, I must warn you that Miss Eleanor can be a sly and manipulative girl when she wishes. If she attempts to befriend you, you must be on your guard against her.'

I was perturbed and a little afraid – I had come as a governess, not a spy – but I couldn't afford to lose this position without another point of refuge so could do no more than nod in agreement.

Mrs Jenson now opened a large account book and pushed it across the table towards me. 'You must also keep a daily record in here.'

I looked at the opened pages in confusion. There were lists of foodstuffs and measured amounts, so that I read, 'Oatmeal – one ounce and a quarter-pint of milk', then underneath this, 'Two slices of beef and two ounces potatoes', which had been crossed through in a different-coloured ink. In a final column, there appeared a series of letters – for example, on 14 March 1871, a large C had been written, which appeared again on 20 March, accompanied by a D. Bewildered, I asked. 'What must I write here?'

Mrs Jenson spoke guardedly: 'When Miss Eleanor is in one of her tempers, she will refuse food to spite us. The doctor has insisted that we keep a record of everything she eats. As you are with her all day, you'll be able to observe the quantities.'

'And the letters, what do they mean?' I asked.

'They are a memorandum for me and her nurse,' she replied. 'The ledger is kept locked in there.' She pointed to a large mahogany cupboard in the corner of the room. 'At seven o'clock, you'll come to my room to complete the entries for that day and make your report to me. The servants will weigh her meals, but it is your responsibility to indicate how much of them she has eaten.'

Concern must have etched itself across my face because she said firmly, 'It's for her own good that she is closely supervised.' Her expression was tightly shuttered and it struck me again that there was something harsh and unyielding about her face and person. She continued, 'If Miss Eleanor says or does anything untoward, I must be informed immediately. That is all you need to know for the time being.'

She rose from her seat, her every action signalling that the interview was at an end. I, too, stood up but, emboldened by the strangeness of her instructions, I dared to ask, 'The carter at the station didn't wish me to continue to the Hall. He said it was a bad place. Why would he warn me?' As soon as the words were out of my mouth, I regretted them. Uncle Thomas Stepford had always said that curiosity was one of my greatest failings and would lead to my downfall.

Mrs Jenson's lips set into a thin line. 'A child was killed here. It was a great tragedy and has brought the family much sadness and created foolish talk in the area. However, it is in the past, more than twenty years ago, and we do not dwell on the matter.' It was clear there was to be no more discussion as she added, 'I'll arrange for a meal to be prepared for you in the servants' hall. I imagine that you will want an early night after your journey.'

Her sitting room was situated near to the kitchen, meaning that our conversation had been punctuated by the clattering and banging of plates and pans, and the occasional knell of one of the brass bells that summoned staff to the main part of the house. She led me into it now. It was a large room, with white tiles and gleaming copper pans hanging by hooks from the ceiling. Off to the side was a door, and I followed her through this into the servants' hall.

A belligerent-faced girl was slouched over the large pine table but quickly jumped to attention when she saw us. Mrs Jenson glared at her. 'Eliza, Miss Caldwell has been travelling for some time and needs food. Tell Mrs Hargreaves to prepare bacon and eggs and a pot of tea.'

Then Mrs Jenson addressed me again: 'Miss Caldwell, I would advise you to ask fewer questions about things that do not concern you, if you wish to keep your position at Teesbank Hall. You would do well to be more careful.' She left the room, shutting the door with a sharp click.

CHAPTER TWO

Eliza pulled a face at her departing back. 'If you really want to be careful, you'd be better off staying away from Mr Wainwright.'

'What do you mean?'

'Well, I'm never alone in a room with him, if I can help it. He can't keep his hands to himself.' And with that parting shot, she disappeared into the kitchen. I sat wearily on the hard wooden chair, as the irony of her comment struck me.

When the bacon and eggs were finally ready, Eliza slammed the plate down on the table. I had heard her muttering to someone in the kitchen and her tone made clear she resented having to wait on someone she saw as little better than herself. The food was swimming in grease and almost inedible, so after a half-hearted attempt, I gave up and instead ate two thick slices of bread and butter. Anxiety gnawed at me all the while, as I considered Mrs Jenson's words about Eleanor. What was her infirmity of mind and why couldn't she be trusted? I wondered, too, about the letters in the ledger – C and D – and what they might mean.

Perhaps this was a bad place, as the carter had said. And if it had been my intention to stay for any long period of time, I might have been frightened but I would remain only until the trail had gone cold and I had saved a little money. Then I would make my next move. I thought of the atlases that had once lined Father's library and told of exotic faraway places. I intended to find a passage on a ship to one of the new worlds I had glimpsed in their illustrated pages. As long as I maintained a steady gaze on my next destination, I could withstand any deprivations of this stopping-place.

Darkness had fully fallen by the time I'd eaten and a housemaid, Agnes, was given the task of showing me to my bedroom. She was about the same age as me and had large, trusting brown eyes, with mouse-coloured hair scraped back from her face. When she smiled at me, I responded gratefully, glad to have some sign of friendship in this vast, strange house. She took two long white candles and a simple brass holder from a kitchen drawer and said she would walk with me to my room, which was at the very top of the building.

She was responsible for checking all the fires had been dampened down for the night, so her route took us into the main areas of the house. Teesbank Hall was filled with expensive pieces of slightly dated mahogany furniture but even the candles placed around the rooms failed to dispel the gloomy atmosphere. Everything was cleaned and polished, but the house felt uncared for – as if the rooms had been put together haphazardly – so that it seemed not so much a home as a soulless museum. There was a deathly hush and we met no one as Agnes checked each room. When I asked whether I might hold the candle as she carried out her duties, she put her finger to her lips urgently. 'No noise,' she hissed. 'The mistress don't like to hear voices.'

I was keen to know why this should be, but as soon as I opened my mouth, she merely pulled a face and continued working in silence.

One of the features of Teesbank Hall was an ornate staircase of carved wood, which curved its way right through the centre of the house. However, when Agnes had finished her work, she took me past this and to a plain dark door at the end of the corridor. Behind it was the servants' enclosed staircase, which ran along the side of the great house and parallel to the main flight, allowing the servants to go about their business invisibly, fetching scuttles of coal and carrying mountains of laundry. The whole house hummed like a well-tuned machine and the owners needed never to be aware of the servants who formed its mechanical parts.

Even on the brightest of days, this staircase was shrouded in gloom, and its narrow, steep steps twisted and turned endlessly. Agnes walked swiftly ahead of me with the confidence of someone following a familiar route, but I was forced to feel my way more cautiously. When we finally reached the attics, I observed that a solid wall ran through the middle of this part of the house and separated it into two quite distinct sections, with four or five rooms facing to the front and a similar number at the back. There was only limited light along the two parallel corridors and Agnes's candle did little to dispel the darkness around us.

Away from the restraints of the main part of the house, Agnes became animated once more. 'Your room is at the front of the building,' she informed me. 'It's been made up for you. It's a good big room. It's the one the governesses always have.' She indicated that I should turn right and follow her.

Something about her tone made me remark, 'That sounded as if there have been many governesses.'

I had made the comment light-heartedly but she turned to me very earnestly and said, 'Ladies don't stay. It's too out of the way here and the life's too harsh.'

'Oh, I'm sure I will survive.' I smiled at her, but her eyes were still serious and she didn't answer me.

As I walked behind her, it was impossible not to notice the deserted nature of the place: all of the doors along the front corridor were closed. In order to break the awkward silence that had descended, I asked, 'Does anyone else live at the top of the house?'

Her eyes widened. 'All us girls live up here but we sleep at the back of the building. They made up some dormitories for the female servants.'

'Is mine the only room used at the front of the house?' I asked.

Agnes had stopped because we were now outside what was

to be my room. She looked determinedly at the floor and said, 'The governess always sleeps at the front of the house. Mrs Jenson says the rooms at the front are better quality and, in any case, most of us girls like to share with each other.'

'But why not have a room to oneself? It seems such a waste to have all these rooms and not use them.'

She fidgeted with her hands, 'It's better to sleep with the others.'

'But why?' I asked, increasingly puzzled at what she said.

'It's dark up here and people say they hear things – see them, too. Not that I ever have,' she reassured me hastily, 'and I think people just like to talk, but still, I'm happier sharing a room.'

'What kind of things? Surely you don't believe in such stories.' I was amazed. Agnes had struck me as being quite sensible and level-headed.

She must have sensed the disbelief in my tone because her next words were defensive: 'I didn't say *I*'d seen anything. But Eliza swears she has. Ghostly things.'

'Is that why no one at the railway station would bring me here?'

'Nobody comes to Teesbank Hall if they can help it. The locals call it Murder House. We're always short of servants because people don't want to work here. I'd leave tomorrow if I could find somewhere else, and I've worked for the Wainwrights for the last three years.'

'Murder House? Is that because of the child who was killed here?' I remembered Mrs Jenson's words.

She nodded. 'But I'm not to speak of it. If Mrs Jenson knew I'd been gossiping, she'd go into a fair rage. You won't say anything, will you?'

'No, of course not,' I answered. 'Perhaps it's because it's so dark and deserted up here, people imagine they see things.' I could understand how the gloomy atmosphere of the attics and the tragic events of the past might give rise to supposed sightings of ghosts and other malign presences.

'Maybe that's the case.' She shrugged. 'Promise you won't say anything to Mrs Jenson, will you? What I said about Murder House and people being afraid to sleep up here.'

I reassured her again, reflecting that she seemed more scared of the anger of the housekeeper than of any super-natural occurrence. Still, I dared to ask her, 'What is your opinion of Miss Eleanor, who is to be my pupil? Mrs Jenson spoke of her strange qualities.'

Agnes shook her head. 'That you must judge for yourself, miss. It's not my place to say.'

'But why must she be watched at all times?'

Agnes looked at me directly. 'I'm closer to Miss Eleanor than most but still I would take care around her. You'll see what I mean in the morning.'

It was hardly a reassuring answer but I must be satisfied with it. Then, just as she was about to go, she paused, as if she were working up her courage to say something important. She opened her mouth to speak but stopped and began again, saying simply, 'Sleep well. You've the candle for your bed-side, just in case. I'd let it burn through the night if I was you.'

'Is anything the matter?' I asked, for she looked so frightened.

'Nothing,' she replied, and walked back along the corridor, quickly swallowed into its gloom.

I wondered what momentous thing she might have been about to reveal to me. But God knew I had secrets enough of my own and didn't need anyone else's. If what she had withheld was significant, I would find it out in time.

My own room. I thought it was pleasing enough, plain but more than sufficient — and certainly not haunted. It was large, and had polished wooden floorboards, partly covered with a clip rug of muted pinks and violets. At the centre was a single bed, with a black iron frame, its covers starched and pristine white. In the right-hand corner stood an oversized wardrobe, which my familiar trunk had been placed alongside, and opposite the window was a small chest of drawers, topped with a mirror and a jug and bowl for washing. The mirror was in the old-fashioned style, with a dark wood surround carved with cherries and swirling leaves; the glass had a slightly green hue and was spotted with age. A strong scent of lavender cleaning wax failed to mask the stale air and I resolved that in the morning I would open the window.

Despite my earlier confidence, I felt very alone after Agnes had left, and hoped I had not offended her with my scepticism about the ghostly nature of the attic. I didn't wish to lose a potential ally so quickly. I imagined — envied, perhaps — the maids giggling and chatting together in squalid solidarity on the other side of the dividing wall. I placed the candle on top of the chest of drawers so I might chase away the shadows, and sat on the bed, facing the mirror.

It was my routine to brush my hair meticulously every night – one hundred strokes with the silver-backed brush. The sepia mist of the mirror reflected my face back at me. My skin was pale and my features were unremarkable. My eyes were dark enough to hide the truth, but my hair was my crowning glory, with its shades of light brown and gold. I usually wore it pinned into a loose chignon, with just a few tendrils escaping their constraints. My figure I knew to be slim and girlish, but my lips were too full and red to be pleasing – Cousin Lucy said it was a sign of my passionate and defiant nature. Perhaps she was right, for I was always unable to accept instruction and behave as Uncle Thomas Stepford demanded.

The obligatory Bible lay by the bed and the sampler on the wall exhorted, 'Remember now thy Creator in the days of thy youth, while the evil days come not, nor the years draw nigh, when thou shalt say, I have no pleasure in them.' (Ecclesiastes 12:1)

I sank to my knees. For me the evil days had come already and what pleasure did I have in the days of my youth? To an observer I might have seemed deep in prayer. However, my prayer was not to God but to myself, my nightly mantra, 'I will not let circumstances destroy me. I will survive this. Everything will pass,' which I repeated until I could begin to believe it was the truth.

Exhausted from the day's travel, I removed my outer dress, splashed cold water from the jug onto my face and clambered half clothed into the narrow bed. In the house in Norfolk, I had savoured these moments before sleep, when I imagined the exotic destinations of my planned escape, the pictures and words of my father's books made flesh, such thoughts blotting out the horror of my day-to-day existence. But that night I was exhausted from my travels, and even the mysteries surrounding Eleanor could not stop me falling straight into a deep and dreamless sleep.

CHAPTER THREE

I woke the next morning to the dull thuds and muffled exchanges of the housemaids. The walls in the attic were thin and cheaply built so even a noise made several rooms away could be distantly heard. I assumed they were rising early to light the fires and begin the tasks that would set the household in motion. The Wainwright fortune was founded on coal, and fires would blaze brightly on all but the hottest summer's day. For the first few moments I lay and enjoyed the warmth beneath the covers, savouring the sensation as I celebrated the first true morning of the freedom I had stolen.

The sharp March sunshine streamed through the curtains. I pushed back the coverlet and went to open the window and let in some fresh air. To my surprise, the large, rectangular window was entirely covered with a fine black mesh, which was secured into place by means of nails placed all around its perimeter. When I asked Mrs Jenson about this later, she explained that birds would fly in and become trapped, terrified in the enclosed space of the attic rooms, so all the windows at the top of the house had been fitted with wire covers. It was the mesh that stopped the easy movement of air into the rooms, adding to the lifeless and claustrophobic feeling in that part of the house.

I dressed hurriedly, as I feared being late on my first morning of employment, and used the stale water in the jug to rub some life into my pale face. Now I was less tired, I began to worry about what I was supposed to teach Eleanor. My own governess's patient lessons would have to be my guide but I suspected it would be easy to see through my lack of experience.

And Eleanor herself. There had been no mention in Mrs Jenson's letters about the dangerous 'qualities' of my pupil or that she must be watched over at all times. I wondered whether I would have taken the position if I'd known that, but the Wainwrights had been the only family to respond to my advertisement in the *Morning Post*. By then, I would have accepted anything.

At the allotted time, Mrs Jenson took me to the library, which doubled as the schoolroom, to introduce me to Eleanor. As we walked along the corridor, I felt my stomach knot with nerves and I almost dared to ask a little more about my pupil, but the memory of the housekeeper's stern warning the previous evening meant that the question died on my lips and we walked together in silence.

I'm not quite sure what I had expected Eleanor to be like, but I was still surprised to find that my charge was taller than me and only a few years younger. She was standing defiantly by the window and barely glanced around when we entered the room.

'Where is Mrs Anderson?' Mrs Jenson asked. 'Why isn't she with you?'

'I sent her away five or so minutes ago. Surely I can be trusted for such a little while.'

'Mrs Anderson knows she must be with you at all times.'

'Then you speak to her for I won't,' Eleanor replied sulkily.

She was very thin, with dark hair, and wore a dark green dress, which hung limply about her boyish figure. The sleeves were long and she had pulled them past her wrists, so that everything about her seemed closed off.

Later, when I had the opportunity to observe her carefully, I concluded her face had a classical regularity about it. Her features were too striking for beauty but she should have been handsome at the very least. She was neither, although I couldn't put my finger on why that might be so – perhaps her chin jutted too far or her blue eyes were too piercing. Certainly there was a scowl permanently stamped across her face. It was clear she had no intention of acknowledging my presence and her whole body was strained towards some point on the distant horizon, as if she were looking out intently for someone or something.

Mrs Jenson changed tactics now and said in a cajoling voice, 'Miss Eleanor, this is Miss Caldwell. She is to be your new governess. Please can you turn around and greet her nicely.'

'I am not a child so don't speak to me as if I were,' she snapped.

I had judged Mrs Jenson to be quite fearless but she apologized immediately and something in her manner suggested she was wary of this young woman. I remembered her warning that I should be on my guard against my new pupil.

Eleanor turned partially towards me, although she didn't look me in the eye. 'I am aware another governess has been appointed but, as must be clear to everybody, I hardly need one.' Her voice registered an icy disdain. 'In any case, I can scarcely see what *she* might be able to teach me.' I feared her withering look must take in the shabbiness of my dress, the grime of the journey that couldn't be sponged away, and my plain, earnest face.

'Now, Miss Eleanor, you've promised you will be good. Miss Caldwell has come a long way so that she might be your governess. I know Mr Henry has written from Durham to request that you be kind and that there should be no more tricks,' pleaded the housekeeper.

This last comment seemed to have its intended effect and Eleanor forced her face into the semblance of a greeting and offered her hand to me. 'I am Eleanor Wainwright,' she announced gravely.

'I am pleased to make your acquaintance,' I replied, and took her hand, surprised at the formality of her gesture.

'There now, that's a good girl,' Mrs Jenson exclaimed. 'I'm sure you will get along well together. Now, I must go back to my duties but I shall return to check that you have been true to your word, Miss Eleanor. You know it is what Mr Henry would want.' With that, Mrs Jenson left the room as hastily as she felt decent, pretending to herself that some kind of truce had been agreed.

In truth, we all knew this wasn't the case, and as soon as she had gone, Eleanor looked at me critically. 'I do not want a governess and I will ensure you do not last long here. That much I can promise you.'

I was determined not to be intimidated and experience had taught me it is always best to face difficulties head on, so I replied, 'I am sure there is much I can teach you. I'm educated in drawing, piano and globe work. My mother was French, from Provence, and I'm able to speak and write the language fluently.'

Eleanor laughed and spoke slowly: 'French is not allowed in this house and, in any case, I have been adept in German, Latin and Ancient Greek since the age of twelve. As for drawing, piano or globe work, I prefer not to waste my time on such trivialities.' Her tone conveyed her total contempt for my suggestions. She gestured around the room at the books that lined its shelves. 'As you can see, I hardly lack education and learning. I have read most of the books in this room, even those that Father and Grandmother consider harmful to the delicate female brain.'

Hot with embarrassment, I replied, 'It's a most well-stocked library, Miss Eleanor.'

She ignored my comment. 'Two or so years ago, I had a tutor, Miss Lilian Howard, who was capable of educating me, but that was clearly far too dangerous for my parents' taste. She was sent away and replaced by a succession of half-witted governesses. Now my brother Henry teaches me what he learns at university so that I am not suffocated by ignorance, unlike so many of my sex.' She glared pointedly at me. 'I intend to sit the General Examination for Women at the University of London. I cannot suppose you have the knowledge to help me prepare for that.'

I feared much the same. 'Perhaps your parents intended me as your companion.'

At that suggestion, she looked at me with derision. 'Surely things are not so desperate that my parents must pay for companionship with someone such as you. I will choose my own friends. Quite frankly, I've no idea why my parents have chosen to appoint yet another governess. I presume they mean you to spy upon me.'

I felt my cheeks burn.

'Ah, yes, I see now. It didn't take me long to find you out. That is what you are, a spy. A horrid little spy. I have been betrayed in the past, but I will not allow myself to be tricked again. And you may tell my parents so yourself.' She turned bitterly towards the window.

I was silent.

'It's obvious you're not used to our ways. You are not from this area and don't know my family's reputation. If you did, I doubt that you would be here.' With that, she resumed her vigil of watching, making it clear that she was tired of speaking to me.

My heart sank at the impossibility of the task ahead of me. 'I suppose we must begin our lessons,' I offered, looking around the room for some form of inspiration as to what I might teach.

Eleanor laughed blankly and mirthlessly. 'I am waiting for my brother to return. I think it will benefit me more to spend my time by the window. You may do as you please.'

Awkwardly, I began to gather together paper and ink. I found an atlas on the library shelves and pretended to myself this would be a good starting point for our lessons.

My thoughts were broken by the sound of the door being opened, and Eleanor exclaimed with joy, 'You are here, Henry, finally you are here! I have been waiting by the window since daybreak and there was no sign of you. How did you get here?'

A deep male voice replied, 'I took the back route across the fields.' Then a pause. 'Oh, Ellie, I'd forgotten I promised to ride in front of the library window.'

'How could you forget? It's what you always used to do when we were younger. I've been watching for you. But it doesn't matter. It has just been so deadly dull while you've been away. There has been no company except for that of our dear parents and grandmother, and I would rather eat bleaching powder than spend more than five minutes with them.'

'Ellie, don't say that!' Her brother laughed.

When I turned, I saw them embracing. Henry pulled his sister away from him and held her at arm's length. 'I really do think you're growing up. You'll be a young lady in no time at all and out in society.'

She frowned. 'You know that I don't care to be a lady. Frankly, I find more enjoyment in my books. Oh . . .' she saw her brother had caught sight of me '. . . this is Miss Caldwell. There is nothing she can teach me after all. She is just the latest of Father's spies. But she is not a very good one and I have caught her out already.'

The brother turned around to face me full on and gave me a cold, disapproving stare. Like his sister, Henry Wainwright was tall and dark but the same features that sat strangely upon her gave him character so he was undeniably hand-some, with dark blue eyes and high cheekbones. His presence dominated the room and I felt myself blush at his natural masculinity. The sum of my knowledge about men was con-fined to my father and my uncle. Although they were very different from each other, they had been familiar, and there was something unsettling about Henry Wainwright. He turned to his sister with a faintly mocking smile playing about his lips. 'She doesn't look very much of a spy, does she?'

'No, she is quite plain and unassuming. At least my last governess Miss Richardson brought the benefit of wit and beauty – much good those did her once Mother found out how Father appreciated her finer qualities! And it didn't matter that she had done everything she could to discourage him.'

'I feel that Miss Caldwell will be safe from such unwanted attentions,' the brother murmured to his sister. She smirked at me.

I felt myself pale with humiliation and it was obvious to them I had caught his words. He had the decency to half bow his head in apology and colour slightly – he had not intended that I should hear the whispered comment. Eleanor, though, smiled vindictively at my discomfort.

I nodded stiffly in return and, attempting to reclaim my dignity, stated, 'Miss Eleanor, we must begin your lessons. I have been instructed—'

'I do not have to take notice of her, Henry, do I? She is just a spy, after all. Tell me all about Durham,' she begged her brother. 'And tell her she can leave the room.'

'I've been instructed that I must be with Miss Eleanor at all times,' I said evenly.

'I will not listen to her,' Eleanor snapped. 'She must understand that I don't need to listen to her.'

'Ellie, we'd agreed that you would be kinder. This must be better than being alone.'

Her response was a hunching of her shoulders and I feared that I ranked alongside her parents and grandmother as her least desired companions.

With a calm air of superiority, he assumed the role of reasonable intermediary, which I found more insufferable than his sister's petulant demands. 'Miss Caldwell, surely you can't object if Eleanor and I sit together by the fire and talk quietly. We've not seen each other for several weeks. You may continue your valuable work sorting the paper and pens.'

This comment brought another snigger from Eleanor. How I hated them both! But, having little choice in the matter, I busied myself by the table and was forced to swallow the torrent of sharp retorts that flooded into my heart. I couldn't risk my position, certainly not for six months, and must learn to assume a calmness of manner that didn't come naturally to me. Brother and sister leaned close together, exchanging confidences and laughing quietly. Every so often, they would glance across at me and I felt myself curl with embarrassment at the thought I might be the source of their amusement.

The day passed with agonizing slowness and I was only relieved of my post by the arrival of Mrs Jenson, who announced, 'As Mr Henry is here, Mrs Wainwright has said you might be excused from teaching Miss Eleanor in order to unpack.'

'Very well. I shall go to my room now.' I nodded stiffly at the brother and sister. 'If you would excuse me.'

'Yes, of course, Miss Caldwell,' Henry replied, with exaggerated courtesy.

'And you have been asked to dine with the family tonight. You must be in the dining room for seven o'clock sharp,' the housekeeper added.

I was quite taken aback at this request so soon after my arrival. It seemed that Eleanor was, too, for she gasped and put a hand to her mouth to stifle a guffaw of disbelieving laughter. She glanced at her brother with a look of annoyance. She clearly had as little desire for me to be at their table as I did. Why had it been requested that I should dine with the family? I would a thousand times rather have spent the evening alone with only my plans and daydreams for company.

I trudged wearily up to the attic, remembering to take the servants' stairs. It was soothing to unpack my small store of possessions and deposit undergarments and stockings neatly in the drawers, place two well-thumbed books on the shelf and hang my dresses in the wardrobe. The simple, rhythmical action brought a kind of relief to my over-charged mind, and when the gong sounded to warn the house that dinner would be ready shortly, I was calm and composed. I had changed out of the worn grey travelling gown and put on a cream muslin dress, which was covered with small sprigs of green and yellow flowers. It had been a favourite of mine and I had managed to hide it during Uncle's searches. My delight at saving it was all the greater because I had managed to thwart him in this, the smallest of ways. I washed, then slowly brushed out my hair. I felt myself to be at least halfway presentable and ready to face whatever this enforced engagement might bring.

I decided to put on my mother's pearl necklace, the only piece of jewellery I owned. Father had given it to Maman on the day they were married at the Église du Saint-Esprit in Aix-en-Provence. A week later, Estelle Artique had left her home and family for ever, giving up everything for the love of my father, a reticent English medical student, whom she had met when he spent the summer learning French at the local university.

Sometimes, at the height of summer, when she smelt the

sweetness of lavender and mimosa, she was reminded of Provence and would fall silent or speak longingly of her childhood home. But seeing how unhappy this made Father, she would force herself to smile and assure him she would make the same choice all over again. And, normally, she was happy, shimmering with life and adventure. She had desperately wanted a son, believing this was what Father desired most, although I believe he was content as we were.

That was why he blamed himself so much when she died in childbirth just two days after my seventh birthday. It was the only time I saw him cry, as their shared coffin was lowered into the frozen ground on a bleak February day. I forced myself to stop remembering. It was not good to dwell too much on the past.

Usually I hid the necklace in a plain white handkerchief, but tonight I wanted to wear something from home. Perhaps I was more agitated than I realized, because I found it difficult to fasten the heavy clasp and, aware of time disappearing, tried to force it into place. My fingers were clumsy and the string snapped, sending dozens of iridescent pearls scattering under the bed. I fell to my knees and tried desperately to gather them together, feeling a sob rise in my throat. A second gong sounded, informing me that I must go downstairs – there was no choice, I would have to find the pearls later.

CHAPTER FOUR

Habit meant I had become accustomed to hiding my true feelings. As I descended the stairs, I breathed slowly to calm myself in order that my outward appearance might reveal nothing of my inner turmoil. I held my head high as I entered the dining room. It was dark, due to the oak panelling on the walls, and lit by an elaborate paraffin lamp, which was suspended from the ceiling. At the centre a large oblong table was set with gleaming silver and white china plates; the family was already seated around it. My delay due to the broken necklace meant I was last to enter the room. I was aware of Eleanor and Henry to my left and my humiliation at their hands in the schoolroom still rankled. The rest of the family were unknown quantities and I assessed them cautiously.

I stood quietly at the furthest end of the room and waited to be introduced and seated at the table, a role which fell to Henry. I suspected I saw bored amusement in his eyes, as I was forced to respond to his polite bow with a stiff curtsy. 'I have already had the pleasure of making the acquaintance of Miss Caldwell, although perhaps we have not had the best of beginnings.' His sister flashed him a look of cold agreement. 'Therefore, may I make amends by having the privilege of introducing you to the rest of my family? This is my mother, Mrs Susan Wainwright.'

She acknowledged me with the slightest inclination of her head and a murmur, which might have been a greeting. A woman then in her mid-fifties, she wore a black silk dress and had eyes the blue of distant skies. Her lack of interest in me and in the rest of the room was obvious. I thought she must have been very beautiful in her youth, but now her face was lined with discontent and her hair, once golden, had faded to white.

As was required of a young woman, I curtsied. Then it was the turn of Mr Matthew Wainwright, a man who was fat with over-indulgence and whose cheeks bore the purple spider veins of alcohol and late nights. He was in his early sixties, and his hair was a shock of pure white. Yet it was possible to trace the ghost of a man who must once have been physically attractive, although there was a harshness about him that meant he was not someone I would wish to cross. As it was, he looked me up and down in a calculating way, before returning to the more interesting contents of his wine glass.

'And, of course, I must introduce you to Grandmother, for it was she who particularly requested you join us at dinner tonight.'

In the far corner of the room, nearest the fire, sat the old lady, Diana Wainwright. She had high haughty cheekbones and her blue eyes burned through the gloom, appraising me carefully before she pronounced, 'This one is no beauty, Susan. You have no need to concern yourself on her account.' She degenerated into a prolonged bout of coughing.

She had spoken of me as if I were not even in the room. I had little enough personal vanity and knew myself to be plain but it was painful to be reminded of it in public. Flushing with shame, I looked down so that I might not see her judgement reflected in the eyes of the others. I wondered whether she had requested my presence at the table solely so she might pass comment on my appearance.

When she finally surfaced from her paroxysm of coughing, she gasped, 'Why is this room always so hot and confined? I cannot breathe here, Susan, you know I cannot.'

'It is you who demand you sit nearest to the fire. Perhaps you would like to leave us for a moment.' Her daughter-in-law shrugged.

Eleanor rose from her seat. 'Grandmother, let me accompany you to take some fresh air.'

Her grandmother waved her hand angrily, 'I don't want *you* near me.' But, with a certain degree of malice, Eleanor insisted. She and Henry half supported and half carried Diana Wainwright from the room.

I was now left alone with the married couple, who faced each other silently along the length of the dining table. Mrs Wainwright crumbled her bread into a neat pile on the plate in front of her and this required all her attention. Mr Wainwright sat for a minute or two, his florid face wavering in the lamplight. He insisted on pouring me a large glass of blood red wine, despite my protests that I did not drink. As he handed the glass to me, his fingers lingered on mine for a moment longer than necessary and I felt my skin crawl with disgust. When I sipped the liquid, it tasted bitter and burned the back of my throat, but the act of drinking at least gave me something to do in the awkward silence.

Meanwhile, he produced a silver box from his pocket and took out a small cigar, which he tapped against the side of the box.

'Matthew, surely you're not going to smoke before dinner,' his wife complained.

'By God, why not?'

'And must you blaspheme as well?'

He laughed sarcastically. 'There is little enough to enjoy here. I might as well take any small pleasures I can.'

'The smell is revolting and we shall have to eat in this room when you have finished.'

He lit the cigar, with a measured relish, and said conversationally to me, 'I'll only smoke Dominican cigars. Most people swear by Cuban but I believe they are vulgar.' The room filled with the dense smell of spiced wood. Mr Wainwright sat back in his chair, while Mrs Wainwright wrinkled her nose and waved the napkin in front of her face. He studiously ignored her. 'I suppose you've heard stories about Teesbank Hall?' he continued.

I thought of the two carters at the railway station and Agnes. 'No, sir, I knew little of the house before I arrived here.'

Mrs Wainwright stopped fanning the air, 'We're not so infamous after all.'

He continued as if she had not spoken: 'We're supposedly haunted – or cursed as the locals will tell you.' I noticed his hand was clenched tightly around his wine glass.

'Matthew, you know what they say is nonsense,' his wife answered pettishly. 'Why do you repeat it? People need little enough excuse to hate us.' She looked back down at the breadcrumbs arranged in front of her – her energy clearly exhausted.

'I'm simply trying to warn the new governess about our home and prepare her against any horror stories she might hear. All the best houses have their own ghost, God knows.' He belched quietly into his napkin and tried to force more wine upon me – again his hand rested too long on mine. 'Have you felt any strange presences, Miss Colton?' He leered.

His foot nudged against mine beneath the table and I moved carefully away. 'It is Miss Caldwell, sir. I have not felt anything strange of note, but I have been warned of the dangers of Teesbank Hall.'

His wife smiled a cold, tight smile. 'I believe Miss Caldwell makes a good point.'

Unlike the dowager, Susan Wainwright and I knew men did not always demand beauty from a woman. Sometimes being poor and vulnerable was enough.

'The local people are all bloody fools. Superstitious bloody fools. There are no dangers here.'

The conversation was broken when Henry returned to the room with his grandmother supported against his shoulder, her bony bejewelled hand clutching at his arm. 'We are quite recovered now, aren't we, Grandmother?'

'Thank you, Henry. I can breathe again. Why do you never air this room properly?' she admonished her daughter-in-law, although Mrs Wainwright simply looked away and refused to acknowledge her words. 'Henry, you and Matthew are the only ones I can trust in this house. You will not let me suffocate. And, Matthew, you're smoking at the table. You know I don't like the smell.'

'I'm sorry, Mother.' He stubbed out the cigar on one of the side plates, where it smouldered for a moment or two longer.

'Hasn't Eleanor returned yet?' Henry enquired.

'We thought she was with you,' replied his mother.

At that moment, Eleanor entered the room, slightly out of breath, her eyes glittering. 'Father, she's here tonight. I can feel her presence again.'

A look of rage flashed across Mr Wainwright's face. 'I'll not have this talk at the table. Be silent, Eleanor.'

She ignored him. 'Something must have happened. She is very strong tonight.' As she spoke, I noticed she was pulling at the material around her left wrist, so that it was all puckered and creased.

'Is she wrong in the head? Stop this now.' Matthew

Wainwright slammed down the heavy crystal wine glass and stood up. 'There will be no more talk of hauntings.' Drops of red spread on the white linen tablecloth.

'Why do you deny it? You know that she walks,' Eleanor said, staring straight at him. 'When she died, she cursed us. And we are cursed. Look at us!'

'No,' he blustered. 'There is no ghost. There must be no more of this talk!'

The white-faced defiant daughter faced head-on the red rage of her father.

He turned to his wife now. 'Can't you control her?'

Susan Wainwright shrugged almost imperceptibly. 'She is your daughter in every way. You are the one who must govern her behaviour.'

'She must learn when to be quiet. And, God help me, if no one else can teach her, then I will,' he threatened.

Eleanor went to speak but Matthew Wainwright moved towards her. Swiftly, unexpectedly, he hit her hard across the face using his open palm. The sound was like the crack of a pistol. Eleanor staggered under the weight of the blow and it seemed she would fall backwards but, at the last moment, she righted herself by gripping the edge of the table.

Henry jumped to his feet. 'Don't you dare touch her.'

Susan Wainwright's hand fluttered to her lips and her mouth made an O of surprise, but she said nothing.

'Don't imagine you can tell me what to do in my house!'

Mr Wainwright swung round and he seemed about to

attack his son but Eleanor cried out, 'No, Henry, please – it makes things worse. Please do not intervene.'

Matthew Wainwright panted heavily. 'Stop her saying those things and I won't touch her again.'

'You have no right—' Henry began, but Eleanor placed herself between the two men.

'No, Henry, stop. I am to blame. I had forgotten we must not speak the truth aloud in this house.' A red mark bloomed on her cheek and her hand went to cover it.

Mr Wainwright stared at her for a moment. 'I'll not eat with her in the room. I'll have nothing more to do with my vexatious daughter until she learns to shut her mouth.' He turned on his heel and left. Agnes and Eliza had been hesitating at the door, balancing a huge tureen of soup between them, but he pushed past.

A terrible silence descended on us.

Then Susan Wainwright said, 'Why did you deliberately anger your father?'

'It was not deliberate.' Eleanor shook her head vigorously. 'I can feel her all around us tonight. I thought you would sense it too. But, Henry, I am sorry. I have spoiled your first evening at home. I should have said nothing.'

'But, Eleanor, you can't allow—'

She cut across him and looked at me: 'Don't say anything in front of her.'

Diana Wainwright murmured, 'Not in the presence of servants, Henry.'

A flush of shame spread from my neck to my face and I saw him glance at me.

Diana took control of the situation. 'Henry, in the absence of Matthew, you must raise the toast. And, you –' she nodded in the direction of the two maids – 'may come in and start to serve.' A solid vegetable soup was ladled into the bowls in front of us and Agnes discreetly covered the wine stain with a fresh white napkin. I wondered if such events were commonplace at Teesbank Hall.

Henry lifted his glass and proposed a toast to the good health of the family. I, the outsider, was not sure whether they raised their glasses in irony or solidarity. The rest of the meal passed uneasily and the food lay heavy on my stomach. Eleanor ate nothing but from time to time she touched the mark on her face. I was surprised to see that she was smiling. Henry turned as if to ask her something but she shook her head.

No one spoke and the only sound was the scraping of spoons against porcelain. Finally, the oppressive silence became too much and Henry asked me, 'Miss Caldwell, have you had the pleasure of visiting the county of Durham before?'

Diana Wainwright cleared her throat to signal her disapproval that I should be included in the conversation but I answered anyway: 'I'm not acquainted with this part of the world, sir. The furthest north I had been before was Harrogate where I took the waters with Father.' The red wine made me bold and I looked defiantly at Diana Wainwright.

Why shouldn't I answer him as an equal? Although my family might not have been as wealthy as the Wainwrights, we were well established in Norfolk. My great-grandfather had been the mayor of Norwich and Father's family had owned our estate – diminished though it might now be – for several generations.

Henry continued, 'We are famous only for our factories and railways but this area has a beauty all its own and I wouldn't live in any other part of the country.'

'Are there any places of interest you would recommend to a visitor, sir?' I asked.

'There is the waterfall over at High Force. It's been painted by J. M. W. Turner no less and is an awe-inspiring sight, especially if viewed in the calm immediately after a storm.'

'I've heard much of his work and would be intrigued to see an example,' I replied.

'We have a colour print of it in the morning room. You must view it tomorrow.'

Although we talked pleasantly and of inconsequential things, the violence of what had occurred simmered beneath the surface of the evening and it was impossible to blot it from my mind.

Henry was in the middle of telling me about his recent visit to York, when Eleanor interrupted, 'Do you intend seeing Edward while you're at Teesbank?'

'I'll probably ride across to Long Newton tomorrow morning.'

'Will you see his sister?' his grandmother asked. 'Rosalind is such an agreeable young lady. You must pass on my good wishes to her.'

Henry coloured. 'I believe Miss Merryweather should be at home. I will tell her you have asked after her.'

'Rosalind Merryweather is the most vacuous woman I have ever met.' Eleanor snorted, looking up from her untouched plate.

'Vacuous? Whatever do you mean by that, Eleanor?' Diana Wainwright asked.

'I mean that she is empty-headed. She talks of nothing but fashion plates, flower arrangements and betrothals.'

'Just because she doesn't have her head in a book every moment of the day doesn't mean she is ignorant.' Her brother laughed. 'Miss Merryweather is very pleasant, just like her brother, who also happens to be my oldest friend, Eleanor.'

'Oh, yes, they are both very *pleasant*, but Rosalind is frighteningly dull and ill-read.'

'Whatever gives you the right to sit in judgement on others?' Henry demanded.

'Well, Eleanor, one certainly doesn't need to look far to see the dangers of excessive learning and the morbid effect it can have upon a young lady's disposition,' Diana Wainwright observed. 'Miss Merryweather is very pretty and that will be of far more use to her in life.'

'Why should her appearance be more important than her mind?' her granddaughter wanted to know.

'It will help her to make a good marriage,' her grand-mother pronounced.

'And, Grandmother, is a so-called *good* marriage to be the only ambition a woman should hold?'

'It is hard to think of a more desirable destiny for a young lady. Now, where have Agnes and Eliza gone? The plates must be taken away and they have disappeared at the exact moment they are needed.'

Eleanor seemed to weigh up whether to respond, but clearly thought better of it and the talk continued about people I didn't know. Henry's comments were now directed solely at his family and he paid very little attention to me from this point onwards. He had fulfilled his responsibili-ties as a host, and the horror at the start of the meal had been temporarily patched over. That meant I could view him dispassionately from a distance. As he spoke, his face was lit by the lamplight, his cheekbones all high angles and his eyes a smouldering blue. He was handsome but there was hesi-tancy, too, and I began to modify my first impressions of him. I wondered if he feared his father. I stopped gazing at him and glanced down at my hands, neatly folded in front of me. When I looked up again and around the table, I saw the eyes of the grandmother boring into me. I turned away quickly.

The meal finally came to an end. I was tired and had hoped to go straight to bed but Mrs Jenson had sent word that she wished to see me. She wanted me to report on my first impressions of Eleanor. By the time our conversation had come to an end, the downstairs rooms were deserted and closed. It was with some degree of relief that I finally started to climb the narrow stairs leading to my bedroom, the flickering candle held in front of me, like a shield against the thick darkness of the enclosed space.

And as I climbed, I began to have the most ridiculous idea that someone was walking just ahead of me and always out of sight. The lightness of step suggested that it was one of the maids, and once or twice I thought I made out the dying flutter of a dark dress. I went to call out to her but something seemed to weigh heavy on my tongue and no words came. I began to walk a little faster, trying to catch a glimpse of her to reassure myself that it was Agnes or the bad-tempered Eliza. But each time I thought I had almost reached her, there was another twist in the staircase and I saw no one at the next turn.

In the chill of the night, I remembered Eleanor's words: 'You know that she walks.' I shivered. I wasn't a superstitious person but as I climbed onwards, up the hidden staircase, a cold fear started to descend upon me. Try as I might, I could not rationalize away my growing apprehension that I was in the presence of something or someone malign. I no longer hurried to catch up with the figure ahead because I dreaded what I might see when I turned the next corner. Longing for the sanctuary of my bedroom, I promised myself I would follow Agnes's advice and let my candle burn through the night so that the room wasn't left in darkness.

When I finally reached the top of the stairs, I was so convinced I would see some ghostly apparition waiting there that I sighed with relief at the emptiness of the gloomy corridor. I ran to my attic bedroom – all the time having the sense to shield the candle's flame with my hand: I was terrified of being without light.

I reached the safety of my room and slammed the door tight behind me, panting as I shut out the darkness and turned the key tight. Carefully keeping the wick free of wax and the flame away from draughts, I put the candle on the chest of drawers. I couldn't risk it going out and being in pitch blackness in that lonely room. The flickering light of the candle threw grotesque shadows around the room and I quickly dressed in my white cotton nightgown.

I sat on the edge of the bed so I might see myself in the mirror and began my nightly ritual of carefully unpinning my hair and brushing it out before sleep. I hoped that by focusing on this simple action, I might block out the terrifying thoughts that flooded my mind.

But there was to be no relief: as I looked in the mirror, I saw a reflection that was me and yet was not me. Released from its pins, my hair hung loose and seductive, snaking its way down to my waist. My eyes were dark and knowing, and as for my mouth (always my mouth was too passionate!), the full red lips were half open and inviting. This image was in the familiar shape and contours of my own face but totally transformed. And what I hardly dared to admit to myself was that I, I who had always been plain and ordinary, was beautiful but it was a debauched beauty and achieved at what terrible cost?

Dread seized me. What if the mirror reflected me back as I really was? Perhaps this was the face I showed to the world. Everyone would know the truth. He had said my destiny was written into the bone and was clearly visible to anyone who observed me carefully. When I looked into the mirror, the proof of his words was there before me.

Terrified, I covered my eyes with my hands, hoping that when I looked at the glass again, I would be reflected back as I knew myself to be, sensible and demure. That it had merely been a trick of the half-light. But the face was still there. I traced her outline with my fingertips; I widened my eyes and she mirrored my action. It was undeniably my face. This was the version of me he had told me about. I had tried to escape but she had followed me here to drag me back down to degradation. With trembling hands, I covered the glass with my woollen cloak. I could not stand to look at myself.

Being without light was frightening but what I could see was more so. With all the moral strength I possessed, I blew out the candle. I was plunged into a total darkness, so tangible I could almost reach out and touch it with my hand.

I climbed into the narrow bed and curled up in a protective ball, rigid with terror. Although I pulled the quilt and blankets close around me, they did little to stop the intense cold that penetrated my heart and made my whole body tremble. Yet the horror of that night was not complete, for in the distance I heard faint sounds of knocking and muffled sobs, as if someone were trapped and trying desperately to escape. I called, 'Can I help you? What is the matter?' but was thankful there was no reply. Only silence. What could I have done? I lay awake, but too afraid to go to their aid. I mumbled aloud my nightly mantra, 'I will not let circumstances destroy me. I will survive this. Everything will pass.'

It felt inadequate against the forces gathering around me.

CHAPTER FIVE

I had not expected to sleep that night, yet in the end exhaustion overcame me. Just as the first glimmers of dawn streaked across the early-morning sky, I fell into a deep state of unconsciousness. It was not a sleep that brought relief. Instead, scenes from the previous night came unbidden into my mind: Mr Wainwright leering towards me and his hand lingering on mine; Eleanor's hysterical excitement; and the sharp explosion of violence as he hit her. Then my face in the mirror.

My disordered thoughts resolved themselves into a kind of narrative and I had the strangest and most vivid dream. I was back in my childhood home, walking in the grounds near the river, when I thought I saw Father ahead of me. He was dressed in black and seemed to be in deepest mourning. I was filled with joy at being reunited with him and called, but he didn't respond and continued to walk briskly away. I hurried towards the figure so I might catch him, but always the distance between us remained the same and always he was just out of reach. I tried to speak, but my voice was low and hoarse, little more than a whisper. And then the man began to shake his head and mutter. I could not hear what he said, but with the certainty of dreams I knew he denied I was his daughter. This filled me with extreme anguish and gave me the impetus to run faster and finally catch him. I tugged on his sleeve, 'Dearest Father, it is your own Harriet.'

The figure turned and it was not Father at all but Uncle Thomas Stepford. He smiled sneeringly and said, 'I knew you would find me in time.'

Then there was that awful blinding light and I was frozen and pinned down in time. I woke with a start and was instantly alert. It was a dream, a nightmare. I was nearly three hundred miles from Swaffham. He could not know I was here. I closed my eyes and, with an act of will, squeezed away such memories.

The rationality of daylight provided explanations. The strangeness of the place, the inebriating wine and the disturbing events of the previous evening, all of these had caused my broken sleep. And were most likely to blame for the distorted perception of myself in the looking-glass yesterday. The sobs had been the heartbreak of a homesick maid carried by the wind. I was ashamed of my foolish hysteria. Yet I dared not remove the cloak covering my reflection in case that face still lurked there.

I untangled the heavy white quilt and climbed out of bed. My mouth was dry and foul-tasting, my head dull and thick. Already the sun was climbing higher in the sky and I feared that I would be late for my seven o'clock start in the schoolroom. The other side of the corridor was silent and the maids must already be long about their duties. The over-rich food of the night before lay low on my stomach and I had no desire to eat breakfast. Instead I washed and dressed quickly, and pinned up my hair in the most perfunctory manner.

I ran down the narrow parallel staircase and entered the schoolroom out of breath. A large, forbidding woman turned to face me: this must be the nurse, Mrs Anderson. Her face was blotched with patches of angry red skin and every ounce of her body spoke of her displeasure towards me.

There was no introduction. 'It's ten minutes past seven. This is not my time. My hours are seven in the evening until seven in the morning.'

'I'm sorry, I didn't wake,' I tried to explain.

'She is to be yours in the daytime hours and yours only. Already you've taken precious minutes from me and I expect to be paid back.' Her accent was harsh and uneducated. 'It's not right and I shall complain to Mrs Jenson.'

'It will not happen again, I promise, and I'll come early tomorrow. Only please don't say anything.' This position was all that stood between me and destitution – I had spent almost every penny I had on the train journey to Eagles-cliffe. Trapped by poverty and my sex, it was impossible to go off and make my fortune in the way that Heathcliff had, and other heroes in the popular romances I liked to read at that time.

'I'll say nowt this time but you've been warned.'

While this exchange took place, Eleanor was working at her desk. The red mark was clear on her face and she touched it from time to time. She seemed indifferent to our conversation and didn't look up from her studies. Her book was written in a series of meaningless squiggles – Ancient Greek, I thought, and decided she must have chosen it because she suspected the tongue was unknown to me. Her face had assumed an aspect of absolute concentration. However, when Mrs Anderson left the room, she stated flatly, 'You are late. She abhors lateness. She is paid well but she does not want to spend a moment longer with me than is necessary.'

'I'm sorry I was late, Miss Eleanor. I'm ready to commence our studies.'

My voice must have quavered. Certainly it registered an emotion that made Eleanor look up again and scrutinize me more closely. 'Something has happened, hasn't it? Are you quite well?'

As I write these words neutrally on the page, they seem to suggest some degree of concern about my welfare. Nothing could have been further from the truth. Her eyes now had the same flash of excitement that had been there last night but her tone was such as one might use in a scientific experiment, when observing the reactions of an insect after poking it with a stick.

My sense of loneliness and the terror of my dream hung heavy upon me and tears stung my eyes as I spoke. Flustered, I answered more candidly than perhaps I should to someone I believed was an enemy. 'My sleep was disturbed and I passed a restless night.'

I now had her full attention. 'They should have locked up that room for ever.'

'Why? What happened in it?' I was frightened my attic bedroom might be linked to the murder in some way.

But Eleanor merely forced a cold, mirthless giggle. 'I am sure you will learn soon enough.' She looked away, her right hand tightly gripping her left wrist and pulling at the cuff.

I couldn't help asking, 'Was it where the child was killed?'

She started with surprise. 'You know of that already? No, the murder was not in the governess's room but I have promised that I will speak of it no further.'

The subject was closed and I searched around for something to do next. I needed to impose a schoolroom routine on our time together or I would be quite lost; the thought of my nightly report to Mrs Jenson haunted me, as did the need to provide details of our activities. 'Shall we begin our studies then, Miss Eleanor?' I suggested.

Her tone cool once more, she said, 'Surely I made it plain yesterday that I will accept no instruction from you.'

'But you must,' I demanded, with a conviction I didn't feel. 'I'm employed to be your governess.'

She met this statement with an infuriating silence and returned to her books, determinedly not glancing up or acknowledging my presence in any way. The heavy tedium of the dull morning stretched ahead of me and time seemed to have stopped. I had reluctantly resigned myself to a foray into Johnson's *Lives of the Poets*, when the quiet was broken by agitated shouts and curses from below, and then the front door crashed shut. The loudness of the noise made me jump but Eleanor didn't glance up, leaving me to question whether my own senses had deceived me.

At twelve o'clock on the dot, Agnes brought in a tray with two plates of food, forks and spoons, and two glasses of water. She shot me a look of sympathy and I was glad to have at least one ally in the house.

Eleanor surprised me by asking of her, 'What was that dreadful noise earlier this morning?' She was aware of what had taken place after all.

'It was your father, miss. Mr Wainwright had to leave unexpectedly to go on business in Newcastle,' Agnes replied.

'Good. I have angered him with my talk of ghosts,' Eleanor said, with a smirk of satisfaction. 'He doesn't like to be reminded of the past.' Her hand reached up to the red mark on her face.

Agnes and I looked at each other again but nothing more was said and the housemaid left the room.

We ate in silence. The meal was plain and almost inedible, a lump of mashed potato, carrots and overcooked beef that had been cut into small pieces, as if we were both small children. When we had finished, I found myself awkwardly checking the contents of Eleanor's plate, so I could record in Mrs Jenson's book what she had eaten. She looked at me and hissed, 'Spy. You are just a spy.'

She crossed to the other side of the room and returned to

the absorption of her studies. Sighing, I reached for *Lives of the Poets*, and the dead hand of the clock counted away the hours. This impasse was to establish the routine between us over the following months. She wouldn't be instructed by me; in fact, she made it clear that the very thought was abhorrent to her and, eventually, I was forced to acknowledge that my role was that of gaoler not governess – there was nothing I could teach her.

We knew implicitly, though, that we must keep up a pretence to the outside world and over time we fell into the strangest unspoken complicity. She would sit each morning at the same desk, surrounded by a large pile of books of romantic fiction and historical epics – the acceptable boundaries of knowledge for a young lady of that time. Secreted within that charmed circle, however, were the forbidden fruits of male learning – the textbooks of Latin and Greek, the advanced squiggles and equations of higher mathematics, even the rudiments of engineering and advancements in farm agriculture. The library had been furnished for her brother, but he took no more than a passing interest in its contents. It was Eleanor who desired and devoured all she could find there.

I would sit a little away, so that I was not compromised by knowing too obviously that she studied what wasn't allowed, yet I had to be near enough that I could pretend to be giving lessons to her when Mrs Jenson inspected the schoolroom. Eleanor and I never discussed this openly, but upon it we seemed to have reached an uneasy truce. Certainly, she glared at me with contempt when I inspected her plate at the end of each meal and I felt shame as I wrote down in Mrs Jenson's book the amount she had consumed at the end of the day.

Over time I realized she ate almost nothing, merely moving her food around the plate. She was painfully thin but animated by a fierce energy that burned through her. When she wasn't studying, she would pace the library for hours on end, relentlessly walking round and round the room until she was out of breath. Once I asked her whether she would like to walk in the grounds.

She laughed at me. 'That's what they want me to do. No, I will stay indoors and choose the times when I am ready to go outside.'

I was so lonely in those first weeks, when I was trapped with Eleanor for twelve empty hours, with only her contempt for company. For the remainder of March and most of April, I was not invited to join the Wainwrights for dinner – presumably the old lady had satisfied herself that I posed no threat to the menfolk of the house – and I saw the other family members only at a distance. In any case, Henry was often out visiting friends or at the university, while Matthew Wainwright was frequently called away on business in Newcastle.

Yet I longed for any distraction that might block out the dark thoughts that constantly intruded upon me. The distorted image in the looking-glass and what had occurred in Norfolk had left me always on edge and nervous. It was as if something menacing was at the periphery of my vision: if

I were to turn around too quickly, I would see it clearly and be forced to confront it and myself.

Sometimes my mind strayed to those places it should not, and it was then, always then, that I felt Eleanor's eyes upon my face. I would look up and catch her watching me. Almost as if she could read my mind. It made me frightened that she might know what had happened and the face in the mirror was the face I showed to the world.

CHAPTER SIX

Eleanor and I were locked together in that hushed library, hidden in the riverbank wood of oak and ash. The weather had been dismal – sheets of grey, spiteful rain fell for most of the daylight hours. Finally, after the early weeks of dull weather, a watery sun blossomed through the thin clouds and, to my greatest astonishment, Eleanor broke her self-imposed silence: 'Would you like to walk in the grounds with me?'

'Yes, of course. I'll arrange for our cloaks to be brought up,' I replied, delighted at a change to the prison of our schoolroom routine, then busied myself with all the necessary preparations. It was near the end of April but the day was cool, so we were both well wrapped up. At the last moment, Eleanor slipped a manila envelope into her pocket. I wondered about the significance of her action but said nothing.

She had decided we would follow an earthen track down to the river, which was reached through an area of trees at the back of the house. The ground was damp and heavy from days of rain, but the hesitant blue of the sky shimmered across the surface of the distant river and the fresh green scents of spring were all around.

Although I had hardly expected us to enjoy a companionable stroll, I was still surprised that as soon as we left the house Eleanor began to walk briskly away without acknowledging me. She looked straight ahead and only occasionally glanced back to gauge the distance between us. It struck me that she had planned this, and there was some reason for what she was doing, but I had no idea what that might be.

Still, I was determined not to lose sight of her – I couldn't forget Mrs Jenson's strictest injunction that I must be with her at all times – but she walked quickly and soon I found myself out of breath. I had a stone in my boot so stopped briefly to remove it and regain my composure. When I began walking again, she was nowhere to be seen. It was then that panic set in.

I heard twigs breaking somewhere ahead of me and plunged into a clump of trees to my left, hoping to either find her there or at least cut off a corner of the walk so that I might reach her more quickly. The thin soles of my boots slipped on the muddy incline of the slope and the low-lying branches of the trees caught in my hair. I tried to keep a sense of my bearings, but the terrain became wild and unkempt once I strayed from the manicured part of the grounds. I looked around at the Hall, which was still visible above the treetops, so I might not lose my way, but its windows glared back at me.

I steeled myself to think rationally. I hadn't gone far. If I used the Hall as a guide point then I should be able to retrace my footsteps and find the way back onto the path. The hem of my skirt was damp and covered with mud, my boots were clumpy with clods of dark earth. Forcing myself to breathe more regularly, I felt fear being replaced by anger. Bit by bit I worked out where the path must be and pushed through the dense foliage. It was close at hand, but in my confusion I had lost all sense of direction. I was determined Eleanor wouldn't outwit me.

The path ahead was empty, snaking down to the river. There was no sign of her but I knew she hadn't just disappeared. If I followed the route I must eventually find her. I was out of sorts and red-faced as I trudged its course, so it was with dismay that I spotted a horse coming towards me and realized Henry was approaching. If I had had more warning, I would have hidden for a moment or two in the wooded area because I didn't want to face his ridicule.

'Miss Caldwell, good day.' He nodded from his mount. I felt sure that his glance took in my dishevelled state. 'Are you quite well?'

'Yes, sir. I am very well, thank you,' I replied, as determinedly as I could. I had last spoken to him at the Wainwrights' dinner table when my voice had found confidence in a glass of red wine. In the sober light of day, I felt awkward and tongue-tied.

'I was told you and my sister had gone for a walk in the grounds and I came to accompany you both. Yet, you seem to be alone.'

'Miss Eleanor walked on ahead and I'm unable to find her.' I realized he might have an idea as to where his sister would be, but I was reluctant to ask for his help and felt certain it would further confirm to him my incompetence.

'A little careless, perhaps, to lose your pupil?' he enquired quizzically and then, to my greatest horror, he began to climb down from his horse. 'Let me aid you in your search, Miss Caldwell. I'm happy to be of assistance.'

'No, no, absolutely not. I'm certain she can't be far and I shall have no difficulty in finding her myself, sir.' My response to his offer was frankly unfriendly but I didn't care. I was already agitated enough and his presence would make me more so. He unsettled me and I wanted to make clear that our dealings would consist of nothing but the most formal of cold politeness.

'Very well,' he said, seating himself back on the horse. Hardly bothering to look at me, he pointed to the right of the river, 'You will most likely find Eleanor in the boathouse. She likes to sit there alone. If you follow the path round, you'll come to it.' He turned the horse and rode off to the Hall.

I followed this direction and, after about ten minutes, reached what I assumed must be the boathouse. It was a small ornate building, positioned right at the water's edge, a miniature stone castle, turreted and Gothic, which was sheltered by a clump of trees and almost impossible to see until you were upon it. It appeared to be shuttered and deserted but I was seized by the conviction that she was hiding there.

It was very silent – not even the sound of birdsong to break the stillness of the day.

'Miss Eleanor, I know you are in there.'

There was no reply.

'I don't know why you're refusing to answer me. Mr Henry told me this is where you would be.'

Although there was no direct response, I thought I heard a murmur of surprise or irritation. I'd had enough of her difficult ways and decided to enter the boathouse and confront her. However, as I stretched out my hand to turn the handle of the door, it struck me how cold I had become: my woollen cloak was inadequate to keep out the deep chill that had settled into my bones.

I don't believe myself particularly sensitive to the atmosphere of places, yet as I stood there, I felt a despair so powerful it threatened to overwhelm me and drag the air from my lungs. It was the most peculiar sensation and I can liken it only to a photographic plate, where silver and mercury capture the living moment and freeze it so that it might be seen and felt for ever. I experienced someone else's anguish, an external thing that was imprinted onto the air itself. The shock of the emotion took me back to the despair of the moment when Dr Williams had told me there was nothing further that could be done: I knew then that Father must die and I must be alone in the world.

To assume a courage I didn't feel, I called, 'Miss Eleanor, why do you play such foolish games? I know you're in here.'

There was no reply, although I sensed her presence and

could hear sharp, rapid breaths. I remembered Mrs Jenson's warning: Eleanor was manipulative and dangerous. I was strangely fearful of her as I entered that dark place – the panting sound put me in mind of a trapped animal. Cornered but still powerful. What if she was to leap out at me, or had lured me to this isolated place to harm me?

There was only limited light in the boathouse, and at first I couldn't make out her hiding-place, but as my eyes adjusted to the half-light, I saw her partly concealed against the far wall. Her face was blank and she stared straight at me, 'You can feel it too,' she said.

I shook my head, frightened.

'I knew you would be able to.' Her eyes flashed intently in the gloom.

My lips formed the word 'no' but my shocked face gave her the answer she wanted.

She smiled with grim satisfaction. 'In some ways, we are more similar than either of us would wish,' she said.

I knew then she must have guessed at something of the fear and darkness that hung about me, try though I might to block the past from my memory.

'Did you see anything as you walked in?' she demanded.

'I saw nothing,' I said. It was the truth but not the whole truth. I hadn't seen, but I had sensed a presence. 'It's a cold and abandoned place.'

'Read this and then you will know what haunts it.' She took a sheet of paper from the manila envelope and thrust it into my hands. It was a crudely printed poster.

Reward

A Substantial Reward is Offered for Information
leading to the Safe Return of Samuel Wainwright who
has been missing since Friday, 10 August 1849 to the
great distress of his parents, Mr and Mrs Matthew
Wainwright of Teesbank Hall, off Jackson Lane in the
Parish of Preston on Tees in the District of Eaglescliffe.

Missing

*Samuel Wainwright, who is Two Years of Age, has not been
seen since the evening of Friday, 10 August, being two days
previous, when he was put to Bed by his Nursemaid. Samuel
has blue Eyes, fair Hair and a pink Complexion. He was
clothed only in his night Flannels, no other Garments
being gone from the Hall.*

Information

Should anyone have Information as to the Whereabouts
of the Infant, they should apply in the first instance to
Seddon and Wilson, Attorneys at Law, the High Street,
Stockton on Tees, and furnish said Information. If this
lead to the Safe Return of the Infant, then a Reward of
One Hundred Pounds will be paid by Mr Wainwright.

'It was a waste of paper,' she said. 'My brother Samuel was
already dead.'

My hands trembled as I gave the sheet back to her. 'I'm so sorry. I didn't know that the child who died was your brother.' I hesitated, unsure of what to say.

'They tell me not to talk of it,' she said. 'But how can I not think of it all the time? Trapped in that house, the place he was taken from. And here –' she gestured helplessly – 'twenty-two years ago, this is where they found Samuel. He had been butchered.' She gripped my arm, turning me so that I was forced to look at her. She was too close and I struggled to be free – I cannot bear people to touch me unexpectedly. Her eyes had a strange exhilaration about them and she didn't seem fully aware of me or our surroundings. 'His throat had been cut almost clean through and that was the fatal wound, the surgeon said, but his body had been stabbed more than a dozen times.'

I gasped with horror. 'He was two years old!' The chill I had felt on entering the boathouse deepened. I asked, 'How do you know these things?'

'I have the inquest papers and other documents too. I had to understand the truth.'

Not wanting to be in this place of death for a moment longer, I tried to persuade her to leave but she dug her nails deeper into my flesh and pushed me down to a seat next to the window. 'I can show you the papers. It was a famous murder and they sold pamphlets of it in the streets. They called it the French Murder.'

The crime was horribly familiar. It had been a notorious

case although Father had protected me from its details. How ironic that my life had once been so sheltered.

'Look,' she insisted, 'this is from the inquest. It will show you how the body was found here.' She placed a sheaf of papers in my hands and I began to read from the first page.

The whole Proceedings before the Coroner's Inquest at Stockton-on-Tees, on the body of Samuel Wainwright, who died of severe lacerations about the body at Teesbank Hall, at an unknown time after 10 August 1849.

Taken in shorthand and edited by S. R. Stocksley

RICHARD DIVINE *called, sworn, and* examined by the CORONER.

Q. *What are you?*
A. *I am a gardener at Teesbank Hall in Eaglescliffe.*
Q. *Is it true that you discovered the body of Samuel Wainwright?*
A. *Yes, Sir.*
Q. *Where did you find the body?*
A. *It was in the boathouse.*
Q. *Was this the first time the boathouse had been searched?*
A. *No, Sir.*
Q. *Why had not the body been found previously?*
A. *It was part buried under some loose earth at the back of the boathouse and had been covered in tarpaulin.*
Q. *What did you do when you found the body?*

A. *I ran to tell the magistrate, Mr Hughes, who was then in the company of Mr and Mrs Wainwright. I said that they should come at once but I was too agitated to tell them why.*

Q. *Is it true Mr Wainwright was the first to arrive at the scene?*

A. *Yes, Sir. Mrs Wainwright is in a delicate condition and stumbled on the rough ground. Mr Hughes stayed back to help her.*

Q. *How did Mr and Mrs Wainwright react when they saw the body?*

A. *(pause) Mr Wainwright became agitated and began to cry out. He shouted, 'God, why have you punished my family in this way?' Mrs Wainwright was silent at first and very pale. I was worried for her because she is near her term. But then she spoke.*

Q. *What did Mrs Wainwright say?*

A. *(considerable pause) This is what vengeance looks like.*

Q. *Were those her exact words?*

A. *Yes, Sir.*

Q. *What did you understand those words to mean?*

A. *I do not know, Sir.*

(The Witness withdrew)

I looked at Eleanor. 'Why did your mother say that?'

'You would have to know the whole story to understand the significance of her words.' Now she took the inquest papers from me before I might read more. 'I will not give away our family secrets too easily. You must earn them.'

'How may I do that?' I asked.

She half smiled, then said, 'The magistrate insisted Samuel's body was left where it had been found until the surgeon might examine it. My family was suspected from the very first of being involved in the murder.'

'Surely that's not possible!' I exclaimed.

Still gripping me tightly, still digging her nails deep into me, she continued, 'My nursemaid Nancy Wilson told me that Mother knelt in the dirt by her son's body and wept that she wanted to return him to his bed. Father paced the floor of this boathouse, like a man deranged, threatening anyone who tried to comfort him.'

'How terrible!'

'Oh, what came later was worse. At least my parents were capable of feeling then. They loved Samuel. There is no love left in the house now.'

'Was the murderer discovered?' I wanted to know.

'Oh, someone was hanged for it,' she replied. 'They dragged her screaming to the gallows at Durham Prison.'

'A woman? How could a woman do such a thing?'

Ignoring my question, she said, 'She claimed she finally wanted to tell the truth. It was a beautiful October morning and she was young. She did not want to die.'

Samuel was murdered in August. Justice had been swift for his killer, I thought.

'What did she mean by the truth?' I asked.

'Oh, it was too late by then. No one would listen – she had been found guilty in a court of law. What more could be said?'

'But why would she kill a small child, little more than a baby?'

'And she cursed us – our family – as she climbed the steps to her death. She would not ask for repentance, saying she was not the one to blame.' A moment's reflection, and then Eleanor added, 'None of the local people think she was the killer.'

'Why not?' I paused. Something about Eleanor's expression made me ask, 'Do *you* think she was the murderess?'

Eleanor released me from her grip and turned away. The exhilaration had gone from her voice and she now spoke in an emotionless monotone: 'When I was a small child and was naughty, my nursemaid used to tell me I must be a very good girl or the dead lady would come back and take revenge on me for what my family had done.'

'What a cruel thing to say to a young child!'

'It was the only way she could control me.'

'What happened to the nursemaid?'

'Oh, she was dismissed once Father knew of the stories she told me. Nancy Wilson had been there when Samuel was taken. He was worried she knew more than she said,' she replied.

'What more could she have known that she wouldn't reveal?'

Infuriatingly, Eleanor refused to answer me but instead continued as if I hadn't spoken: 'Her tales made me wake up screaming night after night. I am sure Father was not concerned at my distress but he does not like to be reminded of the past.'

'It's a horrific crime!' I exclaimed. 'How could anyone forget?'

'Mother does not forget,' Eleanor said, with a degree of certainty. 'She must have found some satisfaction that the punishment was so dreadful. When the judge put on his black cap to tell her that she must hang, he also said that it would be a public execution.'

'Because she was convicted of killing a child?' I asked.

'There is no worse crime,' Eleanor stated. 'Have you seen the gallows at Durham Prison?'

I shook my head.

'The condemned walk along a narrow passageway until they reach a platform in full view of everyone. The hanging of a woman is rare and it attracts the largest crowds. Special trains had been put on so that people could travel from all round the north of England. They said there were thousands of people watching, all come to pelt her with rotten fruit and stones. And as she twitched at the end of the rope, the last thing she heard was the crowd chanting, 'Whore. The governess is a whore.'

'Oh, God.' My hands went instinctively to my face with horror. That word. I could not bear to hear it spoken aloud.

'I think it is why she haunts us. Nancy Wilson believed that she cannot enter Heaven until she has justice.' Eleanor suddenly stopped and fixed her eyes on a point behind me, as if someone had just come into the building. Instinctively, I turned but no one was there.

I was desperate to be out of that dreadful place where blood had soaked the ground so I stood up abruptly. 'We must go on with our walk. The sky is darkening and the rain will come soon.'

She allowed me to lead her from the boathouse but she continued speaking: 'It does not matter whether she was to blame or not, for in the end we were all punished.' And now she stared around her in an agitated manner as if someone was following us and listening to our conversation. I looked in horror as she began pulling at the buttoned-up sleeves of her gown. 'What are you doing, Miss Eleanor? Stop, please!' I begged.

She looked at me, blank-faced, as if she hadn't heard me and continued plucking at the material around her wrists.

'Miss Eleanor, please, you are distressing yourself. We have to return home. Rain is on the way.' Increasingly concerned for her state of mind, I tried to drag her back along the path by holding her right arm but her body was rigid and she was impossible to move. All I wanted was to be back inside Tees-bank Hall and away from her increasing hysteria.

'We cannot talk of it, you know that too. Everyone thinks it was only our wealth saved us.'

I thought of the carter at the railway station and his warning about Teesbank Hall. I thought, too, of how desolate this place was and that there had been no visitors to the door in the weeks since my arrival. 'Miss Eleanor, please, we must go back to the Hall.' With an act of will, I began to force her along the path.

She seemed oblivious to me and muttered to herself, 'My brother was only two years old. They say the shock of his murder made Father's hair turn white overnight and my mother lost her wits with grief. The whole family should have perished that night.'

I recoiled at the horror of what she had said. 'Miss Eleanor, please stop. You are only distressing yourself.'

And then, without warning, her mood changed and her face lost its manic appearance. She looked at me with shock. 'Why are you holding my arm?'

My hands fell limply to my side. 'I – I was worried about you. I wanted to help you return to the Hall.'

She rubbed her sleeve as if it were filthy. 'Do not ever touch me again,' she said slowly and deliberately. Her sudden calm was more chilling than the frenzy of a moment ago.

'Who was the woman found guilty of the murder?' I asked, but already she was walking away from me and would say no more.

CHAPTER SEVEN

I trailed behind her, back to the Hall, shaken by what she had said and by my recognition of the thick despair that surrounded the boathouse. We removed our coats in the hall-way and returned to the silence of the schoolroom. Eleanor looked coolly and critically at my distracted state, before set-tling at her desk and losing herself in the pure abstraction of algebra. There was no such escape for me and I gazed around the vast shelves of the library trying to find something to take my mind off the horrors she had revealed to me.

Finally, I settled upon a volume by the great poet William Wordsworth, hoping the beauty of his lines on nature would transport me beyond the dark thoughts that filled my mind, but his book lay on my lap unread. I couldn't escape the image of the isolated boathouse where Samuel Wainwright's body had been found – so far from the house that his screams would have been heard by no one but his killer. *The Selected Poems of William Wordsworth* fell to the floor with a dull thud. Eleanor looked up at me, her brow furrowed with a frown. 'Be quiet,' she hissed. 'I am trying to concentrate.'

'I can't stop thinking about the murder,' I said.

'We don't speak of it. Speaking will not change what happened.'

I would have returned to my attempt to read poetry, but Eleanor asked suddenly, 'Would you care to see him?'

'Who?' I replied bewildered.

'Samuel. Samuel Wainwright. My dead brother. There is a photograph of him.'

Panic rose inside me. 'I don't want to see it.'

But already she was out of her seat and going to a cupboard by the window. She unlocked it and took out a large photographic album covered with faded grey silk. 'Look,' she insisted, placing it unopened upon the table. 'My brother is pictured here.'

She couldn't have known what it cost me. Even now the familiar sickness rises in me when I am confronted with a photograph, but Eleanor was watching and I forced myself to open the pages of the album. At first, I focused only on the neat copperplate inscription at the front of the album, 'J. Osbourne (East Riding and York) March 1849', and the reassuring regularity of the handwriting. Nothing bad could be contained here, I told myself. Then I slowly turned the heavy card pages, which were covered with rectangles of sepia images.

Eleanor was at my shoulder, breathing hard, impatient. 'Not these ones. You will see him more clearly in the final photograph.' She snatched the book from me. 'On the last page. Look!'

There was a large photograph of the whole household in front of Teesbank Hall. It had been taken at the time when photographers still used the daguerreotype process and the figures in the picture posed stiffly and gazed blankly at the photographer. Mr and Mrs Wainwright were placed at the centre but twenty or so years younger, before life had scarred them with age and grief. They were a very handsome couple, although they sat slightly apart. An infant was cradled on Mrs Wainwright's lap and two older girls, who were perhaps thirteen or fourteen years of age, stood to her left.

I drew her attention to the children. 'Who are they?'

'That is Clara. She was my eldest sister.' A dark-haired girl scowled at the camera. 'Here is Martha, who was two years younger than Clara.'

'What has become of them?' I asked. They must both have been women in their thirties, yet I had never heard their names mentioned before this moment.

'It does not matter. And that is my brother.' Her tone was cold and impersonal, as if she had no family relationship to the three older children.

Even in the posed and blurred photograph, it was possible to see the soft curve of Samuel's baby features. How dreadful that a few months later his body had been left, bloodied and lifeless, in the boathouse. I now began to look more closely at the detail of the photograph, trying to make out the faces of the other members of the household. The print was partly faded but I spotted a grim-faced Mrs Jenson staring out at me, not noticeably different in appearance or nature.

Eleanor stayed close by, watching me. My eyes were drawn to a figure standing a little away from the main family party. She wore a dress of a dark colour, with a neat lace collar. At first her features were indistinct but they began to resolve themselves into a familiar shape – the dark eyes and too passionate lips. I pointed at the book and exclaimed sharply, 'That woman, she looks like me. How can that be?'

Eleanor laughed maliciously. 'I wondered if you would see the resemblance. I thought it from the first time I saw you but I wanted to observe your reaction to be sure.'

'What do you mean? Who is she?' I demanded, examining the photograph more carefully.

Before she could reply, Mrs Jenson stepped into the room. She had been passing the door and now she asked, 'Whatever is the matter? Why are there raised voices?'

'I'm sorry, Mrs Jenson, but it's this.' I held the album towards her. 'For a moment, I thought it was a picture of me.' After my first shock, I had realized that any likeness was only superficial. The woman was the same age as me and had similar colouring but her features were more delicate than mine and she had a soft, haunting beauty about her.

Taking the book out of my hand, she said, 'Such a fuss over a photograph!' Then she stopped sharply on seeing the picture. 'This should not be here! Miss Eleanor, why did you show this photograph to Miss Caldwell?'

Eleanor shrugged and frowned. When Mrs Jenson and I had been talking, she had been watching us greedily, drinking in the drama of our conversation, but now she looked downwards, sullen and silent.

'Well, now that you have both calmed yourselves, I will take care of this.'

True to her word, she removed the album, and when it was returned several days later, that section of the picture had been cut out.

I sank down onto a chair, still shaken. 'Who was the woman in the photograph, Miss Eleanor?'

'It's most ironic,' she said gleefully. 'She was Arielle Marchal.'

'Arielle Marchal?'

'The French governess. She was the tutor to my sisters Clara and Martha. You sleep in the same room as she did. She was from Provence, like your mother. She was a whore. Arielle was hanged for the murder of Samuel.'

Eleanor reeled off her list with relish, and the familiar sick feeling rose in my stomach. Links began to grow between me and the dead Arielle. So many similarities. Even that word, that terrible word, bound us together.

'But you don't think she was the murderess?' I wanted Arielle Marchal to be innocent and then I, too, might be innocent.

'Is it important what I think?' She stopped and considered me carefully. 'I hold documents about the case. They might let you learn the identity of the killer, but they will come at a price.'

'How can you hold papers about the death? Samuel died before you were born.' I feared she would try to trick me in some way because she sensed I was vulnerable.

'Mostly they came from my nursemaid, Nancy Wilson. She was obsessed with the murder and, over the years, she collected anything she could find.'

'So, she showed them to you?'

'It was our secret. Nancy was almost illiterate, and she needed me to read them to her.' She looked distracted again. 'This house is haunted by the past – even the air is sick with memories. But no one would or will talk about it. No one but Nancy. We would sit in the boathouse for hours on end and dissect every last detail. People said the murder had turned Nancy's head –' Eleanor shrugged – 'and I wanted to know the truth.'

'And she gave you the documents?'

'Nancy Wilson?' She laughed. 'No, Nancy Wilson never gave away anything willingly in her life. I took them because they were mine by right – they were my family's secrets. When she was dismissed, Mrs Jenson watched her pack and Nancy could hardly stuff her case with stolen papers. I promised I would keep them safe and return them to her, which I did not intend to do, of course.'

'And you will let me see those documents, so I can unravel what happened?' I asked.

'Perhaps. I have other records too, which I stole from Father's study. He wants to forget and has become careless. I think he still doesn't know they are missing. But, as I have said, you must earn the truth.' She smiled coldly. 'If I allow you to know our sins, I expect to be given something in return.'

'What do you want?' I suspected she had long known the demands she would make. The trip to the boathouse, tempting me with snippets of information, even the photograph, all had been planned to arouse my curiosity.

'I will trade you my knowledge for a sliver of freedom. I crave only half an hour away from you, time without always being watched over. If you grant me that tomorrow, then I will let you see the rest of the inquest papers.'

I bit my lip. It was the strongest instruction Mrs Jenson had given. Miss Eleanor was not to be left alone. Not even for a moment. And she was manipulative too – Mrs Jenson had said that also and that I must not trust her. Already I could see how bitter and tormented she was and, worse, she hated me and would not hesitate to destroy me if she could.

Even now I wonder why I agreed to her bargain when it placed me in so much danger. Uncle Thomas Stepford had told me that curiosity would prove fatal to me and I should ask fewer questions. Perhaps he was right. It's true that I was desperate to know the story of what had happened here but it was more than just mere curiosity. There were so many parallels between me and Arielle Marchal, both governesses to this hostile family and both alone, that we seemed mirror images of each other. Superstitiously I believed that if I understood what had happened to her, I might be able to make sense of my own experiences. And, in truth, it was easier to lose myself in someone else's story than to think about my own past.

She saw the shadows of doubt that crossed my face. 'You must decide now. There can be no promise that I will make this offer again.' She laughed. 'See it as the serial of a Charles Dickens novel. Each week, I will provide you with a new instalment in return for half an hour of freedom.'

'What if you are seen alone? Mrs Jenson will know I've let you out of my sight.'

She realized then that I had agreed and she had got her way. 'I promise I will be careful. No one will see me.'

The next day, true to our words, we walked to the boathouse. 'We will not be disturbed here,' was her simple explanation for the choice of venue.

As was typical of spring, spells of bright sunshine were followed by sudden bursts of rain and the weather's changeability reflected my own lingering doubts over our agreement. We were silent and in step with each other. From a distance we must have looked as if we were close companions – I suppose it was our bargain alone that united us. Eleanor carried the same manila envelope as yesterday. I felt the thrill of anticipation but also dread about the revelation of secrets from that blood-soaked night so many years ago. Meanwhile, her eyes darted around, as if she was calculating what she might do with the freedom she had been promised.

When we reached the boathouse, I hesitated. The place carried an air of abandonment, being so far from the main house. I dreaded opening the door – perhaps it would be better not to know the details of the case.

Eleanor said contemptuously, 'You dare not enter now you know what occurred here!'

I wouldn't be accused of cowardice by her so I pushed the door open quickly and walked in. It was only a place, I told myself, damp and gloomy, perhaps, but only a place, no more than that. I couldn't pretend I was comfortable there and it was difficult to block out knowledge of its history – but the visceral horror of the previous day was gone.

She gave me the bracelet watch from her wrist. 'You may check me to the minute, but I promise I will be gone no more than half an hour.'

'No more than half an hour,' I echoed. It was too short a time for her to do any harm.

Then she handed me the manila envelope. 'It is here. You can begin to piece together what happened.'

'Will this tell me the truth?'

'It will tell you what they said happened,' she replied.

Once she had gone, I sat down on the small window seat at the front of the boathouse. It gave on to a view of the river Tees, washed clean by the earlier rain. The scene's loveliness made it possible to block out the horrors of what had happened there, but as soon as I opened the envelope, I was plunged into the darkness of many years ago. I ignored the questioning of the gardener Richard Divine, which I had seen yesterday, and instead began to read from the second page, which related to the condition of the body and the cause of death.

The Inquest

THOMAS FULLER, *called, sworn, and examined by the* CORONER.

Q. *Are you a regular Surgeon, and admitted at the College?*

A. *I am a regular Surgeon, and I am admitted at the College.*

Q. *Did you ever see Samuel Wainwright?*

A. *The day his body was found.*

Q. *Did you ever see him while he was living?*

A. *No, Sir.*

Q. *At whose request did you go to see the body?*

A. *I was solicited to do so by the Magistrate Mr Hughes.*

Q. *What was the state of the body when you saw it?*

A. *It had been wrapped in a length of fine white silk and hidden beneath a quantity of tarpaulin. The body had been partially buried and there was some soil about it.*

Q. *When you undid the coverings, could you see any wounds on it?*

A. *Yes. There was a deep cut across the throat, about three inches long and two inches deep.*

Q. *What was the appearance of this wound?*

A. *It was livid, and the head was partly separated from the body.*

Q. *Do you believe Samuel Wainwright died in consequence of this wound?*

A. *Yes. I believe this wound caused the mortification.*

Q. *When do you believe death occurred?*

A. *On account of the putrefaction of the body, I believe that death took place either on the night of 10 August or the morning of 11 August.*

Q. *Were there any other wounds on the body?*

A. *Yes. There were a number of deep cuts, which had bled heavily.*

Q. *Do you believe the murder took place in the boathouse?*

A. *Yes. There was a large quantity of blood found at the back of the boathouse and no blood was found in Teesbank Hall.*

Q. *Were there any other injuries apart from those you have already mentioned?*

A. *No, Sir.*

Q. *How do you think Samuel Wainwright came to be in the boathouse?*

A. *I believe the attacker must have accompanied him because of the distance from the house and the young age of the deceased.*

Q. *And there was no sign of bruising on his body, for example, around the arms, indicating that he was taken to the boathouse against his will?*

A. *No, there was not.*

Q. *What conclusion would you draw from this?*

A. *I would conclude that Samuel Wainwright went there willingly, most likely with someone he knew.*

Q. *Are there any other matters you wish to bring to our attention?*

A. *Yes. I am no expert, Sir, but the white silk around the body was of a very fine quality and I do not believe it would be available locally.*

(The Witness withdrew)

Irrationally, I couldn't help scrutinizing the ground, wondering whether it still bore witness to what had happened. But all bloodstains had long since been washed away and, greedy to know more, I turned the page and read the statement from the next witness to be called.

WILLIAM BLACK called, sworn, and
examined by the CORONER.

Q. What are you?

A. I am the butler at Teesbank Hall in the Parish of Preston-on-Tees, in Eaglescliffe.

Q. Did you observe anything unusual on the morning of 11 August, which may be relevant to the murder of Samuel Wainwright?

A. Yes, Sir. The scullery door to the garden was unlocked and the key was missing from the board next to the servants' staircase.

Q. Is this believed to be how the child left the house?

A. Yes, Sir.

Q. Are you sure that the door was locked the previous evening?

A. Yes. Each evening at nine o'clock, I check all the windows and doors that lead to the outside. I also make sure that all the keys are placed on the board.

Q. Did you carry out this check on the evening of 10 August?

A. Yes, Sir.

Q. Who would have access to this key board?

A. (after a considerable pause) Anyone who was in the house and knew where the keys were kept.

Q. Would Samuel Wainwright have been able to take the key himself?

A. No; it was placed too high and the lock itself was too heavy for an infant to open.

(The Witness withdrew)

As I read on to the longest piece of testimony, there was a familiar name:

NANCY WILSON, called, sworn, and examined by the CORONER.

Q. What are you?

A. I am the nursemaid at Teesbank Hall.

Q. Was Samuel Wainwright the sole child in your care?

A. He was at first but when she — the French governess — left, I looked after Miss Clara and Miss Martha until a new governess could be found.

Q. Were you the first person to notice that Samuel Wainwright was missing?

A. Yes. I went to wake him on the morning but his cot was empty. I was not alarmed at first because I thought he must be playing with his sisters.

Q. When did you become alarmed?

A. I spoke to his sisters and they had not seen him. He didn't answer when called for. So I told Mrs Jenson, who is now the house-keeper at the Hall.

Q. What happened as a result of this?

A. All the servants began to search the Hall.

Q. Why did you not inform Mr and Mrs Wainwright immediately?

A. *We did not inform them until we was sure Samuel was missing. Mr Wainwright can become angry if disturbed for no reason.*

Q. *When was the last time you saw Samuel Wainwright?*

A. *When I put him to bed the previous evening.*

Q. *Can you tell us what happened on the previous evening?*

A. *The children had tea in the nursery and then I took them down to say goodnight to Mr and Mrs Wainwright. But Miss Clara was very petulant and would not leave so we was later to bed than usual.*

Q. *What was the cause of Miss Clara's bad temper?*

A. *Because he would not pick her up.*

Q. *What do you mean by that?*

A. *Mr Wainwright, Sir, was making a fuss of young Samuel and picking him up and pretending to throw him over his shoulder. Miss Clara asked if he would do the same with her but he said she was far too old to be treated as a baby.*

Q. *And this caused the bad temper?*

A. *Yes, Sir. Master Samuel is such a favourite with everyone. (Pause). I mean was such a favourite. Mrs Wainwright said it was a terrible shame Samuel was the only one in the family worthy of Mr Wainwright's affection.*
(There was a break in the inquest's proceedings.)

Q. *What did you do when you reached the bedroom?*

A. *We said our prayers and then I put Samuel to bed. His sisters is old enough to look after themselves and so I stayed with him.*

Q. *Samuel slept separately from his sisters?*

A. *Yes, Sir.*

Q. *Can you describe the sleeping arrangements to the proceedings?*
(NANCY WILSON *shook her head and there was a considerable pause.* MATTHEW WAINWRIGHT *approached the* CORONER *and showed him a sketch of the rooms he had hastily drawn.*)

Q. *Is it correct to say that anyone entering Samuel Wainwright's bedroom would have to pass through your room first?*

A. *Yes, Sir.*

Q. *Were you aware of anyone entering or leaving your room that night?*

A. *I don't know, Sir.*

Q. *Is it correct to say you were the last person to see Samuel Wainwright alive?*
(*A voice from the crowd, shouting, 'For shame! Are you saying a young lass would do such a terrible thing?'*)

A. *Why, Sir, except for them who has done this deed, I would have been.*
(*Further general shouts of 'It's the family you want to question. Not Nancy.'*)

Q. *Do you have knowledge of who might have carried out this murder?*

A. *Yes, Sir.*

Q. (*Pause*). *Who do you believe is the murderer?*

A. *It was Arielle Marchal, the French governess.*

Q. *Why would the governess wish to kill Samuel Wainwright?*

A. *Revenge, Sir. She hated them all, all the Wainwrights. They got rid of her because she was a whore.*

Q. (*addressed to Mr Wainwright*) *Is this true, Sir?*

A. *(spoken by Mr Wainwright) It is true.*

(Mrs Wainwright fell into a deep swoon and there was much jostling and shouting in the room. The Coroner insisted that Mrs Wainwright be taken to a place of rest. The inquest was adjourned.)

CHAPTER EIGHT

I was so lost in the bleak facts from the past I had forgotten the time. When I looked at Eleanor's bracelet watch I was shocked to see that almost thirty minutes had passed. Panic set in – what would I do if she failed to return? I had so much to lose if I was dismissed. It had been foolish to let her bribe me. I jumped up from the window seat and went to the door. My fright was over in a moment as, on the very dot of her agreed time of return, she appeared and came into the boathouse.

She had the same feverishness I'd seen yesterday and immediately asked, 'Did you find what you wished in the papers? Did you see that it was the governess who was responsible?'

'She was accused of the murder but that doesn't mean she was guilty. The magistrate seemed to suggest Nancy Wilson might have been involved. Perhaps she was shifting the blame – the child must have left through her room.'

'Nancy was not capable of murder.'

'She was cruel to you, with her stories of a ghost punishing you from beyond the grave for the slightest thing.'

'Nancy was certainly malicious, but she was too dull-witted to get away with murder. It cannot have been Nancy.'

'But could she have hidden the identity of the true killer?' I asked. 'And why did people in the crowd say your family should be asked about what hap—'

She cut me off: 'You can hardly expect me to answer that question.'

'No, I'm sorry.' We left the boathouse and stepped out into the sharp April sunshine. I walked slightly behind her now, trying to reflect on the significance of what I'd read in the courtroom documents. I didn't want to share my thoughts with Eleanor and there was some detail that nagged away at me.

She stopped. 'You don't believe it was the governess, do you?'

'Was Nancy Wilson's word the only proof? Surely that wasn't enough to condemn her to death.' I shivered as I thought of the gruesome public gallows where she had breathed her last. 'She had no reason to kill your brother.'

'Mrs Jenson always used to say that Nancy Wilson and Arielle Marchal were as thick as thieves. She wouldn't incriminate her friend unless she was guilty.'

I shook my head and then it struck me. 'Nancy Wilson said that the French governess had been dismissed from the house?'

'Yes, she was sent away in disgrace,' Eleanor replied.

'The house was locked up. The butler swore only someone inside the house could have had access to the key for the scullery door.'

Eleanor smiled a tight smile, as if rewarding me in some way for my cleverness, but said, 'She was tried at the Durham Assizes, only a few weeks after the murder. The judge stated the evidence against her was overwhelming. He said that she was an unnatural and degenerate woman.'

'But she was not inside the house,' I insisted. 'She wouldn't have had access to Samuel. Why didn't she say that in her defence?'

'She refused to speak at her trial. She stood mute on the witness stand and would not say a word. The jury took her silence as guilt.'

She held an obvious defence, one that must have been apparent on even the most superficial examination.

'If she wasn't the murderess, then the true culprit went undetected,' I said.

'And is living among us, you mean,' Eleanor murmured.

'Yes. Why was everyone so ready to believe she was guilty?' I said.

'Possibly it was convenient, I don't know,' Eleanor replied. 'But if she was not the killer, surely she would have spoken out.'

'She said nothing at all during her trial?'

'She confirmed her name, no more. Perhaps anyone can kill if they have a strong enough motive.'

'Did she have a motive?'

'I have already told you, Miss Caldwell, I will barter my knowledge for a portion of freedom. You may see the next instalment whenever you wish. I need only thirty minutes.'

I longed to know the story of what had happened, but the price Eleanor set was high and the panic of a moment ago was still fresh in my mind. I mustn't prove the truth of Uncle Thomas Stepford's warning and allow curiosity to destroy me. I shook my head.

She looked annoyed. 'I don't like to be crossed, Miss Caldwell, and what I ask for is really very little. In any case, I know you will change your mind in the end.'

With that, she turned in the direction of the Hall and I followed reluctantly.

Once we were back in the library, she acted as if I wasn't in the room. She sat at her table and began to draw, all the time humming tunelessly. I wondered what it was that demanded so much of her concentration – I found out when Henry came in.

'Henry, look at the likeness. Don't you think I've captured her exactly?' She presented the sheet of paper to him.

He peered at her drawing, then glanced across at me. He half laughed with surprise and recognition. 'Ellie, that isn't kind.'

'But it is her, isn't it? Perhaps I should have added a spyglass to complete the look.'

He was a little embarrassed and quickly changed the subject. 'Ellie, Edward and his sister are riding over from Long Newton this afternoon.'

'Rosalind Merryweather?' Eleanor interrupted, with a stricken look. 'Coming here?'

'Yes, coming here,' Henry repeated, refusing to acknowledge her obvious horror. 'I wonder if you'd like to join us for a walk in the grounds and then take tea.'

'Most definitely not. I've already been for a walk today, just ask Miss Caldwell.' She nodded across to me. 'It will do my complexion harm to spend too long in the sun and I don't like tea.'

'Since when have you cared about your complexion, Ellie? Miss Merryweather is a very pleasant young lady and could be a good friend to you. She lives only four miles away.'

Eleanor mumbled something, possibly words to the effect that she wished it were a further distance but then said determinedly to her brother, 'Unfortunately, I am far too tired to walk again today and will remain at my studies.'

He was obviously unhappy at her response, but said simply, 'Very well, Eleanor, but I will bring them up to the library. It would be rude not to see them and it's not good to cut yourself off in this way. If you were to give Miss Merryweather a chance, I'm sure you would find you had things in common.'

Eleanor refused to acknowledge his comment, but Henry's news had clearly put her into a foul mood.

As he left the room, he said, 'For my sake, at least pretend to be civil towards Edward and Rosalind.'

While this conversation took place, I had moved to the

window. I wanted to be as far away from them as possible and had no desire to be ridiculed. However, when Henry left the room, she pulled a face and sauntered across to me. 'Miss Caldwell, you have quite inspired me to be an artist. Perhaps you would like this keepsake of yourself.'

The picture she thrust into my hands was the cruellest kind of caricature. It was recognizably me, but with all my least favoured features accentuated: my plain face, the dark secretive eyes; and the familiar concerned expression that played about my lips. They were all there – jostling for the audience's attention, so that if someone might – out of kindness – have ignored my physical failings, they would see all my defects clearly before them. And it bothered me that Henry of all people should see me in this light. The costume I wore wasn't my own and, with a start of recognition, I realized it was the dark dress, with a neat white lace collar, I had seen on the French governess in the photograph.

She saw I had remembered. 'I thought the costume most appropriate for you, Miss Caldwell, but I must apologize. The picture is not yet finished. It lacks the most important detail.'

She took it from me and, with a neat stroke of her pencil, added a noose about the neck of my likeness. 'There, see. It is perfect now, Miss Caldwell.'

I refused to reply to her or even register any emotion because I knew that would provide her with satisfaction.

'Here take it, Miss Caldwell. It is a warning.' She stood very close to me, so that her face was only a few inches from mine and it took all my nerve not to flinch away from her. She was breathing heavily. 'If you insist on staying here, even though you are not wanted, you must face the consequences of your choice.'

'I have no choice,' I said, and turned away from her.

We sat in total silence for over two hours until the library door opened, and Henry came in with a young man and woman. They were all laughing and seemed in a very good mood.

'Eleanor, as I promised, I've brought Edward and Miss Merryweather to see you. I know you wouldn't want them to leave without welcoming them.' He looked at her warningly, as if daring her to state her true feelings.

'Oh, Eleanor, Henry told us you were unwell. It's such a shame you weren't able to walk in the grounds with us.' Just as Diana Wainwright had said, Rosalind was very pretty, with golden hair and unclouded blue eyes. She looked around the room now and exclaimed, 'And what a charming room, but there are so many books here! Surely you haven't read all of these, Mr Wainwright.'

Henry shook his head. 'No, I haven't but Eleanor probably has.'

'You must be so clever, Eleanor,' Rosalind continued. 'I do mean to read more but I am bored after half an hour of sitting down, then have to be up and doing something interesting.'

Henry clearly feared the direction the conversation might

take after her remark and turned to me. 'This is Miss Caldwell, Eleanor's governess.'

Edward and Rosalind bowed in acknowledgement and Rosalind smiled very sweetly at me. 'Oh, how admirable to be independent and make your own way in the world. You quite put me to shame and, if you're a governess, you must be very clever too.'

'It is better than being ignorant,' Eleanor growled.

Rosalind went slightly pink and Henry was forced to say, 'As I told you, poor Eleanor is unwell and that has affected her mood. Let us go to see my grandmother. She particularly wished to speak to you both.'

In a moment they were gone, Eleanor and I left alone. 'Five minutes in Rosalind Merryweather's company always makes me feel like vomiting,' she declared.

'But she seems very nice,' I replied.

'Exactly.' And with that, she returned to her book of Latin grammar.

CHAPTER NINE

A few days after this, Mrs Jenson came into the library and said she needed to speak to me. My first thought was that Eleanor had told her how she had been left alone and I would be sent away in disgrace, but she said, 'I'm going to Stockton-on-Tees tomorrow and wish you to accompany me. I have some provisions to buy for the household and it will be useful for me to have a companion to help with any carrying.'

'What about Miss Eleanor?' I asked.

'Agnes can be freed from her household duties for a few hours and will be able to take care of her while you're away. Stockton is a market town and quite sizeable. You may find it of interest.'

'I'd like that very much then, Mrs Jenson.'

It would be good to be away from the claustrophobic atmosphere of Teesbank Hall. I had been there only a short time and already I felt as if the world had closed in around me. Its setting was physically remote, with very few people living nearby. There was a hunting lodge a mile or so away, which was owned by Lord Londonderry, but it was usually empty, but for a skeleton staff of the housekeeper and groundsman. In any case, they would have nothing to do with us – the servants regarded Teesbank Hall as cursed, and the established Londonderry family saw the Wainwrights as social inferiors.

'I hoped you would agree. It'll give us an opportunity to discuss Miss Eleanor's behaviour away from any interruptions.'

So that was the real reason for the invitation.

The next day was fine and cool, and Mrs Jenson and I set off in the Wainwrights' carriage. There was something of a holiday air about the proceedings and she was dressed in her best clothes, her hat worn at a rather jaunty angle. Much to my horror, her pampered spaniel accompanied us and insisted upon lying across my feet, so that they were pinned to the floor. He was named Albert in honour of the dead prince and suffered from the most severe flatulence, due to his over-rich diet, which meant the carriage windows had to be open throughout the journey, even though there was a chill to the April air.

At first, we talked of general things such as the weather and places of interest to a first-time visitor to the town. However, once we had exhausted these pleasantries, she asked me directly, 'So, Miss Caldwell, how have you found your time at the Hall?'

I hesitated, uncertain of my reply. If there had been anything at all maternal about Mrs Jenson, I would have revealed to her the muffled sobs and bangs I had heard on my second night, possibly even the image I had seen in the mirror, although I wasn't quite sure how I could put that into words. If there had been any sign of softness in those black eyes, I might have told her about my homesickness and how I found Eleanor's contempt difficult to bear. Instead I replied carefully, 'My room is very comfortable, thank you. I have everything I need.'

'You have slept well at Teesbank?' she asked.

'I . . . I . . . Yes, I have slept well.' The grey circles under my eyes gave the true answer to that question but I couldn't confide in the housekeeper. Her questions felt like an attempt to trick me into some revelation, so I continued, 'Teesbank Hall is very removed from society.'

This seemed to satisfy her because she nodded. 'The house is quite out of the way and not to everyone's taste, but I have been here for over twenty years and it has suited me well enough.'

I knew she had been there at the time of the murder. Her grim face had stared out at me from the formal photograph of the household. I dared not speak such thoughts aloud but instead asked how long we would spend in Stockton.

'I have a number of merchants to visit and then I intend to see my sister for an hour or so. You'll be at liberty to explore the town, if you wish.' She paused. There were clearly other matters she wished to discuss. 'You have now been Miss Eleanor's governess for more than a month and no doubt you'll have formed an opinion as to her character.'

I nodded cautiously and she continued, 'Mr and Mrs

Wainwright wish to know whether you have observed any undesirable traits in her behaviour in that time.'

What was I expected to say in response? Everything about Eleanor's behaviour seemed undesirable to me yet Mrs Jenson and the other servants accepted it as normal. 'I'm afraid Miss Eleanor doesn't much like me and there seems to be nothing I can teach her. She's made it clear she wants me to leave.'

She ignored this last comment and said, with a note of annoyance. 'Mr Henry has indulged Eleanor with her book-learning, but what I must ask of you is ... have you seen any qualities that would give you cause for concern? Has she done or said anything you might consider strange or unseemly?'

Again, I did not know how to answer. 'She can be wilful at times.'

'That she can. Only Mr Henry has any real power over her and even he does not know the half of what she is capable of. She is a close and secretive girl.' Mrs Jenson then continued, 'So there is nothing particularly upsetting in her behaviour for me to report upon?'

'She took me to the boathouse.'

Mrs Jenson's face closed down. 'She will be spoken to about that.'

'The murder. She told me of the murder of her brother, Samuel Wainwright.'

Mrs Jenson looked away. 'Yes,' she said. 'But it's in the past now. It only causes harm to speak of it. The family have all suffered for what happened then.'

I couldn't help asking, 'Why didn't they move away from Teesbank Hall after his death? By staying they must be constantly reminded of what happened.'

She considered for a moment, and I remembered that first day, when she had warned me against asking questions, but finally she spoke: 'I believe Mrs Wainwright was desperate to leave, but the senior Mrs Wainwright would have none of it and Matthew always follows his mother's wishes. She and her husband Joshua built the Hall and she refused to live anywhere else.'

'Yet it must hold such terrible memories.'

'She said it would look as if they were running away, if they left. She's not a woman to be intimidated by anyone.'

Surprised by Mrs Jenson's openness, I dared to ask, 'Miss Eleanor has had a number of different governesses, I believe.'

'Yes, there have been several. One of the young women, Miss Lilian Howard, proved to be very unsuitable and was told to go.' Distaste flashed briefly across her face.

Miss Lilian Howard. I had heard the name before. She was the only governess Eleanor considered capable of educating her.

'Also, as you know, Miss Eleanor can be difficult and the house is isolated. Not everyone wants to live far from a town, so others chose to leave.' She then weighed up what should be revealed next. 'Perhaps you would not judge her so harshly if you knew a little of her childhood.'

'I don't judge . . .' I said, but Mrs Jenson waved away my words.

'As a small child, she was left in the sole care of Nancy Wilson, who was a feckless and vindictive girl. It had a most detrimental effect on Miss Eleanor.'

From Eleanor and the inquest report, I already knew who she was but pretended ignorance so that I might find out more from Mrs Jenson. 'Nancy Wilson?'

She puffed out her cheeks. 'She was the children's nurse-maid for many years and should never have been allowed to stay after Samuel was taken. She was careless and the mur-der warped her mind.'

'Why was she kept on, then?' I dared to ask.

'The house was in such confusion. Mr and Mrs Wain-wright were so lost in their own grief, I think they ceased to care very much what happened. Certainly, the two girls, Clara and Martha, were overlooked and ran wild. They were sent away to a boarding school in the end.'

'Are Clara and Martha Miss Eleanor's elder sisters?' Ghost names from the inquest papers. Blurred faces on a sepia pho-tograph. They were never mentioned by anyone and Eleanor had refused to tell me what had become of them.

'Yes, they were the two older Wainwright girls. Both gone. This house has been visited by much sorrow.' Mrs Jenson closed her eyes briefly and was silent.

Only Henry and Eleanor remained, I reflected, a whole earlier family dead and buried.

'And Nancy was obsessed with the murder. She talked about it constantly. She used to take Miss Eleanor to the boathouse –' Mrs Jenson nodded at me – 'where she took you, and they would sit there together, picking over all the gruesome details of the killing.'

'But Eleanor was only a young child. Why did nobody intervene?'

'Nobody knew. Mr Henry was away at school and she's never been close to her parents. She didn't tell anybody what was happening and it wasn't until she began to have night terrors that we knew something was wrong. She made herself ill because she was afraid to sleep. Finally, the doctor was called. It didn't take him long to work out what was wrong with her.' Mrs Jenson stopped, then continued, 'They got rid of the nursemaid after that, but the damage was done and the poor girl's mind had been warped. And it is my belief there were other consequences. That is why she must be constantly watched.'

'And the house too. Surely living in the house where her brother had been murdered must have affected her.' I remembered Eleanor telling me how Teesbank was tainted by the secrets of the past.

Mrs Jenson wouldn't be contradicted. 'It was the behaviour of Nancy Wilson that turned her mind. She grew up knowing more about the dead than the living and remains convinced the Hall is haunted. That is a sore trial to her parents. They can't bear the past to be spoken of.'

I didn't wholly believe Mrs Jenson's account and so was silent. After a while, we fell back into polite conversation, but neither of us had our heart in it.

We were both relieved when we arrived at our destination

and Cooper, the coachman, asked us to jump down so he could take the carriage to a meadow on the outskirts of town. He would rest the horses there and take the reluctant Albert for a walk. Cooper was then to return in a few hours' time and pick us up from the Shambles, a covered market dating from medieval times, which was at the centre of the high street.

Stockton is a bustling town, with many striking examples of Georgian architecture, similar in some ways to Teesbank Hall but without its grave-like hush. From the very first moment, though, it was impossible to ignore the strange reactions of the people we encountered. Many passers-by stared at us, whispered comments were made, and a woman with pursed lips dragged her young son across the road and away from us.

'People can be ignorant,' Mrs Jenson commented. She walked briskly along the high street, seemingly immune to the effect our presence had. In the butcher's and grocer's, she spoke in a firm tone – instantly complaining if she felt she were not being given the finest quality and asserting defiantly that she was buying on behalf of Teesbank Hall so her account was valuable.

When we had finished visiting all the shops on her list, Mrs Jenson said, 'I've arranged to meet my sister at her house in Finkle Street, which will allow you some time to explore by yourself. The walk from the parish church along the river is pleasant and should take you an hour or so.' She waved to the left. 'I expect you to be by the Shambles at one o'clock prompt, Miss Caldwell.'

With this, she turned and walked away. I was glad to have some time alone and hoped I might be more anonymous without the company of Mrs Jenson to mark me as attached to the Wainwright family. The path by the Tees was easy to find and I followed the meandering route of the river, enjoying the feel of the sun against my face and taking in my surroundings.

Suddenly my daydreams came crashing to a halt at the sight of two men walking in my direction. They were deep in conversation and hadn't noticed me. There was the horror of familiarity. Uncle Thomas Stepford. Father's only brother. Having disgraced the family name, he used his stage name to hide his true one. He was dressed in the greasy black coat and tails of the showman.

The sun shone brightly behind him, but his frame blotted out the light and his face was thrown into darkness. My whole being was centred upon the shadow of his looming figure and I felt the blood drain from my face.

Even now, with the gap of several decades, I can smell again the fear of seeing him – an acrid, bitter stench. He was tall and thickset, towering over those around him. Yet the power he held was more than physical. It was there in my dreams – the blinding light that shot through everything, leaving my brain dazzled, showing me in negative.

Oh, God, I had run so far – surely he could not have found me.

He was wealthy now, living in my father's house and a respected scientist, or so he said. I knew he was no more than a charlatan, who had earned his living as a performer, travelling the length and breadth of the country, attracting gawping crowds as he displayed the art of phrenology. His fraud was cloaked in the language of science. The brain itself was made up of different organs, or so he claimed, each related to a different aspect of human nature. The skull grew to accommodate these organs: someone who was particularly benevolent would have a large forehead, for that was where the seat of benevolence lay, while someone who was marked as argumentative would have an indentation behind the right ear. In his eyes, character could be reduced to the lumps upon someone's head.

As Cousin Lucy and I sat trapped in the rigid formality of the dining table, he would repeat that the skull was the key to the soul. He had a stock of endless tales, of criminals who had been betrayed by a protuberance on their head. Or lovestruck women who married badly because they had ignored his advice about a prominent bump denoting avarice in their suitors. We were forced to listen attentively and would giggle afterwards, when he left the room, stuffing our fists into our mouths to mask the sound. But I did not tell her about the other things that happened. I could not.

I leaned against an old gateway to stop my legs giving way beneath me. There was no hiding-place and I stood helplessly, watching the figures advancing up the path and accepted my fate. Yet as they turned out of the shadow I saw I had been mistaken and it was not Uncle Thomas Stepford at all but a much younger man who was of a similar build. Only in my terror at being discovered had I confused him with my uncle. His power over me was such that his existence haunted my mind – I saw him everywhere and traced him in the features of strangers.

My shock must have written itself across my face for the nearer of the two men approached me and asked whether I was quite well and if they could be of assistance. I shook my head weakly, too overwhelmed to speak, and they carried on walking. It had not been Uncle Thomas Stepford this time, but I knew he would try to track me down – he was a determined man and I was too valuable to him. I must let this shock remind me of what I was running from. Although Teesbank Hall was a bleak place, it was a sanctuary and there were worse terrors to be faced.

My peace of mind was gone and I returned to the Shambles to await Mrs Jenson's arrival. When she came back, I was in no mood to talk and told her I felt ill. We sat in silence on the journey back to the Hall. When she asked me to accompany her to Stockton the following week, I refused. I suspected this angered her, but I couldn't risk being seen. It was better to remain hidden away.

CHAPTER TEN

That evening, I couldn't face being alone in my bedroom and decided to sit in the servants' hall, where at least I could guarantee company. Mrs Jenson rarely went there, preferring the solitary dignity of her sitting room, but Mrs Hargreaves, the cook, usually occupied pride of place by the fire and could be relied upon to provide a stock of stories and ready opinions. I came and sat down quietly near to the door.

Eliza glared across at me and muttered, to no one in particular, 'What's Miss High and Mighty doing here?'

Agnes nudged her and said something quietly. After that, Eliza left me alone and I was able to lose myself in the soothing chatter of the other women.

Mr Wainwright had just returned from one of his frequent business trips to Newcastle, and his lurking presence threw a shadow over the lives of all the young female servants. Eliza had warned me about him when I first arrived, but an hour in his company was evidence enough to avoid him whenever possible. He drank heavily and reeked of wine mixed with the spiced wood scent of Dominican cigars. His favourite strategy was to creep up unawares on a lone servant, knowing that his position as master of the house made it almost impossible to protest at his wandering hands and muttered innuendoes. I probably suffered the least from his attentions because I was in Eleanor's company all day, and that was the one place he could be guaranteed to avoid. His lecherous ways were a staple of the servants' hall gossip.

The target of his worst abuses was Mary, a very pretty shy girl who had just started at the Hall. There had been some incident the previous evening when he had come into the kitchen where she was alone and pretended to be looking for something. 'And when I handed the glass to him, he put his hands upon me just here.' With an air of embarrassment, she pointed to her breasts. 'He was stinking of the drink and he said the most terrible thing.'

'What did he say?' Eliza demanded to know.

Mary blushed. 'I don't want to repeat it but Mrs Jenson came in just then, and if she hadn't, I don't know what would have happened.'

'Oh, he's a dirty old pig,' Eliza said. 'I've taken to eating lumps of raw onion so if he comes anywhere near me I just breathe on him, strong as you like, and say, "Ha!" then watch his face crease with disgust.'

'Oh, I'd never dare do such a thing,' Mary said.

'Well, more fool you, Mary. It's always the quiet ones who get caught.'

'But, Eliza, how can you bear the stink of onions all day

long? It's bad enough when I can smell them on my fingers after chopping for Mrs Hargreaves,' Agnes added.

'I'd rather eat onion than have that beast with his hands all over me,' Eliza answered.

'What about his wife?' Mary said. 'Surely she must see how he carries on. Why doesn't she say anything?'

'I'm sure she knows exactly what he's up to but I reckon she's just happy it's not her he's chasing after.' Eliza laughed. 'The pair of them can't even bear to be in the same room. Can you imagine them in the same bed?'

They giggled together and Mrs Hargreaves looked up from her knitting. 'Now, girls, you know it's not proper to speak of the master and mistress in that way.'

'And you know we're saying no more than the truth!' Eliza retorted.

Mrs Hargreaves put down her needles. 'They're such an ill-suited couple, although both were very handsome when they were younger. That's where the attraction must have been. When I started, nearly thirty years ago, a lot of the maids were sweet on Mr Wainwright.'

This shocked us all, as we contemplated the possibility of Matthew Wainwright ever having been anything other than a raddled, overweight menace.

'And Mrs Wainwright, well, she was always expecting, with one confinement after another, although most never came to term.'

'I'd have chopped Mr Wainwright's whatsit off years ago, if I'd been her,' Eliza interjected.

'Stop there, Eliza. That's going too far,' Mrs Hargreaves scolded, quickly changing the subject. 'Why, Mrs Wainwright nearly lost Master Henry. He was born a month early, what with the shock of the murder. God rest poor Samuel's soul.'

The door opened and Mrs Jenson came into the room. We all sat up a little bit straighter and she marched straight over to Eliza. Without any greeting, she demanded, 'How many times have you been told that the knives must be counted after every meal? Especially after supper.'

'I always count them, Mrs Jenson. All the knives were there tonight.'

'In that case, how do you account for this?' Mrs Jenson brandished a fish knife at her and Eliza's face went scarlet. 'This was under the table when I was checking the room, so clearly all the knives weren't there.'

'I'm ever so sorry, Mrs Jenson. I must have counted wrong.'

'Well, don't let it happen again or you might well find yourself looking for a new position.'

The housekeeper left the room and there was a moment's silence before Agnes said, 'It's an easy mistake to make, isn't it? Mrs Jenson does go on a bit.'

She glanced across at Mrs Hargreaves, who picked up on the previous conversation. 'Mind, Mary, you need to be careful. There was another girl, shy just like you, about seven or eight years ago. He wouldn't leave her alone, always jumping on her. She ended up in the family way, and her little more than a bairn herself.'

Mary looked shocked. 'Oh, the poor thing.'

'Her family would have nothing to do with her – her not being married and that – and she had nowhere to go. She died in the workhouse giving birth.'

'It's not right, is it?' Eliza exclaimed. 'Why should she suffer and him carry on with no punishment whatsoever?'

'Oh, I think he has been punished. There was that other one . . .' Mrs Hargreaves paused. 'I think he loved her, but his mother put a stop to it, and then all the terrible things happened.'

Eliza and the others were desperate to know what Mrs Hargreaves meant by this, but she shook her head and was so definite that the subject was dropped. Instead, Agnes turned to me and asked, 'How have you found Miss Eleanor?'

I was quite surprised to be included in the conversation but, after a moment's hesitation as to how honest I should be, I replied, 'She can be difficult and I find her moods hard to judge sometimes.'

'Well, that's putting it mildly,' said Eliza. 'I'm more than happy to stay working in the kitchen if it keeps me out of the way of her tantrums.'

Mrs Hargreaves tutted at Eliza, then said, 'The eldest one, Miss Clara, was much worse, mind. And I'm not saying Miss Eleanor isn't bad but that other one . . . There was something about her that wasn't right.'

'What d'you mean?' Eliza wanted to know.

'It's not my place to say, but there were times when I was frightened of her. Still it's all in the past now, and in this house, it's best not to talk about the past.'

'My mother didn't want me to come and work here. She said Teesbank Hall is cursed and the Wainwrights are a blighted family,' Mary added. She had gone very pale and left the room a few moments later, breaking up the conversation.

I was the last to go to bed that night, hoping tiredness would chase away memories of Uncle Thomas Stepford – but he was persistent.

CHAPTER ELEVEN

That heavy, thick breathing and the catch of desire. The light that was always too bright. I held up my hand to shade my eyes and made out the familiar dark shape standing over me. 'I can't,' I said. 'I can't.' My skin was already sweating at the imagined touch. I would be sick. The nausea rose in my throat. He would be angry. 'I can't.'

'It's what you want. I knew you would find me in time.' He was always so certain.

'I didn't look. I didn't try to find you.'

'But I was always there. Written into you. Written into your bone.' The dark shape was coming closer and I was terrified I would be suffocated by it. I had to escape but I was frozen by the light and couldn't move. 'I can't!' I was shouting now and my whole body was alive with terror. 'I can't!'

There was an insistent knocking and a terrified voice, 'Miss Caldwell, Miss Caldwell. Are you all right, Miss?'

I stopped shouting but my heart pounded so loudly it

filled the room. I was not in Swaffham. I was not in that room. It was nearly three hundred miles away.

'Agnes?' I asked, trying to stop my voice from shaking. The candle had burned out and it was still the middle of the night.

A moment's hesitation. 'Yes, miss. Are you all right? Can I come in?'

I dragged the white quilt about me and unlocked the bedroom door. She was standing there. 'You was shouting out so loud I thought someone must have been murdering you.'

'It was just a nightmare.' My skin was still clammy and Swaffham was more real than Agnes, standing there in front of me.

'Just as long as you're all right, miss,' she said, and turned as if to leave.

'Agnes, please don't go.' I didn't want to be alone. If I was alone, those thoughts would come back into my head. 'Couldn't you stay a while and talk? I don't think I can go back to sleep.'

She came into the room. It was cold in the middle of the night, so we wrapped ourselves in the quilt and lay squashed together on the narrow bed. Agnes's teeth were chattering and her feet were two blocks of ice against mine. 'I used to have nightmares too – lots of us did in the workhouse.'

'I didn't know you were in the workhouse,' I said.

'Me, yes, and Eliza too. We were at the workhouse in Bishop Auckland together.'

'You were friends before you came to Teesbank, then?'

'Yes, I suppose so, as much as anyone could be in that place. She came to work here a few months after I did.'

'What was it like? In the workhouse.' I was desperate for Agnes to keep talking. Her words might blot out the horror of my nightmare.

She said wryly, 'I learned to scream quietly when I had nightmares, otherwise I'd be told to shut up. No one ever came to comfort me. That's why I needed to see if you was all right.'

'That's terrible!' I exclaimed.

'I was there right from when I was born. I didn't know any other life until I came here. Maybe that's why I can put up with Teesbank Hall better than most,' she said.

'Is the workhouse as hard as people say?'

She seemed thoughtful. 'No, probably not as bad. Life there was just nothing, I suppose. Nothing.' She was silent for a while and I thought she wasn't going to add anything else but then she said carefully, 'Bishop Auckland workhouse wasn't an awful place, not like some are. I was rarely hit and we were never starved. The superintendent was enlightened.' She laughed. 'Yes, that's what he called it. We had lessons every day in reading and writing and arithmetic. I'm probably better learned than those who grew up outside the workhouse.'

'And yet what?' I prompted.

In the darkness, I felt her face turn towards mine. Her words were so quiet, I had to strain to catch them. 'I was just lost. There were so many other children there and I was such a mouse. People couldn't be bothered to remember my name half the time. No one was cruel but no one cared much about me either. I've no memory of what it is to be loved by a mam or dad.'

'Oh, Agnes, I'm so sorry.' No matter how bad my life had become, at least I'd known what it was to be loved.

'Thank you, Miss Caldwell, but I've learned to be tougher. At first, I was too scared to stand on my own two feet and stayed on at the workhouse as a general maid, even though I was miserable there. But by the time I was eighteen, I wanted to see the world, so I left to go into domestic service.'

'And you came here?' I said incredulously.

'If there's anywhere in the world that it's possible to get a position, it's here – no one in their right mind would choose to work in this place,' she said bitterly.

'That makes two of us.' There was a moment of recognition, and then we talked of other things. It was safer that way.

After a while, I asked her, 'Why does Eleanor hate me so much?'

'It's not you she hates in particular. It's just that she knows the governesses spy on her. The last one, Miss Richardson, made this big pretence of wanting to be friends with Eleanor, then told nasty tales on her to Mr Wainwright. She got her into real trouble.'

'But that's not my fault!'

'No, but she's learned not to trust anyone. It's a lonely life for her. She was really close to one of her governesses, Miss Howard, but then she had to leave.'

'Why?' I asked.

'There was some kind of problem. I'm not sure what,' Agnes said vaguely. 'I think she left under a cloud. No one talks about it. After that the Wainwrights got a nurse in for night times and Eleanor wasn't allowed to go out anywhere by herself.'

'Poor Eleanor.' It was strange to pity her. I dared to ask, 'Mrs Jenson always wants to know whether Eleanor's done anything but I don't know what she means. Have I seen the worst of her behaviour?'

'No, not really. You wouldn't ask if you had.'

'What is it she does that's so terrible?'

'Oh, Miss Caldwell, I wish you wouldn't ask so many questions. It isn't my place to say anything. I've got to be up at five and must get some rest.' With that, she turned away from me and pretended to fall asleep.

I lay awake in the darkness and wondered why everyone was reluctant to tell me the truth about Eleanor.

CHAPTER TWELVE

By the time I presented myself in the schoolroom at seven, I already felt weary and my spirits sank further when I saw that Henry was there in place of Mrs Anderson. We nodded at each other coldly before he returned to his discussion with Eleanor. They were talking and laughing – how unlike the sullen silences she shared with me.

She glanced briefly in my direction, 'Henry is here this morning. You may go now. He will sit with me.'

'You know I must stay, Miss Eleanor, unless Mrs Jenson releases me from my duties.'

She pulled a face. 'Well, then, you should find something to busy yourself with and not disturb us.'

Sighing, I sat quietly in the corner as they talked together. I had set myself the task of reading the complete works of William Shakespeare and was just at the point in *Hamlet* where the Danish prince was confronting the ghost of his dead father. Dramatic though the story was, I couldn't keep my mind on the play. Henry and Eleanor were speaking about a trip he had made to London, and snatches of their conversation allowed me glimpses of an outside world, far from the confines of Teesbank Hall.

Eleanor was animated, her voice enthusiastic. 'There will be the lectures too, Henry. Remember the spring before last, when I heard Thomas Huxley speak at Owen College in Manchester with Lilian – I mean Miss Howard?'

'Yes, Ellie, I remember,' he smiled, 'but—'

'According to *The Times*, one of the Tuesday evening lectures is to be about Darwinism. Can you imagine being able to debate the great theories and ideas of our time?'

I couldn't help interrupting: 'I've met Charles Darwin.'

They both looked at me, astonished, and Eleanor asked, 'How could *you* have met Mr Darwin?'

I reddened slightly. Perhaps I had said too much. I didn't want to draw attention to my past, but as both Henry and Eleanor were now looking at me expectantly, I continued, 'Father was in correspondence with him for many years. They were contemporaries at Cambridge and both maintained an interest in farming practices. He came to stay at our house once.' That would have to satisfy them. I would say no more.

However, Eleanor was intrigued and looked at me with a grudging respect. 'You have met Charles Darwin?' she repeated, astounded. 'What did you speak of?'

I hardly liked to admit that his only words to me had been praise for the quince jam made by our cook – I knew Eleanor well enough to realize that that would not impress her. Instead I murmured something about his very interesting ideas on how drainage could be improved in the Fens, which she found intriguing, but when I was unable to expand on the topic, she resumed her talk with Henry, although every so often she glanced across, as if reassessing me.

Henry had just been to South Kensington and had seen the site where the London International Exhibition would be based in the coming months. 'I would like more than anything to go to the exhibition, Henry. There will be designers and manufacturers from all over the world, bringing with them new ideas and technologies. Everything is changing so rapidly and I want to be part of it, not buried alive here.'

'It will all be reported in the newspapers. You can read about it there, Ellie.'

'But I want to see it! Reading about it is not the same as experiencing it. Would you beg Father that I might be allowed to accompany you to London?'

He shook his head reluctantly. 'You know I've tried many times. The answer is always the same. Father believes you need the peace of Teesbank Hall.'

'What peace does he think there is for me? It's worse than death, being trapped in our family's past and not allowed—'

'Ellie, stop!' Henry insisted. Although I was looking down at my book, pretending to read, I was sure they had both glanced at me.

Eleanor was silent for a few moments. When she spoke again, she was more composed. 'I would promise to be with you at all times. Father might allow it then. You have my word nothing would happen.'

'It's not as simple as that, Ellie. You know what Father says. You'll have to wait until you are well . . .' His voice trailed away.

'I will never be what he calls well, Henry. We both know that.' Her voice carried a note of such despair that I couldn't help but look at her.

At that very moment Eleanor caught my eye. 'Oh, God, Henry,' she exclaimed, 'it is insufferable! She is watching me again. I cannot do anything – I cannot even think – without her spying upon me.' Her voice shook with distress. 'All of this, everything, is too much to bear but she makes it a thousand times worse with her quiet prying. I will not speak another word. I will not cry in front of her. She will write it all down so even my thoughts are not my own. But what of me? How can I live like this? I am shut out from any kind of life.' Eleanor stumbled from the room, slamming the door behind her.

Henry and I stood up in the same instant. My heart was pounding and I was sickened at the truth of what she had said, but I knew my job was to follow her and check upon what she might be doing.

Henry blocked my way to the door and demanded of me, 'How can you lower yourself to mistreat my sister in this way? Do you have so little sense of morality that you think it's acceptable to spy on her and take away the small portion of freedom she has? Eleanor has been pushed to the point of despair and you allow yourself to be a part of this.'

Now I felt anger rise within me. 'It is you who are in the wrong! I didn't choose to spy upon her. I came as a governess, nothing more, and now I'm forced into a role where it is my poverty alone that buys my compliance.'

He was stunned: until this point, I had covered up my feelings.

'You are wealthy – you are a man and may travel freely in the world. But I am a woman and I must support myself. I'm in a position that I did not choose – that I would not choose,' I said bitterly. 'Please don't presume to judge me because I am poor and destitute. If you must allocate blame, then look to your parents for it is they who demand Miss Eleanor should be watched at all times.'

I stopped. I had said too much. Cousin Lucy had always warned me I was too defiant and would suffer because of it. It was inevitable that I would be sent away. My hand went to my mouth as if I could take back the words I had spoken.

Henry stood shocked and silent. Then he said, 'I am sorry, Miss Caldwell. I didn't understand the difficulty of your position. As you say, our situations are very different. I will find Eleanor and try to make her return to the schoolroom.'

After he had left, I sank down in my chair.

The incident marked a turning-point in my relationship with Henry because, from this time onwards, he was increasingly courteous towards me and more respectful – there was no more of the whispering with Eleanor and glances thrown in my direction. I suppose he had seen me as a willing accomplice in the spying. Even she was sometimes less dismissive and hostile, and I suspected Henry had spoken to her, asking her to treat me more kindly.

Henry attended the newly established University of Durham, which was within easy reach of Teesbank Hall. I learned from Mrs Jenson that he had chosen this institution over the more ancient Cambridge so he might be close at hand if occasion demanded. I took this to mean if Eleanor needed him. He was studying mathematics but had some hopes he might take up a position in the Church, an unlikely aspiration in the light of his father's fierce hatred of religion.

When Henry was at home, he spent time in the library talking to Eleanor. He would sometimes try to involve me in the conversation, as if to negotiate a friendship between Eleanor and me and lighten the dark atmosphere of our schoolroom. But I knew, as he seemed not to, that she was already angry enough that my silent presence encroached upon their time together. If I were to be included in their discussions, there would be no limit to her disapproval. Therefore, when he asked my opinion on the actions of Garibaldi or Otto von Bismarck, or the architecture of the newly opened Royal Albert Hall, I would answer only cautiously, sometimes feigning a lack of interest and continuing with whatever task I had to hand. In fact, I longed for conversation during those hours, and he was the only person who showed any inclination to speak to me, but I feared Eleanor's retaliation more than I desired the pleasures of friendship.

My previous life had been secluded. I had no living siblings and Father didn't want to send me away to school, so I was educated at home with a governess. But I was a happy child, although perhaps a little serious. I liked the familiarity of our routine, meeting with Cook to plan meals, the treat of accompanying Father on his medical rounds, and occasional visits from friends he had made through his scientific interests. We had lost contact with Mother's family over time, they were too far away, and Father had only one surviving relative: Uncle Thomas Stepford.

Even when the terrible times came – I refused to think of them in more detail – I had the consolation of my friendship with Lucy. As Father and Uncle Thomas Stepford were estranged from each other, we didn't meet until after Father's death. She was unlike anyone I had ever encountered before and made me giggle at the most ridiculous things. I was both shocked by and admiring of her audaciousness. She told me she'd had to grow up quickly in the world of travelling showmen and it was dangerous to be too timid. 'You must never trust anyone,' she told me solemnly.

She had a sweet prettiness, with hair so fair it was almost white and jade green eyes. When spoken to by her father and other adults, she would answer in a dutiful voice and look demurely at the floor, but once we were alone together, she would talk for hours on end and laugh at the foolishness of whoever she had succeeded in charming.

Lucy said I was the only person in the world with whom she could be herself – for everyone else she played a part. I remember once she'd hugged me so fiercely that I couldn't breathe and exclaimed, 'I'm glad we've found each other. You are my only true friend.'

'And you're mine too, Lucy. I can't stop laughing when we're together.'

She smiled at that and, still holding me tightly, said, 'Promise me we'll never be apart.'

I paused for a moment. 'Of course we'll never be apart, not now that we've finally found each other.' How could I tell her I was already planning my escape? It would be impossible to explain the full extent of her father's behaviour towards me.

'Harriet, we could be sisters. We're similar in so many ways.'

Inwardly I was flattered because she was much more adventurous than I, and I protested, 'But we're very different. I've always lived in Swaffham and you've toured England with your father's show and seen much more of the world.'

She shook her head. 'All I've seen is cheap lodgings in one town after another. In the end, the places merged into each other. In truth, I was just as isolated as you. I've never really known someone of my own age.'

'Yes, we are similar in that,' I agreed.

Lucy had an amazing talent for mimicry and reduced me to helpless fits of giggles, with her impressions of Cook complaining about soured milk or her father pontificating on phrenology.

Once Father's lawyer, Mr Braithwaite, came to visit the house. He was a very kind man, but quite timid and with a pronounced stammer, which became worse if he was flustered. In his will, Father had arranged a small annuity for my old nurse, but there had been some problem and she hadn't received the money. Mr Braithwaite wished to speak to my uncle about the matter and, I think, use it as an excuse to check on my welfare. Lucy and I were called to the sitting room. The two men had clearly been arguing immediately before we came in and Uncle Thomas Stepford stood glowering in the corner.

'M-my dear Harriet, how are you?' Mr Braithwaite asked.

'I'm well, sir. It's very good to see you,' I replied, feeling a pang for the lost life his reassuring presence represented. Would it be possible to reveal something of my true situation, with Uncle watching so closely?

'And y-you. It's several months s-since we've met.' He smiled kindly at me.

I was about to answer when Lucy stepped forward. 'I-I am Lucy, H-Harriet's cousin. W-w-we h-haven't met before.' Somehow she'd caught his voice exactly. She glanced across at me and I felt myself on the verge of giggling.

He looked at her, unsure whether she was mocking him, and a pink flush rose steadily upwards from his neck. 'I-I-I h-hope all is w-w-well,' he asked me, his stammer becoming more pronounced.

'Yes, Mr Braithwaite, thank you, and I hope your family is well.'

'I-I-I h-hope s-so too,' Lucy cut in.

Poor Mr Braithwaite was beside himself with embarrassment and left quickly after that, closely followed by Uncle Thomas Stepford, who wanted to make sure he was gone.

'Lucy, you've driven him away. It was unkind,' I exclaimed.

She stopped suddenly, the blood draining from her face. 'Whatever do you mean?'

'He knew you were mocking him and he is such a good-hearted man.'

'Harriet, I'm so sorry. I didn't mean to cause any offence. Sometimes my desire for fun runs away with me and I don't think about what I'm doing. I promise I won't behave like that next time.'

There was no next time as Mr Braithwaite didn't return to the house, but instead conducted all his business through his office in the town and I didn't see him again.

It was the thought of Lucy that made me most homesick in those early months. Eleanor would never replace her as my closest friend, but I wanted to create some relationship between us. The family took *The Times*, which would be delivered to the library after Mr and Mrs Wainwright had finished with it. I had taken to reviewing the pages and circling articles I thought might be of interest, which we could discuss together. When Mr Wainwright was away, the newspaper would always be delivered to us untouched, Mrs Wainwright having no curiosity about the outside world.

It was in this way that we began to feed our fascination with events happening far from Teesbank Hall. Eleanor was particularly enthused by the London International Exhibition, which was then taking place at the South Kensington Museum. On this particular topic, she could talk for hours about the wondrous advances in science and the exotic offerings from far-flung countries around the globe. We began to speak tentatively on this subject together and were able to establish some common ground. It was better than the long, gloomy silences that had existed between us previously.

I found, too, that Eleanor was very widely read, and we had similar taste in novels. One day we were sitting close together, talking animatedly about George Eliot's *The Mill on the Floss*, when Agnes came into the library. She looked shocked, so much so that I laughed. She asked me later what was funny.

'It was your face, Agnes. You were a picture of surprise.'

'Well, Miss Caldwell, I didn't think you and Miss Eleanor were friends. It's been a while since I've seen her act so amicable with any of her governesses. Not since Miss Howard left.'

Agnes's comment made me reflect. Could Eleanor and I be called friends? The coldness of our relationship had thawed a little, I supposed, but she was still unpredictable. We might talk with warmth one moment and at the next she was distracted and snapped at everything I said.

That evening, when I made my daily report to Mrs Jenson, she seemed in a particularly sour mood and commented on how pallid Eleanor was. 'Why don't you take her into the grounds for more walks, Miss Caldwell? It is good for her to be outside and physical exercise leads to good moral health.'

'Most days, I try to persuade her to go out but she will not.' It was unfair to be blamed for Eleanor's refusal to leave the schoolroom when I wanted so much to be in the fresh air. Any further discussion was cut short when Mary dashed into the room. 'Mrs Jenson, you're needed at once. Archie has been kicked by one of the horses and he's in a bad way. Mr Snowdon wants you to see if we should get the doctor out.'

Mrs Jenson left the room immediately and didn't lock the mahogany cupboard, as was her usual habit. I finished writing in the account book the tiny quantities of food Eleanor had eaten that day and went to return it to the cupboard, reckoning that this was safer than leaving it out on her table. As I did so, I knocked over a pile of books, leaving one half open on the floor. I picked it up and saw that it was a small account book, with the first entry dating from over twenty years ago. Regular payments were recorded to a sole recipient, 'Gate Helmsley', and the amount involved was substantial: it had been twenty-five pounds per month in the last few years, a sum equivalent to half my annual salary. I shook my head, bemused, but had no time to think about it for I heard footsteps outside. I jumped to my feet and shoved the books back into the cupboard. Mrs Jenson entered the room and I must have looked guilty because she frowned. 'Why are you lurking around the cupboard?'

'I went to return Eleanor's ledger.'

'Don't presume to go near there again. It holds the personal documents of the Wainwright family and nothing there is any business of yours.' She shut the door and turned the key. 'You may leave now, Miss Caldwell, but I would strongly advise you against prying.'

I left the room hastily, thinking over the significance of what I had found and what else might be contained in the cupboard.

CHAPTER THIRTEEN

It was rare that anyone came to Teesbank Hall. The house
was less than six miles from Stockton-on-Tees, which was a
bustling industrial town, but we might as well have been in
the middle of the remotest heath. This meant that any visit
or new face at the Hall was a significant event. One morning in the middle of May, I came down to breakfast to
a warm smell of baking and a feeling of industry about
the kitchen. Mrs Hargreaves was flustered and snapping at
Mary to hurry with whisking the eggs.

Once the cook was out of the room, I asked Agnes what
was happening.

'Mrs Crawford is coming to visit. She lives with her son
Luke out Ripon way but before that she was at Teesbank for
years. She was the cook when Mrs Hargreaves started as a
kitchen maid.'

'We always do well when she comes to visit. Mrs Hargreaves thinks she must impress her,' Eliza commented,

stuffing her mouth with toast and jam. 'When was it she was last here?' she asked Agnes.

'Getting on for nearly two years ago, I think.'

'Well, she's a canny woman, and even Mrs Jenson can just about manage a smile when she's around.'

I reflected it was rare to hear Eliza praise anyone.

That evening, I came into the servants' hall after finishing my day with Eleanor, and the two older women were drinking tea by the fire. Mrs Crawford was a tiny woman, with white hair and a face as wrinkled as a walnut shell. She was introduced to me and Mary, who had also started at the house since her last visit. When Mrs Hargreaves said I was the governess to Miss Eleanor, I saw them exchange glances.

'Have there been any more incidents, since all that carry-on?' Mrs Crawford asked.

'They've got her a nurse, Mrs Anderson, who's with her when Miss Caldwell isn't. It seems to be working well enough. Certainly it's been a bit quieter.'

Mrs Crawford shook her head. 'Now, what about Mr Henry? He was always a good lad. You'd never take them for brother and sister.'

'He's in his final year at Durham University but is often back, especially when there's a problem with Miss Eleanor.'

'It's not right how his parents let the responsibility fall on him. A young lad can't be left to bring up his sister. Neither the mother nor the father had sufficient care for their own children. I spoke to them about it,' she said.

'Oh, I know,' Mrs Hargreaves nodded, 'and at least they listened for once.'

It was peaceful to sit in the glow of the fire in the servants' hall and listen to the reassuring murmur of conversation. After a while, their talk turned to the past, to people and servants who had been at the Hall long ago.

'They were better days,' Mrs Hargreaves said, 'before everything happened. There were at least eight more servants in the house and we weren't always rushed off our feet. And it's got worse and worse – no one wants to stay. You left at the right time, Mrs Crawford.'

'After that terrible thing happened, it was never the same again. A darkness fell over this house. Mind, I never took to Matthew Wainwright and I can speak my thoughts aloud now I no longer work here.'

'Well, nothing's changed in that respect,' Mrs Hargreaves said, with a significant glance in Mary's direction. 'He's got more dissolute in his ways as he's got older.'

'Aye, his mam spoiled him and let him get away with whatever he wanted. I blame her, I do. The old master, Joshua Wainwright, I respected. He was strict but he was a hard worker, too, and earned every penny he had.' She turned to the younger servants. 'He started as no more than a clerk at the colliery and within fifteen years he owned the pit.'

'He married the pit owner's daughter and that didn't hurt him,' laughed Mrs Hargreaves.

Mrs Crawford was forced to agree but added, 'Well, at

least Joshua and Diana Wainwright were in love with each other – not like the son and his wife.'

'They hardly knew each other when they married, had only the flame of youthful attraction to bind them together and that burned out quickly enough. Then they had to face each other in the cold light of day.'

'I reckon it took them all of half a year to realize they couldn't even sit in the same room without upsetting the other and it was too late by then. The vows had been made in church and she was already pregnant.'

'Was there ever a moment when she wasn't?'

Nodding, Mrs Crawford said, 'Still, the way he went on with the French governess – it wasn't right. Everyone knew about it. Right under Mrs Wainwright's nose. I don't know how she could bear to get through the day, seeing him flaunting that girl in front of the whole household.'

Mrs Hargreaves agreed. 'It was all wrong. The mistress, as is now, would eat upstairs alone. She'd be crying into her food and Mrs Diana – they hated each other even then – would tell Mrs Wainwright she was a failure because she couldn't keep her husband's interest.'

'They used to go to that boathouse, with the two girls Clara and Martha trailing behind them. Matthew Wainwright claimed he wanted to oversee their education.'

'Oh, aye. Mr Snowdon, the head gardener, once told me that he found the two girls standing outside the boathouse and Clara was peering through the window and sobbing. Miss Marchal and Mr Wainwright were nowhere to be seen, but there were sounds coming from the boathouse and they didn't leave much to the imagination.'

We were all aghast at the revelation.

'Oh, he's such a pig!' exclaimed Eliza.

'And she started to get airs and graces, didn't she, that Arielle Marchal? Thought she'd be the next mistress of the house. Do you remember when she sat right there, just where you're sitting, and said the meat was tough so you must find something of finer quality to serve her?'

Mrs Hargreaves laughed. 'I remember that well. I took it back, spat on it, then served it with a bit of gravy, saying it was a more tender piece of meat. Arielle Marchal was a woman who needed taking down a peg or two. She was little more than his whore, but she acted like she was mistress of the household.'

'She suffered in the end, mind,' Mrs Crawford said quietly. 'Remember when Mrs Wainwright threw her out of the house and she had to walk through the kitchen. Everyone fell silent. We all knew what life awaited her.'

Mrs Hargreaves surprised me by making the sign of the cross, 'Aye, God rest her soul. She paid indeed.'

'And those two girls. Clara and Martha. They ran wild. No one much cared what happened to them.'

'Well, that's not altogether true. Before Samuel was born, Mr Wainwright spent hours with the girls. He could be a loving father – more so than a loving husband – when he put his mind to it. But once Samuel came, Matthew Wainwright absolutely doted on the child and had no time for his sisters.'

'I think that's what turned Clara,' Mrs Crawford said.

I longed to ask what they meant but felt shy in their company. Eliza had no such qualms. She turned to Mrs Hargreaves. 'You said the eldest sister Clara had a dreadful nature.'

'Well, I didn't exactly say that, Eliza!' Mrs Hargreaves exclaimed.

'Why not? It's true. Clara *was* a bad girl and she wouldn't be crossed in any way.'

'She was vicious. Very free with her hands and thought she could slap us servants and get away with it,' Mrs Hargreaves grumbled.

'All the servants were frightened of her. One day, young Samuel had a really nasty cut on his arm – red with blood, it was, and with bruising coming through. They said he'd fallen and hurt hisself but I've never seen an injury like that from a fall.'

Her story was interrupted as Henry came into the kitchen. 'Mrs Crawford, I heard you were here and couldn't let you leave without saying hello.'

'Oh, young Mr Henry, haven't you grown? It's good to see you.'

'It's good to see you too. How have you been? And how is Luke?'

'He's very well, thank you, sir, just started in a new position at Chambers and Sons. On more money.'

'It was the right decision for him to leave Teesbank Hall.'

'Aye, it was, but he still talks about the pranks the pair of you got up to when you were both young lads here.'

Henry laughed. 'It feels a long time ago now. You must send him my best wishes. I still remember your shortbread, Mrs Crawford, and cups of tea. I was always sure of a kind greeting in your kitchen.'

'You was always very welcome, sir.'

Suddenly, I had an image of Henry as a child, lost in the big house, his parents wrapped up in their own misery, and forced to creep down to the kitchen to find company and warmth.

Their meeting was interrupted by Eleanor's arrival. It was as if a cold tap had been turned on. In a moment, all the good feeling disappeared and we sat awkwardly, as she glared around her. 'Henry, what on earth are you doing in the servants' hall?' she demanded.

'I heard that Mrs Crawford had come. I was away at university the last time she was here.'

Eleanor ignored the visitor, not even turning in her direction. 'You are going back to Durham tomorrow and you promised that we could ride together along the river to Yarm.'

'Ellie, we can do that once Mrs Crawford has gone.'

'It will be too late then,' she insisted. 'Really you must come now.'

Nevertheless Henry refused to leave and she walked out of the kitchen slamming the door behind her. There was a moment's stunned silence. Then Mrs Crawford said, 'Perhaps you'd best follow her, sir.'

Henry replied, 'No, no, not at all.' He tried to continue

the good humour, but the mood had cooled and Mrs Crawford left soon after. When she went to stand, I saw that she suffered with rheumatism and grimaced with pain as she used the table edge to heave herself up. Agnes jumped forward to help, but the older woman waved her away. 'I can manage, dear. I'm not that ancient yet, but thank you. Mrs Hargreaves, it has been good to see you – just like the old times.' The two women embraced each other with genuine affection and Mrs Crawford left by the scullery door.

A few minutes later, I went to retrieve my book from the library and happened to glance through the large windows. Mrs Crawford was walking down the main driveway from the house. To my surprise, Eleanor appeared, walking swiftly behind her. She must have called the older woman's name because she turned around. Eleanor moved closer to her and, to my horror, kicked Mrs Crawford swiftly and viciously in the ankle. She stumbled to the ground and looked up at Eleanor with an uncomprehending expression.

For a moment, I stood at the window in shocked disbelief and then I hurried down the stairs and outside.

'Mrs Crawford, are you all right? Are you hurt?' I helped her to struggle to her feet and dust down the skirts of her dress.

She took a deep breath and stood up straight. 'Thank you for helping, my dear. I'm not really hurt, she just caught me a little off balance. It's that one –' she turned to Eleanor who was standing and watching us – 'it's that one you should be asking if she's all right, for truly she is blighted, and her family's money won't protect her for ever.' Having said these words, she walked slowly away.

I couldn't stop myself turning on Eleanor. 'How could you do that? I saw you kick Mrs Crawford. She is defenceless and old, and your actions are unforgivable.'

'I don't care what you think. It was no more than she deserved. She has always tried to come between Henry and me, just like she did this evening.'

'She only delayed your ride together,' I said, aghast. 'She didn't stop you seeing him.'

'It was more than that. You don't know what she did to me, even though she had always pretended to be kind.' I was astonished to see that Eleanor's eyes had filled with tears. 'She told my parents it was cruel Henry hadn't been sent away to school. That woman claimed it was ruining Henry's life to leave him at home looking after me.'

I remembered Mrs Crawford's earlier conversation. 'But she only wanted what was best for Henry.'

'And what about me? I was seven years old and separated from the only person who cared about me. The first time he went away to Rugby, Father had to restrain me from running after him. I screamed for a week and refused to eat.'

'But that wasn't—' I began, but Eleanor interrupted me.

'I was left here, in this house, this terrible house, with only my nursemaid, Nancy Wilson, for company. And at night I had dreams, so powerful I thought they must be real. Yet it was never Henry I dreamed of, but always my dead brother. Oh, God!' She put her hands to her face. 'They would not let me escape, like Henry, because I was a girl and must remain here at Teesbank Hall.'

'I'm sorry—'

'I don't need your pity, Miss Caldwell.' Any tears had disappeared now and her tone was hard. 'I will always hate Mrs Crawford for her part in taking Henry away from me, but she taught me a valuable lesson – to be careful of whom I trust. And I will always fight for what is rightfully mine.'

I felt then that I had seen a glimpse of the Eleanor everyone spoke of in hushed voices.

The next evening, when I completed the ledger in Mrs Jenson's room, I told her I had something to report about Eleanor's behaviour.

'What has she done?' Mrs Jenson asked.

When I recounted what I had seen and Eleanor's reaction when I confronted her, she said thoughtfully, 'She can be a vicious girl, there is no mistaking. There is bad blood flowing in this family's veins.'

But she would say no more on the subject and I became even more wary of Eleanor.

CHAPTER FOURTEEN

The fragile blue of May's forget-me-nots had melted into the warm pink of June's roses, but little else had changed, certainly not my daily routine of long, airless hours spent in the schoolroom. It was much easier for Henry and Mr Wainwright, who were often away from the house and in the wider world, but the three women of the family and I were trapped together in the cold comfort of Teesbank Hall.

Mrs Wainwright was a woman who had fallen into a permanent decline and did very little with her days. She had contracted a fixation with playing whist, which she had learned in childhood, and which demanded four players. One evening, Mr Wainwright had left for Newcastle unexpectedly, and a game could not be made up.

The older Mrs Wainwright had long ago declared card-playing to be the work of Satan, for no other reason than that she wished to spite her daughter-in-law, and would retire to her room in a state of indignation, clutching an unread Bible to her bosom. Mrs Jenson was an indifferent player and Eleanor refused to take part unless someone more competent could be found. I was forced to acknowledge that I knew the game well and was requested to join Mrs Wainwright, Henry and Eleanor in the drawing-room. Mrs Anderson, of course, relished the nights when cards were played, as she would escape several hours of Eleanor's company, only reappearing to collect her at the end of the evening, smelling faintly of gin and speaking too loudly.

The four of us sat around the card table and Henry shuffled the cards. Mrs Jenson was there too, and he chatted with her about the new vicar, who had just been appointed at St John the Baptist Church. She sat a little away from us, with Albert the indulged spaniel flopped at her feet. Supposedly, he would be miserable if left alone in the evening so he had inveigled a prime spot by the fire, while the housekeeper fed him pieces of tender cooked liver. Strange rumbling noises intermittently sounded from his corner of the room.

'The weather was very dull and dreary today,' Mrs Wainwright commented, in her hesitant voice. 'It seemed overcast for a good part of the day.'

'Perhaps it will be better tomorrow. Mr Snowdon is hopeful we're in for a spell of fine weather – he said his gardens have already had more than enough rain,' Henry replied.

Mrs Wainwright nodded. 'I may take a walk, if the weather is to improve.'

At this, Eleanor snorted. We all knew Susan Wainwright never left the house.

'The gardens are beautiful now, Mother. The roses have come into bloom and the air is filled with their scent. We could walk together along the river. We might even take Albert with us.' Henry gestured at the dog, which growled softly at the suggestion.

Susan Wainwright seemed to agree for she nodded dreamily. 'Roses were always my favourite flower. From June to September, Father would insist the house was filled with great vases of pink roses, so we had their fragrance through all the summer months.'

'Then, Mother, you must certainly walk with me tomorrow.'

'Oh, Henry, it is still too chilly. We may walk there when the weather is a little warmer.' She pulled her shawl around herself for emphasis. Her eyes were already drawn to the pack of cards on the table in front of us because she had had no real interest in the conversation. Now that the demands of politeness had been met, she returned to the true matter at hand. 'Henry, would you deal the cards for us?'

Bowing, he replied, 'Of course, Mother.'

Hand after hand of cards we played, until the darkness of night began to encroach upon the clear light of the long northern evening. As we played, I saw Mrs Wainwright's eyes sharpen and gain a focus they didn't usually hold. So distant and distracted for most of the day, she now seemed wholly intent on reading the direction of the game and the prophecies foretold in her hand. Henry and I attempted to make conversation about the concerns of the household and of the wider world. He proposed taking a walking tour with Edward Merryweather and another friend in Scotland later that summer and we marvelled at how it was possible to catch a train from the local railway station right up into the Highlands. Mrs Wainwright interjected occasionally, although it was the game that held her true attention. Eleanor refused to join in this trivial talk, but instead used calculated strategies, focusing solely on winning. She had an intimate knowledge of the most obscure rules and employed these ruthlessly, so it was impossible to enjoy playing.

And there was a further hindrance. As the evening progressed, an obnoxious and familiar smell began to waft in my direction. I remembered the unfortunate journey into Stockton and the carriage windows that had been opened as wide as possible to disperse the foul smells emitting from Albert. As if to remind me, the indulged spaniel looked in my direction and, in so far as it was possible for a dog to do so, positively smirked with malice. The pained expressions on the rest of the group's faces suggested I was not the only person to be aware of Albert's contributions to the evening. No one said anything although Eleanor began to cough very loudly and obviously, and Mrs Wainwright reached for her scented handkerchief.

Mrs Jenson was more used to Albert's bodily functions than the rest of us but even she became unable to ignore the foul vapours any longer. Jumping to her feet, she declared, 'I might open a window or two. As Mr Henry has pointed out, it would be the perfect time to enjoy the scents of the roses.'

I had been battling to stop myself giggling, as we all tried to ignore the pungent whiff. At that very moment, I happened to catch Henry's eye and the impossible occurred. I realized he, too, was on the verge of convulsing with laughter and Mrs Jenson's euphemistic declaration was the final straw. He guffawed loudly, a sound he tried to turn into a sneeze, masked by his large white handkerchief but I could bear it no more and broke into peals of uncontrollable laughter. And then we were both laughing helplessly and in unison. The inappropriateness of the situation and the disapproval of our elders made it all the more impossible to stop. It was liberating in this gloomy house to laugh, and to remember I was young and that darkness would not last for ever.

'I don't see what is so funny,' Mrs Wainwright said disapprovingly. But the fact that she had to make this statement while wafting a scented handkerchief in front of her face, merely added to our amusement.

'Albert has a very sensitive stomach,' Mrs Jenson grumbled, opening the windows as far as she could. 'It's no laughing matter that he suffers with his digestion. Young people will laugh at the most serious of things.'

We were both suitably chastened and Henry opened his mouth to apologize but then he looked at me and spluttered out, 'The scent of the roses . . .'

'It would be the perfect time,' I agreed, and we began to

giggle all over again. It was impossible to speak or even to explain what was so funny.

Mrs Wainwright and Mrs Jenson sat tight-faced and un-amused. Meanwhile, Eleanor played on coldly and brought our merriment to an end by slamming down an ace and observing, 'I have won. The game is over.'

I was not asked to play with them again.

CHAPTER FIFTEEN

As a reaction against the enforced confinement of the schoolroom, I started to take lengthy evening walks, right along the riverbank, until I reached the boathouse and was quite out of breath. Then I would turn back before it was too dark to make my way easily through the woods. I wished to exhaust myself because I dreaded night-time, when either sleep eluded me or I was haunted by terrible dreams. Although mercifully, their contents were usually obscured, they would always end in the same way, with that blinding light, and I would sit up, shaking, my nightgown soaked with sweat. I was not in Norfolk, I told myself, re-assured by the hundreds of miles that lay between me and Uncle Thomas Stepford.

One particularly beautiful June evening, I walked for several miles and returned home feeling quite light-headed. The riverbank had been a riot of wild flowers and the air was heady with the scent of meadowsweet and dog roses. The whole universe seemed to hint at the possibility of new beginnings and fresh starts. In the long light of the far north, even the enclosed servants' stairway did not seem so gloomy. Perhaps I was happier because Eleanor was not so ill-disposed towards me or perhaps it was because Henry offered me some form of friendship. Whatever the cause, I finally felt it might be possible to escape the past and have hope for the future.

Once back in my room, I sat at the dressing-table. There were still glimmers of pink and gold in the sky, so I hadn't lit a candle. I reached for my silver-backed hairbrush and, as I did so, my arm must have caught the cloak covering the mirror. It slithered down onto the floor, leaving the mirror naked. Immediately I looked away. I hadn't dared to glance at my reflection since that terrible March night when the other self had haunted me.

I clasped my hands tightly. It was foolish to be frightened of an image, a trick of the light. On the night I had seen her, I had been exhausted and confused after my long flight from Uncle Thomas Stepford. Now there was a distance of time and place from the events that had scarred me, even happiness might be possible. I wondered if I dared to confront the mirror. I sat down in front of it resolutely but with my eyes closed. I opened them slowly. She was there. The phantom girl was there. How could she not have been? We stared blankly at each other – the same and not the same.

The same dark eyes, holding the most terrible of secrets, the snake-like hair and the too-passionate lips, partly opened. I didn't want to let the image intimidate me. I lit the candle and it threw soft shadows around the room, veiling the harshness of those eyes that had seen too much. Her pale skin was warmed by the candle. Seductive yet beautiful. I gasped a single word, 'You!' The girl in the mirror mouthed it back. We each accused the other. She was the self I had escaped but her presence suggested she had never left me.

I needed her to know I wasn't frightened and I had chosen to leave. With my finger I traced her features. My gaze lingered for too long in the total silence of a summer night.

And then my thoughts were broken, smashed apart by the sound of heavy footsteps in the corridor outside. A man's footsteps. I jumped, my shock all the greater because I had been so absorbed a moment ago. Even the maids rarely came here and men were forbidden to enter this part of the house.

'Who's there?' My question reverberated in the air but there was no response.

I felt exposed, as if the intruder might sense how I had been drawn in by the creature in the mirror, had traced her features and known them to be my own. Ashamed now of my reaction to the face, I sprang up, determined to confront whoever might be there. Surely if their intention had been innocent, they would have answered my question.

As I went to open the door, I heard the sharp strike of a match against flint and then a warm odour filled the enclosed space of the attic. The spiced wood of Matthew Wainwright's Dominican cigars. I froze, horrified. He had come here to the attic. My heart pounded within me and the

familiar sickness came. My silent lips mouthed, 'I can't.'
And then I feared it was me, just as Uncle Thomas Stepford
had told me. I had conjured up the master of the house when
I had seen the depths of my soul reflected in the mirror. The
door handle rattled and the smell seeped its way through the
thin gap beneath the door.

The first time Uncle Thomas Stepford had felt my head,
he said the bumps there denoted a licentious and wanton
nature. It was written in my bone. He said it was my fault
he behaved as he did, because I had the qualities of a whore.
And here was the proof: Matthew Wainwright waiting outside my door. I tried not to breathe. Nothing. Absolutely
nothing that might indicate I was in the room. I sat against
the door, curled up in a ball and would have cried silently if
I hadn't been so afraid that it might betray my presence.

His feet paced the corridor outside, back and forth. If
he knocked on the door, what would I do? I remembered
the other times, when I had heard the sly knock, as quiet as
a breath, so I could begin to fool myself that it had been
nothing, block my ears and pray. Until the knock came
again, more insistent, and I had known with certainty that
he lurked outside.

And now I prayed but still the footsteps came closer to
the door. He stopped outside. I could hear his harsh, ragged
breathing. I tensed for what was inevitable. Desperation
made me brave and I screamed out. Perhaps he feared the
noise might wake someone because, at the last moment, he

turned sharply on his heel and I heard the footsteps disappear down the corridor.

I was overcome with relief, but I needed to know he had gone. I couldn't bear the thought of Mr Wainwright somewhere in the attics, choosing his moment to strike. Silently, I left my room and saw a man's dark outline ahead of me, being eaten up by the gloom. It was only a fleeting glance, but I was no longer as certain it was Matthew Wainwright. I waited a moment. I decided to edge along the corridor to check that all the rooms were empty. I stood on the threshold of the first, too terrified to enter, in case someone jumped out at me.

It was in this distraught state that Agnes found me. 'Miss Caldwell! Whatever is wrong? I heard you scream ever so loud.'

I pointed, horrified, in the direction she had come from. 'There was a man. He was waiting outside my door. Can you help me see whether he's still in the attics?'

'Whoever would come up here?' she asked.

'I don't know.' Something stopped me naming Mr Wainwright. I hadn't seen him properly and I didn't want to accuse the master on so little evidence.

She looked at me oddly but agreed to help and we worked together, entering all the rooms at the front of the house. All empty.

'But this is impossible, Agnes. He was on the landing minutes ago. I saw him with my own eyes. If he isn't in any of the rooms, then he must have escaped down the servants' staircase.'

'Miss Caldwell, I've just climbed up the stairs. There was no one there. No one passed me.'

'Are you sure of that?' I pleaded with her. 'How can he have just disappeared?'

She repeated, 'Miss Caldwell, there was no one. The candlelight can play tricks with your eyes.'

'But I didn't just see him – I heard him. I heard his footsteps outside my room – as clear as anything. Oh, Agnes, I know that a man was here.'

She was now trying to manoeuvre me back into my room and was reluctant to look at me. 'You must have imagined it, you really must. No one was there.'

'How can that be possible?' I asked.

'You said yourself, didn't you, that the darkness up here will make people think they see things? And there are so many stories . . .' She trailed off. 'Eliza said she'd seen something a few times, but it was never a man.'

I didn't protest further, but I knew what I had seen and what had happened. Once Agnes was gone, I locked the door and jammed a wooden chair beneath the handle, so it was impossible to open from the outside. I climbed into bed and lay there rigid with terror. I was fearful of the darkness and let a candle burn throughout the night. But still sleep eluded me and the thought of seeing Mr Wainwright the next day made me sick with worry.

The following morning, I spoke to Mrs Jenson at

breakfast and asked if I could see her alone, as I wanted to confide something.

'I hope it won't take too long, Miss Caldwell. I have a lot to do this morning.'

'I would prefer to speak to you in your sitting room.' I could see Eliza lurking sullenly in the corner of the room and didn't want her to hear our conversation.

Mrs Jenson stood up, her face sour, making a great show of sighing. 'Eliza, can you sit with Mary? I'll be back as soon as possible.'

Once we were in the privacy of her room, I told her about the man in the attic, but she shook her head. 'That is simply not possible.'

I was adamant. 'I know what I heard and saw.'

'I can assure you that you are mistaken. The men servants would not dare go up to the attics. Their quarters are below stairs, and they know it is out of bounds for them.'

'There was a man outside my bedroom door last night.'

'The only other men in the house are Mr Wainwright and Mr Henry. I presume you are not suggesting they were sneaking about the attics?' Her voice was cold and dismissive.

'I'm not saying—'

She cut me off mid-sentence: 'Was there another witness to this man?'

I was forced to admit I was the only person who had seen anything and that Agnes had been on the stairs but he hadn't run past her.

'Well, I think you have your answer there, Miss Cald-well. It is very likely you had a bad dream and have made something more of it than it really was. Now, I have urgent matters that won't go away and Miss Eleanor must be attended. It's almost seven and Mrs Anderson will not be best pleased if you are late.'

There was nothing more I could do. I walked reluctantly to the library, haunted by the thought that I had let loose my own demons. Eleanor was sitting at her table and I nod-ded at her before going to sit quietly by the window, but I couldn't forget what had happened. I vowed to keep the chair jammed against the door and the mirror covered with its cloth, in case the ghost girl should appear again. Logic-ally I knew it was foolish, but my imagination insinuated that I had somehow conjured up an evil presence when I had tried to confront my fears.

In contrast to my silence, Eleanor was strangely exhila-rated and desperate to drag me into conversation. Finally, she burst out, 'Father has gone away this morning. I think he will be gone for quite some time.' She smirked.

'Has he gone on business?' I asked mechanically.

'You could call it that.' She laughed.

When Agnes came at midday with our lunch, Eleanor jumped up straight away and went over to her. 'Tell me what's happened, I need to know everything.'

Agnes was downcast. 'It's bad, miss. Mary's mother is com-ing for her this afternoon. She won't work here no more.'

'What did he do?'

'Miss, if you must know, he grabbed her as she finished for the night and there was no one around. He pushed her against the wall and did things he shouldn't.' She shook her head with disgust.

'Everyone knows that what he did was wrong,' Eleanor said bitterly.

'Yes,' Agnes replied, 'but it's not him who'll pay.' I was surprised to see a look of anger flash across her face – she was always so meek – but then I remembered pretty shy Mary and shuddered at how he might have hurt her.

It was impossible to settle that day. The presence of the man in the attic and what had happened to Mary brought back all the thoughts I tried to suppress in my waking hours. By three o'clock, I could bear it no longer. Memories of Uncle Thomas Stepford and Swaffham crowded out every-thing else. I couldn't allow him to overwhelm me again: I needed to be lost in another story. Arielle Marchal, my double. I wanted to know what had happened to her and see if it might predict my future. 'Will you show me more documents from the murder?'

Eleanor looked up from her writing. 'You understand the price? I must have thirty minutes alone.'

'Yes.' Anything was better than being trapped inside my own head.

Eleanor retrieved the manilla envelope from its locked cupboard and then we walked to the boathouse where she gave me a document, which was written in faint blue ink and torn in parts. It related to the arrest of Arielle Marchal.

ACCOUNT OF THE ARREST OF ARIELLE
MARCHAL (16 AUGUST 1849)

Prepared by: William Hughes (Magistrate for Stockton-on-Tees and its surrounding areas)

This is written in the hand of William Hughes (Magistrate for Stockton-on-Tees and its surrounding areas) on 17 August 1849.

Nancy Wilson, the nursemaid at Teesbank Hall, in the Parish of Preston-on-Tees, Eaglescliffe, has sworn under oath that Arielle Marchal, formerly the governess at the above-named residence, was responsible for the most brutal murder of Samuel Wainwright, such event having taken place between the night of Friday, 10 August, and Monday, 13 August, when the body was found.

On the Coroner's direction, I (William Hughes) and Jacob Moore were given responsibility for apprehending Arielle Marchal so that she might be questioned in the matter.

Arielle Marchal had been dismissed by Mrs Wainwright from her position as governess at Teesbank Hall on the morning of 29 July. It was established that immediately after she had walked to the neighbouring town of Yarm. A number of people living there were able to vouch that she had asked about employment as a general maid and one witness added that she seemed to be most distraught and was crying and pulling at her clothes. When asked why she had left her previous employment and why she was unable to furnish a letter of recommendation, the young woman began to cry most piteously and said that she had been sorely used.

It was obvious to all from the swelling of her belly that there was a baby on the way and, she being a comely young woman, it seemed that someone had gained her love with false promises and deceit. Further, she wore a small pearl ring upon her wedding finger, although all who knew her vowed that she was without a husband, and called herself Mrs Wainwright, presumptuously using the name of her former mistress, so that she might cover the shame of her unmarried condition.

None wanted her in their home because of her fallen state. However, she had walked on to Appleton Wiske, a hamlet some seven miles or so from her former place of employment. There she spoke to John Fletcher, who has a farm of fifty acres, which he runs with the help of a single farmhand. His wife had died of the scarlet fever five weeks previous, and left him with four children, the oldest of whom is only eight years. With dire need of help in the house, he agreed to take on Arielle Marchal to work there in exchange for her board and lodging, but it was made clear to her that she could not stay for longer than two months due to her condition.

John Fletcher was concerned that her presence would give rise to slanderous thoughts among his neighbours, who might believe that he was responsible for her sad and sorry state. For this reason, he insisted that she sleep in a rough room that was above the barn, so that she might not be in the house itself and therefore would not be a moral danger to his young children. He described her as a hard worker but said she was very quiet and often tearful.

We had arrived at Fletcher's farm at a little after nine o'clock in the evening of 16 August, and he showed us to the barn, which truly was a desolate and lowly place and fit only for animals. She,

Arielle Marchal, was in a makeshift bed in one corner of the room and when we arrived, she gasped with horror and cried out. She demanded that we leave, but we showed her our warrant, which had been signed that morning by the Coroner.

While Jacob Moore began to search her belongings, I informed her that she had been accused of the murder of Samuel Wainwright. She seemed most shocked and said, 'I had nothing to do with that thing.' She claimed that she had loved the boy and said, 'She has told you this, yes?'

When I told her that Nancy Wilson had made a statement of her guilt to the inquest, Arielle Marchal became visibly distressed and responded, 'Nancy is my friend. She would not say such a thing.'

I then asked her why she had left the employment of the Wainwrights, and she answered that if I was here, then I would know the reason. When I asked her where she had been on the night of 10 August and the early morning of 11 August, she said that she had been in this room but that no one could vouch for her because Mr Fletcher and his children had gone to visit his parents.

Jacob Moore was then looking through a small valise that belonged to Arielle Marchal and he shouted out and held up a piece of fine white silk, saying, 'This is just the cloth used to wrap the body of the murdered infant.'

At these very words, Arielle Marchal made a dash for the ladder that led from her room and would have been all the way down if I had not caught her by the hair and dragged her back. It was clear to us that this was a sign of her guilt and we then put restraints upon her so that she might not attempt escape again. She was in a most hysterical and distressed state and said repeatedly, 'I have done nothing wrong, I swear upon my life. I do not bear the guilt for what has happened.'

We have brought her to the cells, ready to be taken to Durham Prison. When we came back to Stockton-on-Tees, we have placed together the white silk taken from her lodgings and the bloodstained cloth from the murder. They are identical and have been cut from the same bolt of cloth.

Nancy Wilson – and the Wilson family generally – are known to be of a low and dishonest nature and I was heartily relieved to have such confirmation of Arielle Marchal's guilt.

Signed and dated: **William Hughes, 17 August 1849**

When Eleanor returned, she said, 'See, it was not only the word of Nancy Wilson. The white silk incriminated her.'

CHAPTER SIXTEEN

Two or so weeks after this, Mrs Jenson came into the library unexpectedly and took Eleanor to one side. She spoke to her quietly and a look of disgust crossed Eleanor's face. 'Why do I have to endure their presence? I'll refuse to speak to them. Mother knows that I will.'

'Now, Miss Eleanor. It would make your mother very grateful if you behave well,' Mrs Jenson pleaded. 'Mr Wainwright and Mr Henry are away and your grandmother can sometimes be ill-disposed on these occasions. Mrs Wainwright will need you to support her. She doesn't like to receive visitors.'

Eleanor turned away her face and settled herself into a ferocious sulk that was to last most of the morning. 'I have my studies to complete,' she complained, 'and afterwards I will be tired.'

I wondered who on earth could be coming to the house and why it should upset Eleanor so much. I found out later that day when Mrs Jenson returned to the room and, after a quick glance at Eleanor, said to me, 'The new vicar from St John the Baptist Church, the Reverend Mr Sterling, and his wife are paying a visit to Teesbank Hall this evening and Mrs Wainwright has asked that you are in attendance.'

Eleanor now flung down her book in disgust and pulled a face. 'Why do they have to come here? Why doesn't Mother just refuse?'

Mrs Jenson continued speaking to me alone, as if she had not heard this interruption. 'He arrived at the parish five weeks ago. As Teesbank Hall is one of the grandest houses in the area, he wishes to pay a visit.'

Before I had a chance to respond, Eleanor exclaimed, 'I hope he is not such a fool as the last vicar – with threats to pray for our souls and requests we attend church! I will not endure him, Mrs Jenson!'

The housekeeper merely nodded.

I was surprised to be invited, but in the absence of anyone else, Mrs Wainwright had been forced to enlist my help against this unwanted intrusion from the outside world. If Mr Wainwright had been there, I'm sure he would have refused to allow the vicar into the house and have damned the consequences, but Mrs Wainwright was too weak to say no outright. For my part, I was very glad at the thought of new faces and how they would break the monotony of the house's routines.

When evening came, we were seated uncomfortably around an arrangement of small tables in the sitting room. Mrs Wainwright looked nervous and her eyes darted around the room, as if seeking out an escape route. Meanwhile Eleanor glowered with thinly hidden anger.

At the last moment, Diana Wainwright came in, having thought better of her previous refusal to be present. She complained, 'Susan, I can't believe you've allowed them to come to the house. I cannot abide the clergy and would never willingly let them cross the threshold.' She glanced at Eleanor, who was slumped rebelliously in a chair by the fire. 'You might at least sit up and attempt to smile, Eleanor. Your appearance is displeasing enough without any deliberate scowling.'

I was relieved that she ignored me.

Mrs Jenson brought Mr Sterling and his wife into the room.

The vicar beamed. 'I'm very pleased to make your acquaintance and only sorry we've not visited before. Elizabeth and I are just starting to find our way around the parish. Why, we were at the Merryweathers' only the other day and what a charming family they are!'

'Indeed,' Diana Wainwright said, glancing at Eleanor. 'My grandson Henry is very close to the son and daughter of the family.'

'They are very pleasant young people,' he responded. 'But it is such a pity your husband is not here too, Mrs Wainwright.'

Given what I knew of Mr Wainwright's opinion of the Church, I couldn't help but reflect that the vicar should be grateful the master of the house wasn't there.

Mrs Wainwright nodded in response and looked down at her fingers. Eleanor stared resolutely out of the window. The older woman, however, stood up and extended her hand, 'I'm delighted you have been able to visit. I was only saying to Susan that we must invite you to Teesbank Hall. Wasn't I, Susan?'

Mrs Wainwright continued to look at her left hand, as if there was a point of incredible interest upon it and said nothing.

The vicar responded with the innocent smile of a school-boy, who is desperate to please everyone. 'That's splendid. Quite splendid!'

I suspected his wife was a little sharper than he was and there was something in Diana Wainwright's tone that made her glance across, as if judging what to make of her.

He then turned to me and pressed his damp, eager hand into mine, saying, 'Miss Caldwell, I am pleased to make your acquaintance. I understand that you, too, are a new-comer in this part of the world.'

'Yes, sir, I have come from Norfolk,' I replied. It could not matter to be specific – it is a large county.

'And how do you find being so far north? Mrs Sterling and I perceive the landscape as most picturesque but the weather rather cold. We are used to London.' His voice was boundlessly enthusiastic and a little high-pitched.

I agreed it was a very beautiful location before a dull silence descended upon us all. The vicar coughed awk-wardly into a large white handkerchief, then launched into conversation again. 'I cannot help but notice that, apart from Henry, the Wainwright family is not to be seen at church. In fact, my deacon has told me your family has not attended for many years.' He left his observation hanging in the air, hopeful that the mere statement of the fact would draw a contrite response from us. However, as Mrs Wainwright made only an indecipherable noise, he blundered on unhindered, 'It would be of great benefit for the ordinary people of the parish to see you among them at prayer.'

'As is obvious, Mr Sterling, I am too old and infirm to go to church,' Diana Wainwright responded. 'However, you must ask my daughter-in-law Susan why she chooses to ignore her religious duty.'

'I cannot attend church. I cannot leave Teesbank Hall,' Mrs Wainwright said desperately.

There was a moment's further silence before Mrs Jenson defended her mistress: 'Mrs Wainwright suffers with her nerves. It's not possible for her to attend a public place and she can't be in large groups of people. She will make amends with God behind closed doors.'

So final and definite was Mrs Jenson's tone that he dared ask no more and, seeing the closed-off face of Eleanor, decided I would be a better focus for his missionary work. 'Miss Caldwell, are you of the Anglican faith?'

When I confirmed I was, he continued, 'And we have not seen you among our congregation either.' His tone suggested genuine upset at my absence and concern that I should take part in the services. 'Why, Miss Caldwell, other servants from Teesbank Hall are at services most regularly. Surely you are able to attend.'

'I would be very glad to come to the service on Sundays,' I replied. 'If that's acceptable to you, Mrs Wainwright.'

In the circumstances, she could hardly refuse, and I looked forward to an opportunity to escape Eleanor, if only for an hour or so. It was decided that Agnes would watch over her while I was away for the morning. She seemed able to calm Eleanor when others could not and would talk quietly with her for hours at a time.

The conversation continued in a desultory way, with some comments about the weather and the inconvenience of the building works then taking place around the railway station. Socially, Mr Sterling seemed out of place, as if trying too hard to please and ingratiate himself with the company in which he found himself. I knew that some of the rougher servants mocked him and his fine accent, but I believed him to be a kind and sincere man, who only wished to do good.

His wife was slightly taller than he was, with frank blue eyes and a forthright manner. She had been largely silent until this point, but now interposed, 'Mrs Wainwright, it may not be my place to say this, but I understand your family has been afflicted by a great tragedy. You have our sincerest sympathy for the death of your son. The people of the town still speak of it, despite the passage of time.'

'What do they say?' she whispered.

'That a terrible sorrow came to Teesbank Hall.'

I looked at Mrs Wainwright. Her face was drained of colour. Her mother-in-law got up and walked to the other side of the room. I found it hard to believe the vicar's wife had talked so openly of Samuel Wainwright's murder, here in this house of silences. It must strike Mrs Wainwright with the sharpness of a knife that the family's suffering was openly discussed, even with newcomers such as the Sterlings.

Foolishly, Mrs Sterling failed to read the expression on Mrs Wainwright's face and so she continued, 'Surely there would be great consolation to be found in regular attendance at the church. You would have the grace of God and the sympathy of others at your loss.'

The wound opened was too great. Even I, then only twenty-one and with all the social gaucheness typical of that age, felt compelled to change the course of the conversation. 'Mrs Sterling, you and your husband were in London before you came to Eaglescliffe. You must find it quite different here?'

My interruption was abrupt but had its intended effect – perhaps she realized she had been too blunt in her comments – and she responded, 'Yes, it is different. We had become quite used to the activity and bustle of the city. My husband held a ministry in Holloway in north London. I don't know if any of you have visited the district?'

We all assured her we had not, and she continued, 'There is much poverty, and it's a sad irony that many go short of the most basic necessities in what is the wealthiest city in the world.'

'I hope you're not one of those radicals, with absurd ideas about equality,' Diana Wainwright commented. 'There will always be the poor because some people choose an imprudent life and must suffer the consequences.'

Mrs Sterling's cheeks flushed pink. 'There are very few, Mrs Wainwright, who I believe would wish to live in poverty. It's the circumstances of their birth that dictate their life.'

'Nonsense. My late husband, Joshua, was born without a penny to his name and made a fortune through sheer hard work. He didn't bleat about his birth or other such foolishness.'

'He is to be commended for his industry and good fortune, Mrs Wainwright, but it cannot be the case for everyone. Before my marriage, I worked at the St Mary Magdalene House of Charity in Highgate. We helped fallen women and gave them skills that would allow them to leave behind a life of vice.'

'A life of vice! You or I or any right-thinking lady would hardly behave in such a way. Too many excuses are made for such women.'

'They are women who had very little choice in the matter,' said Mrs Sterling, with increasing anger.

'Of course they have a choice. We all have a choice,' Diana Wainwright asserted disapprovingly. 'In any case, I hardly think this is a proper subject for discussion in front of a young lady like Miss Eleanor.'

Eleanor laughed, her first contribution to the conversation.

Her grandmother looked at her sourly.

'Mrs Wainwright,' Mrs Sterling said earnestly, 'many of the girls at St Mary Magdalene were even younger than Miss Wainwright.'

I was in the furthest corner of the room and partially hidden, something for which I was grateful. It was impossible to hear a discussion on such a topic without feeling discomfort.

'They are all the more to be blamed, then. To fall into a life of sin at such an early age shows a hardened predisposition for immorality of the most alarming kind.'

This was too much for Mrs Sterling and, despite many sidelong glances and desperate coughs from her husband, she launched into an attack. 'Mrs Wainwright, I'm shocked that you can say such a thing! They are vulnerable and have been sorely abused by the very people who should care for them and have their welfare at heart. They are not guilty parties in what occurs but rather the helpless victims of a cruelty that is hard to comprehend. They need our support and not our condemnation.'

Mrs Sterling cannot have known the effect of her words upon me. This was something to be treasured and thought over when I was alone in my room. I felt a dark shadow begin to lift from me.

'Your views seem reprehensible for the wife of a vicar,' the old lady responded. 'I shall continue to condemn where I find moral degeneracy.'

Mrs Sterling looked resolutely ahead of her and didn't answer.

Diana Wainwright now glared at the fire. 'It is ridiculous, Susan, how you insist on having a fire in the middle of summer. It is wasteful.' Her daughter-in-law opened her mouth to protest. 'No, I shall hear no excuses. I am much too hot and uncomfortable and will retire for the evening.' She walked out of the room without acknowledging anyone, other than Mrs Sterling, whom she looked at with pure hatred.

Poor Mr Sterling coughed once more into his handkerchief and cast around desperately for a conversational topic that would not offend. Finally, he hit upon something. 'We chose to move to the parish in Eaglescliffe because we have a number of connections in the north of England. My parents live in York and we wished to be a little closer to them.'

Mrs Wainwright surprised us all by speaking: 'York is the city of my birth,' she said. 'I left when I married Mr Wainwright.'

Clearly relieved to have gained a response, he exclaimed, 'You grew up in York! We might have acquaintances in common.'

Her reply was vague: 'I moved away many years ago. Only my brother and his family and one of my dear sisters live there now.'

'Do you visit the city at all?' Mrs Sterling enquired. The distance between York and Eaglescliffe was about forty-five miles, a lengthy but not impossible journey, certainly not since the coming of the railway.

Mrs Wainwright shook her head. 'I have not been there for at least twenty years. The travel would be too difficult.'

The vicar asked, 'Did you meet your husband in York?'

Susan Wainwright looked into the distant air as if seeing a faraway past. She put her hand to her face for the briefest time. 'He was a business acquaintance of Father. He was often at our house.'

The vicar felt on more secure ground now. 'Your love for Mr Wainwright must have been very strong to persuade you to leave your family and the beautiful city of York.'

'We hardly knew each other,' she said abruptly. 'I was only seventeen when we married with full ceremony at the Minster. I don't think we spent one moment alone together before our wedding day. My mother or aunt was always in attendance.'

Eleanor spoke, glancing vindictively at her mother. 'It took them a matter of months to discover they had nothing in common and they have been unhappy ever since. Father keeps a mistress in Newcastle and he is with her now. She calls herself Mrs Wainwright but her true name is Margaret Smith and she has no more right than I to describe herself as married.'

The vicar and his wife looked at each other, clearly appalled, but Mrs Wainwright continued as if Eleanor hadn't spoken, 'My father had five daughters and only one son. It was our fate to be married off as quickly as possible, whether there was love or not. I thanked God on the day each of my sons was born.' The fast-falling night hid her face and I think that is why she spoke with a frankness I had not heard before.

'Of course, you have a son, Henry, and—' The vicar broke off, realizing with horror how his sentence must end.

'I had three sons, Matthew, Samuel and Henry, and three daughters too. And now only Henry and Eleanor are left to me. All the rest are gone.'

'Mother, why are you crying?' her daughter demanded to know.

Susan Wainwright put her hands to her face. 'I paid heavily for the choices I made.'

A silence fell upon us all, broken only when Mrs Jenson got up to say that night was now here, and began to draw the curtains. We sat for a moment in the darkness, before the lamps were lit and the shadows chased away. The internal gloom we felt could not be dissolved so easily with the soft paraffin light. And Mrs Wainwright sat, still weeping silently. I saw how she twisted and turned her hands together in her lap and wondered at the thoughts that haunted her.

Very soon after this, the vicar and his wife left. Mrs Sterling asked her most sincerely whether there was anything she could do to help ease her unhappiness. Susan Wainwright shook her head hopelessly and said no.

The following morning, Eleanor told me she had more of the story to give me, so I followed her to the boathouse. She handed me an envelope. 'Father strayed for the first time with Arielle Marchal. Perhaps he loved her. This letter was sent by Mother's younger sister Eveline.'

26 July 1849

My very dear Susan,

Many thanks for your kind parcel of assortments and with most especial thanks for sending me the yellow silk gown of yours that I so admired when at Teesbank Hall in the spring. I wore it to the Hemingways' Thursday last and received many compliments upon the colour and material and et cetera.

I hope that this letter finds you all well and that the stifling heat has abated – it is so worrisome, especially in your *delicate condition*. We continue well in London, although Father frets and says he would like to return to York as soon as possible, although Mother still holds out until at least one of her girls has made a suitable match!

I fear I must be the bearer of some news which may cause you unhappiness and have much debated whether to tell you. But I am convinced that you have been most sorely used and have the right to know exactly how.

When I was at the Hemingways', I spoke at some length with Mrs Angela Baker – it was she who recommended the French governess (Arianne? Arielle?). She asked me at great length how this woman got along at Teesbank Hall and when I quizzed her as to the reason for her most particular interest, she confessed she asked the girl to leave because she had found her *in a compromising situation* with Hugh, their sixteen-year-old son. And not – as she had told you – because her daughter Christabel had outgrown governesses. In fact, Christabel does have a new governess, who is a very plain, stout thing by all accounts.

When I rounded on her and asked why she had suggested this woman to you, she had looked very shame-faced and said she wanted her out of the house quickly and, there being no unmarried men in your household, she had thought there would be no danger of anyone falling for her wiles.

As you can imagine, I was quite short with her after this and she was very apologetic et cetera. I am sure there is no possibility of Matthew being seduced by such a young woman. However, it seems to me that she is *a moral threat* to your household and to your peace of mind.

Please forgive me for communicating this to you. I have, as ever, your best interests at heart.

I am and remain your most loving and dear sister,

Eveline
53, Hampstead Grove,
London, NW

'Mother received this letter a day or two after it was written. She showed it to Father and insisted that Arielle Marchal leave the house immediately.'

'Did he agree?' I asked.

'Yes. Nancy Wilson told me she believed Father was tiring of Arielle, who was, in any case, pregnant and an inconvenience. He was to be away on business for several days and it was agreed that Mother alone would dismiss her from the house. He was too much of a coward to be there.'

'Was it your father's child?'

'I think there was no doubt of that. Nancy Wilson said Arielle doted upon him and had no interest in any other man. She would have faced almost certain destitution, pregnant and friendless as she was.' She paused. 'For such an insipid woman, Mother has a great capacity for hate.'

CHAPTER SEVENTEEN

Following the vicar's visit, I was to attend church that Sunday. Mrs Jenson was of the Methodist faith and attended the squat red-brick church in the town of Yarm. Many of the maids, gardeners and stable lads were Anglican but the social hierarchy of Teesbank Hall meant I wasn't expected to walk with them to church. I was condemned to go the dusty few miles alone, ahead of the others of the household. I hoped the maids didn't imagine I considered myself above them. In truth, I was quite shy then and felt awkward in their company. I was envious of the familiarity with which they laughed and confided in each other and longed to have that ease of friendship. The kitchen-maid Eliza had taken a particular dislike to me and had given me the name Miss High and Mighty, which the other servants dared not say outright to my face, but I saw them giggle and snigger among themselves.

The church of St John the Baptist has stood in Eaglescliffe village since the twelfth century and overlooks the river Tees. It's a simple building in the Norman style and nestles in the green shade of yew trees, cradling within its hallowed grounds the remains of the dead dating back for several hundred years. The walk had left me parched and it was a relief to enter the cool of the church after the heat outside. I had a few minutes alone, as the other servants had not yet arrived and only the most devout of parishioners were in church so early.

The place smelt strongly of incense and of the pink and cream roses that were arranged prettily in vases on the altar. As befitted a leading family in the area, the Wainwrights had their own pew. Yet, while the servants of the household presented themselves scrubbed and in their Sunday best each week, the Wainwrights, with the exception of Henry, hadn't been to the church for many years and the pew was often empty.

I suspected Mr Wainwright had a sacrilegious belief that God Himself was responsible for Samuel's murder. It was written down in the inquest papers that he had said, 'God, why have you punished my family in this way?' Mrs Wainwright would not be seen in public, and Eleanor was too strong-willed and stubborn to be forced to do anything she didn't want to do. She might believe in ghosts, but it was Darwin not God whom she worshipped.

For myself, I found a welcome peace in the church, with its soothing rituals and prayers that had been said over and over again for so many hundreds of years. There, I could gain a perspective on my own life – so insignificant in the great scheme of things. Looking around the church, I thought of those who had knelt there before me, taking comfort in the belief that they, too, might have struggled with the greatest of traumas and the most difficult of dilemmas, but ultimately death and God must judge us all. The things I feared most might never arise, hidden so far north and so far from home. Surely I was safe from detection and harm.

At the end of the service, the vicar stood at the church door to greet his departing congregation. When he saw me there, he pressed my hand warmly and said with sincerity how glad he was that I was able to attend and that he hoped he would see me there the next week. It was a beautiful summer's day and a bliss of blue skies and sweet-smelling flowers. I was reluctant to return to the prison of Teesbank Hall. It was the Sunday in the month when the afternoon was mine to do with as I wished and I decided to use my freedom to enjoy some time alone.

However, having freedom and knowing what to do with it were two quite different things. Other than the vicar and his wife, I knew nobody in Eaglescliffe and, because I belonged to Teesbank Hall, it was likely that I was distrusted. I knew from my experience with the carters that the very name of the place was enough to provoke the most extreme of reactions. And I had hardly a penny to my name. Until six months had passed and I received my wages in arrears, my poverty kept me trapped at the Hall.

The money I needed for the journey to Eaglescliffe had been stolen. For five desperate weeks I had riffled through pocketbooks and wallets, even the strongbox in Uncle Thomas Stepford's study. My thefts had become more reckless as my desperation grew. I knew only that I had to escape, and this single thought drove out every other terror. In truth, it would only have been a matter of time before I was caught. The letter from Teesbank Hall saved me from discovery.

With the absence of an alternative, I walked in the graveyard of the church. Although that might sound a melancholy thing to do, it was in fact the prettiest of spots, shaded by the green leaf of trees in all their summer glory. There could have been no better place to continue my reflections on our insignificance, where each headstone told a story of lives lived well or badly and reminded us that all our hopes and earthly achievements will end in the grave. I thought of the words of the great bard – truly we are but a 'quintessence of dust'.

With such thoughts playing through my mind, I walked along the narrow path that wound around the church. It was with a start of surprise, that I found myself at the Wainwright family tomb. It was set a little apart from the rest of the grounds, a great marble monument to the family, not as weather-beaten as the gravestones of those longer established in the area. They were relative newcomers. It was less than sixty years since Joshua Wainwright had built the Hall on the sweat of the Durham coalfields. This marked them out as an oddity in an area where most could trace their ancestors back across several generations, some as far as the Domesday Book.

Etched into the solemn stone, I saw the briefest of

histories. The names were already becoming fainter with time, so I traced them with my fingertips. There was Joshua Wainwright, who had built Teesbank Hall, with the intention that his family might join the ranks of the gentry. He was taken from this life in 1851 and was greatly mourned by his loving wife Diana, but his epitaph assured the world that he had died in the faithful hope of resurrection.

Much more poignant than the adult deaths were the dates of the births and deaths of the Wainwright children. Here, carved into stone, was the pitiful story of Susan Wainwright's life. Each neat, chiselled name represented all the hope and potential of a life come to nothing. There was an oldest son, who carried his father's name of Matthew, and died in 1840, not even seeing his first birthday; Martha had been carried away by tuberculosis at her school in Pooley Bridge in the same year as her grandfather. From the gossip in the servants' hall, I knew that the births were woven through with pregnancies not come to term. Then, most sad of all because of his unnatural death, Samuel Wainwright. In this peaceful graveyard, there was no sign of the savagery of his end, merely the words, 'Samuel Wainwright, Born 12 February 1847, Taken from us on or about 11 August 1849, Beloved son of Matthew and Susan Wainwright, Sorrow without end.'

The words of Mrs Wainwright, spoken into the darkness of a summer evening, came back to me: 'And now only Henry and Eleanor are left to me. All the rest are gone.' I stood a while in the shade of the trees and offered up a prayer for those departed souls before beginning my slow and reluctant walk back to Teesbank Hall.

Yet a haunting doubt followed me out of the church grounds. The names of Matthew, Martha and Samuel were written on the tombstone, alongside their pitifully short lifespans, but the name of the one daughter was not. Clara Wainwright. The girl who was named in the inquest papers, the girl who was in such a bad temper on the night of the murder that Nancy Wilson testified to it before the assembled crowd. The girl, too, who had frightened Mrs Hargreaves.

There must be some reason for this. Why hadn't she been buried with her brothers and sister?

Now a new idea began to form in my mind. Clara would have been around fourteen at the time Samuel died, old enough and jealous enough, perhaps, to hate the younger child. Matthew Wainwright had been a good father to his daughters before the son replaced them in his affections. He was the longed-for heir, she the useless elder daughter who must be married off at expense to the family. And Clara had a capacity for violence – the servants still gossiped about it and about how she had attacked her younger brother so viciously that he was cut and bleeding.

At the inquest, the surgeon had suggested the infant left the house willingly with someone he knew. It would have been easy for his sister to lure him from bed with promises of a game or a treat. Her bedroom was close by her brother's. The French governess had been sent away; she was nowhere near him. But Clara's arrest would have brought even more sorrow to the broken family, and Matthew Wainwright struck me as ruthless enough to allow his former lover to take his daughter's place on the gallows.

He had been at the inquest and Nancy Wilson would never have dared to accuse his daughter of murder, certainly not to his face. It might be common knowledge among the locals that Samuel had been killed by a member of his family, and only their status protected the killer. It would explain the mood of the crowd, whose angry shouts had been diligently noted in the court transcript. When Nancy realized that the Coroner's questions seemed to implicate her, she was forced to cast about for someone else to blame. And the easiest person of all to name was Arielle Marchal. She was friendless and destitute. No one would speak up for her.

I became convinced Nancy Wilson held the key to the truth about the murder. She had told Eleanor dreadful stories about the vengeful governess. Perhaps her own guilty conscience had made her believe Arielle had returned to haunt her for lying at the inquest and condemning her friend to death. Whatever the truth, her voice was there in the narrative, always a heartbeat away and always knowing more than she was prepared to reveal. She would know why Clara Wainwright had not been buried in the family grave, I reflected.

Teesbank Hall was a place of unanswered questions. There were too many things I didn't understand. Reluctantly, I started back there, when my thoughts were interrupted by the clatter of horses' hoofs and the wheels of a carriage, and then a cry of greeting: 'Miss Caldwell, how are you?'

I turned and was surprised to see Henry, with Rosalind and Edward Merryweather, all in an open carriage. They smiled in my direction.

'Miss Caldwell, how lovely to see you!' Rosalind exclaimed. Even though the day was hot and the road dusty, she was perfectly serene in a silk dress that matched the blue of her eyes. 'You're very well met, because Edward and I must turn off for the Long Newton road and now Mr Wainwright will have someone to walk with on the dull journey back to Teesbank Hall.'

'Would you allow me to join you?' Henry asked, jumping down.

'Yes, of course, sir,' I said, and felt myself blush slightly. 'I didn't expect to see you.'

'We've been out to Yarm. It's impossible to stay inside on such a hot day,' he replied.

'Oh, yes,' Rosalind agreed. 'And, of course, we've had lots of plans to make.' He smiled up at her and she touched him lightly on his arm.

'Why don't you come over in the next day or so?' Edward said. 'Father will be home and we can look at dates.'

Henry agreed and, with that, we wished them goodbye and their carriage set off at a fast pace.

He turned to me and observed, 'I see you've managed to escape from Teesbank Hall.'

'Only for two hours or so. I went to the service at St John the Baptist and then walked for a while in the churchyard.'

'What do you think of Mr Sterling and his wife?' he asked. 'Eleanor told me you were there when they visited last week.'

'I liked them. I thought they were a pleasant and principled couple, Mrs Sterling especially.'

He laughed. 'That's not quite the word Grandmother used but, yes, I agree with you. They seem very sincere and are a good addition to the parish. I would have been at the service myself, if I hadn't been with Edward and Miss Merryweather planning the trip to Scotland.'

'Is your holiday still to take place?'

'Yes, we're going in August and were talking about possible routes. We've booked the train to Inverness and it seems Miss Merryweather and her parents will be able to meet us there for a few weeks, which is splendid.'

'That will be nice,' I said mechanically, thinking of how different Rosalind's life was from my own.

'And then Edward, Richard and I hope to get across to the Isle of Skye – the new Kyle of Lochalsh Line will take us to the ferry port. We might go climbing, if the weather holds.'

'Is Richard a friend from university?'

Henry chuckled. 'Well, yes. He's supposedly studying theology, but is usually to be found on the rugby pitch or in the Shakespeare Tavern. He's very good-natured but definitely no scholar. The dean's put him back a year and now they're threatening to throw him off the course.'

'How awful! He must be worried.'

'Richard? Not at all. The Wardhaugh family owns half of Northumberland, so it doesn't much matter whether he gets his degree or not.' He paused. 'When I return from holiday, I'll have to decide what to do next, now that I've graduated.'

'Do you know what you want to do?'

He was suddenly quieter and said, 'Knowing and being able to do it are quite different.'

We were both silent. Determined to change the topic of conversation, I said, 'The Isle of Skye is supposed to be very beautiful but aren't there lots of midges in August?'

'Everyone tells me so. Supposedly eucalyptus keeps them away, but I can't stand the smell and would rather be bitten.'

'Lavender is meant to have the same effect as eucalyptus.'

'I didn't know that. Before I leave, I'll invest in some lavender, as long as you can assure me it will keep me free of bites.'

'I can't guarantee it but you'll certainly smell sweeter.'

We continued chatting in this way and arrived quickly back at the house.

'Thank you for walking with me,' he said, and went off to speak to one of the stable lads.

CHAPTER EIGHTEEN

As I entered the cool of Teesbank Hall, my skin still glowed with the warmth of the sun. I had a whole afternoon of leisure ahead of me and wondered what I might do with it. However, Eleanor and Agnes were waiting for me. It was obvious that something had happened. Eleanor's face was feverish with excitement, while Agnes was downcast and subdued.

'What has taken you so long, Miss Caldwell?' Eleanor demanded. 'We were looking out for you from the library window and you have taken so long.'

'I spent some time in the graveyard. It's a pretty spot and shaded on a hot day like this.'

'And you walked back with my brother. Did you impose yourself upon him in that creeping, quiet way you have? Poor Henry! We often laugh together at how plain you are.'

At her words, my good mood began to deflate and disappear.

She gave me a strange look, but then continued, 'You will be glad to know that you are needed for once!'

'What do you mean, Miss Eleanor?'

She smiled secretively across at Agnes. 'We are going to have a séance and summon the spirit of Arielle Marchal. We can ask her what we must do to take away the curse upon Teesbank Hall.'

I was horrified. 'We can't do that. It wouldn't be right.' The suggestion chilled me, coming as quickly as it did after the time I had spent contemplating the gravestones in the churchyard.

'Agnes knows all about séances. She and the other servants had one in the attics last week.'

I looked at her, startled, but she nodded. 'It's true, miss, we did. Eliza's sure there is something evil in the attics so she made us all hold a séance. Her auntie from Consett used to fancy herself a spiritualist.'

'You don't believe in that, do you?'

Agnes looked shame-faced. 'When we did it, something happened. We asked if there was an unquiet spirit in the room and Eliza went into a trance and the glass on the board went mad – it kept spelling out "Yes"! I've never been so frightened and afterwards Eliza didn't remember anything about what happened.'

'Oh, Agnes, it's all trickery,' I said. 'Eliza will have feigned the whole thing. Anyway, if she's such an expert, she can be involved in your séance. I certainly won't.'

'Eliza refuses to do it again. She was scared. Proper scared.'

The idea appalled me. 'I don't want to take part. I want nothing to do with it!'

Eleanor had been quiet but now she spoke: 'You must, Miss Caldwell. We can hardly hold a séance with only two of us.' She had that strange feverishness about her again and I noticed her tugging at her buttoned sleeves.

'Well, I won't be a party to raising the dead. It's unchristian.' The darkness of the human world already hung over Teesbank Hall. It did not need the spirit world to be added.

'You must take part,' she said sulkily.

'No.' I was adamant.

Eleanor looked at me carefully. 'Surely, you don't want Mrs Jenson to know that I have bribed you to leave me alone and unwatched.'

With a sinking heart, I realized the power of her threat.

'I am happy to reveal all. I will tell her how you left me for hours at an end, so you could wade through the secrets of my brother's murder.'

'That's not right,' I protested.

'If you take part, I'll not tell how you abandoned me. That must be our bargain.'

I remembered Mrs Jenson's words. *She is a sly and manipulative girl.* I realized she had spoken the truth and Eleanor had trapped me.

'Where will the séance be held?' My question was an acceptance that I would take part.

'We can use one of the rooms at the front of the attics. Nobody goes there. It must be in the dead of night.'

Agnes and I nodded at the grim inevitability of her response.

'What about Mrs Anderson?' I asked. 'She'll know you've gone.' I clutched at the smallest of hopes.

Eleanor laughed. 'By midnight, Mrs Anderson will be fast asleep and snoring her gin-sodden dreams. You do not need to worry about her.'

And so, at around twelve that night, there was a faint knocking on my bedroom door. I opened it to see Eleanor and Agnes.

'Perhaps we could hold it here. In this room,' Eleanor said. 'It was Arielle Marchal's room. Her spirit will be very strong here.'

My refusal was so definite that Eleanor said no more and we crept by candlelight into a large room further along the corridor. It had been used to store discarded bric-a-brac, and piles of unused furniture lined its edges. At Eleanor's request, Agnes had found a small oval table and three wooden chairs. In the centre of the table was a talking board – what we would now call a ouija board – an oblong tray covered with all the letters of the alphabet. Eleanor carefully closed the door behind us. 'No one must know. We cannot be caught. Father would not want us to invoke the past.'

The three of us sat around the table, unsure of what to do next. The room felt cold, even though it was a summer's night. Apart from the single candle on the table, it was in darkness.

'What happened when you had the séance with Eliza?' Eleanor asked.

Agnes thought for a moment. 'We placed the glass in the

middle of the board and Eliza began to ask questions. Just straightforward ones at first, like was anybody there, and then we tried to find out who it was.'

I could see even Eleanor felt frightened and unsure as to what we should do. 'Agnes, you must ask the questions.'

'But, miss—'

'You know what to do. Neither Miss Caldwell nor I have been at a séance before.'

That seemed to decide it and I was glad that at least I was not responsible for calling up the dead. The glass was placed at the centre of the board and all three of us placed one finger upon it, so lightly that we were almost touching pure air.

We looked at each other in the candlelight. Unified in silence. Then Agnes asked tentatively, 'Is anyone there?'

There was no response. Instinctively, I glanced down at my hand but could see nothing in the semi-darkness. The minute stretched itself out to eternity. 'See? It's nonsense. We are sitting here like fools. We should stop now,' I said.

'No,' Eleanor replied sharply. 'Ask it again.'

'Does anyone from the other side wish to speak to us?' Agnes whispered.

Again there was nothing. Then I felt the faintest tremor. We held our breath and the dead furniture around us seemed to crowd in to observe. The glass beneath our fingertips began to move across the board, slowly at first and then faster, as if rushing to complete its message. Y–E–S. We looked at each other in terror.

'Who is it?'

Again there was a moment's stillness, and then the glass was travelling rapidly across the letters. First to the G.

'What is it saying?' Eleanor demanded.

We watched in silence as the glass spelled G–O–V–E–R–N–E–S–S.

'She is here. Arielle is here!' Eleanor exclaimed excitedly. 'Ask her if she is a good spirit or an evil one?'

Agnes repeated the question but this time the glass stayed firmly in the centre of the talking board. 'She doesn't like that question. I don't want to make her angry,' she whimpered.

'Ask her who she is, you fool. Then we'll know for definite whether or not it is Arielle Marchal.'

But Agnes would ask no more, so it was Eleanor who demanded into the darkness, 'Who are you?'

There was a moment's pause and then the glass began moving. At first, hesitantly, it settled on the W but then more confidently crossed and re-crossed the board. I knew already, even before the glass moved through all the letters, the word it spelled out

'Whore!' Eleanor exclaimed triumphantly. 'That is what they shouted at her as she was dying. Two words, "GOVERNESS" and "WHORE".'

It was too much. I could bear no more. It was not Arielle Marchal the dead spirits addressed, it was me.

Whore. The word that Uncle Thomas Stepford said.

'No!' I screamed, leaping up and pushing away the table so that the board and everything on it fell to the floor.

Agnes and Eleanor looked at me aghast.

'I cannot stay here.' I ran to the door and grappled with the handle, my panic making me clumsy so that I couldn't open it.

'Miss Caldwell,' Agnes gasped, 'we didn't mean to upset you. It's only a bit of fakery, you said that.'

I was hysterical now and they had to calm me. Even Eleanor looked worried. 'Be quiet! You must be quiet or we will all be in trouble for this. If Father knows . . .'

Finally I was silent, although I sobbed.

Agnes dared to say to Eleanor, 'You've gone too far. You shouldn't have made her do it. Miss Caldwell, I'll take you back to your room.' She put her arm around me awkwardly and spoke in my ear: 'I'm so sorry, miss. I didn't expect this to happen, but it's impossible to refuse Miss Eleanor when she's in one of her moods. I wish I'd never talked about Eliza's séance in front of her.'

I nodded. I refused to believe in ghosts, but this place, with its terrible secrets, had eaten away at my nerves.

CHAPTER NINETEEN

My room was as I'd left it. The white cotton nightgown lying neatly on my bed, the silver-backed brush waiting on the dressing-table. All was ordered and neat, but I felt like an aberration in the room. Agnes moved the nightgown to one side and sat next to me. 'I told Miss Eleanor that we shouldn't dabble with the dead, but she wouldn't listen.'

I was unable to speak. I was sick to my core and the images I always tried to push to the back of my mind were playing out now. The blinding light was there. That sense of deep unease and terror, too, as I tried to make sense of the unthinkable.

'But, Miss Caldwell, no one expected you to have such a turn. Why did you take it so bad?'

I had to answer. If I did not, it would create more questions and I didn't want attention drawn to me. But I must decide how much of the truth I should portion out, offer to Agnes so she wouldn't probe further. 'Someone once called me that. Whore. I find the word offensive.'

Agnes looked at me bemused. My reaction had been so extreme.

I was trembling still but forced myself to say, 'It was in the past and he was a very ignorant man. I will not see him again and we don't need to speak of it further.'

Agnes went to ask more questions, but I shook my head. I had no more to say. After a moment's reflection, she haltingly changed the subject. 'Miss Eleanor is obsessed with the murder and with Arielle Marchal. It's not right. That's why she was so desperate to have the séance.'

'She lures me with stories about the past,' I whispered, although my thoughts were in another place. Another past.

'It's best left alone most of the time,' she replied, and looked at me significantly. 'Now, Miss Caldwell, will you be all right to be left?'

'Yes. Thank you for your kindness. Please call me Harriet.'

'Yes, Harriet.' She smiled.

Once she had gone, it was impossible to settle. I turned on my side, so I faced away from the looking-glass and the face that haunted me there. But it was not so easy to turn away from myself. Uncle Thomas Stepford. It had taken just one word and I was trapped in Swaffham again.

Phrenology was a discredited branch of science. I knew that. Father had often spoken disparagingly of his younger brother. And he was a man who rarely spoke ill of anyone. Father's money had freed Uncle Thomas Stepford from the monotony of his travelling shows. Now he could take his research in new directions. One of his first actions when he moved into my home had been to set up an unwieldy box camera. It had taken pride of place in Father's study, now transformed into Uncle Thomas's workshop, where Fowler's *Practical Phrenology* overthrew Shakespeare and Milton.

He declared that human nature was not written merely on the human skull but on the human body. Destiny and social class might be read in the turn of an ankle, the slope of the shoulder or the curve of a bosom. Gladys, the scullery maid, and I were to be the subjects of his scientific enquiry, to compare how social class and breeding were reflected by our bone structure. Both of us were bound by poverty and dependence – impossible to protest against the degradation of the weekly routine, she on Monday afternoons and I on Thursday, when we had to present ourselves separately at the door of Father's former study.

Uncle Thomas Stepford's photographic machine sat at the centre of the room, a huge box of beech-wood, shrouded in a cloak of black. It was aimed at a heavy linen sheet pinned against a wall, upon which various lines and measurements indicated different parts of the body. The machine worked only on the brightest of days and I would pray for storms and dark clouds, so that his plans would be thwarted.

He had a box of scientific instruments and measuring apparatus: the strange circles of metal that were used to check the size and shape of our skulls, the measuring rods to calculate our height to the closest inch. The procedure would always be the same. I would be told to disrobe behind the makeshift screen that he had erected against the wall and put on a thin, almost transparent white shift. He would disappear behind the curtain of the photographic apparatus and issue commands about how I should stand, or he would emerge from his tent and move my body, so that I was correctly aligned. All the time he would be sweating and panting, and I saw him furtively put his hand inside his trousers and rub himself. When I tried to protest, he told me I was an ignorant girl and didn't understand the demands of the natural sciences, using terms from Latin to cloak the depravity of what he did.

Finally, there would be the dazzling bright flash and I would be photographed against the white sheet, standing frozen, motionless in time, so that no movement might blur the lines of the carefully arranged photographic impression to be added to his collection. Later I saw the pictures of myself, staring dead-eyed into the bleakness of the future he was preparing for me.

My height was recorded meticulously in a parallel line to that of Gladys. We were four months apart in age, but I spiralled at least three inches above her, which pleased him endlessly. No doubt it gave justification to what he did. I tried to speak with Gladys. I knew from the markings upon the white sheet that she was forced to submit to the same indignities as I, but when I asked her directly once, she merely looked at me with dull grey eyes, shrugged her shoulders and turned away. I think she might have been crying.

One week she was ill with influenza. That Friday was the first time there was a sly knock on my bedroom door. He had brought a book to show me. 'Look at the pictures,' he said. 'They are women just like you. They have an immoral nature, too. They are whores.'

I said, 'I can't. I don't want to.' But he forced the book in front of me and I looked at the photographs with a fascinated horror, as he turned the pages breathlessly. How to describe what was there? Anonymous women in a state of undress, sitting, lying, standing, looking at the camera with the same blank stare that I recognized as my own. Further on, there were pictures of men and women contorted together in ways and shapes I couldn't comprehend and that seared themselves onto my mind.

'You could be beautiful, just like them,' he panted hoarsely. 'It is written into your bone.'

'I don't want to look like those women.' I pushed the book away.

'You're just not ready yet, but you will be, given time. Gladys refused at first, but when she considered the life she would be driven to, with no character and no position. Well, now there is nothing she will not accept. I have the photographs, if you need proof.'

The colour had leached from my face. 'I'm sorry but you must leave now, thank you. I am very tired.'

In this unknown territory, I fell back on the banalities of polite conversation, having no knowledge of how else to respond. And, strangest of all, he followed the rules of social conduct and went. Once he was out of the room, I shook uncontrollably and was violently sick into the chamber pot. It was then that I learned to barricade my bedroom with a chair jammed under the door handle. To dread the sound of footsteps and the soft whisper of my uncle outside my room.

But he found me in the dining room, morning room or garden, seizing his moment when no one else was in earshot and murmuring, 'You're just not ready yet, but you will be. You're just like the women in those pictures. You are a whore, Harriet. You will find me in time.'

I looked him directly in the eye and said if he touched me I would tell the world the kind of man he was. He laughed at this. We both knew I was trapped, and the threat was as fragile as the ancient lock on my bedroom door. I didn't know how long it would hold.

I had to escape, and quickly.

Father's solitary nature meant we had lived a secluded life. He had a small circle of friends, who had mourned him at the funeral, but they were scattered around the country and I had no way of contacting them. There was also Mr Braithwaite, the family lawyer, who had overseen the probate of the will. He had looked at me with sad eyes as its contents were fully revealed and I passed into the keeping of Uncle Thomas Stepford, under his guardianship until I reached the age of twenty-five. He might have been able to assist me in some way, but he no longer came to the house.

By the luckiest of coincidences, my former governess and I shared a Christian name, so I took her surname and history for myself and placed an advertisement in the *Morning Post*. Each morning I waited with bated breath, determined to be first to catch the post and see if I had a response. Uncle Thomas Stepford went to bed at two or three in the morning and didn't rise until noon, so I hoped he would not be aware of any packages directed to Miss Harriet Caldwell, the departed governess.

Although none of the servants dared to support me openly, I thought they wouldn't betray me. The only reply I received was from Teesbank Hall, which requested I furnish a letter of recommendation and provided some limited details about the post. My carefully forged documents were sent away and I can still remember my joy when the appointment was confirmed. I had found employment. I packed my trunk secretly in the night and crept out before the sun rose to catch the train north. I did not even tell Lucy – how could I reveal the monster her father was? Instead, I thanked God as I silently shut the door of the house in Swaffham.

I could never return.

Although I prayed for numbing sleep, the bells of St John the Baptist counted out the bleak hours and still I was awake as the chimes told four o'clock. I must have something to think about that wasn't Uncle Thomas Stepford and wasn't Swaffham. From Father, I had inherited a tendency to make lists whenever I was unsure of anything. He would counsel me to draw up both sides of the argument, so that I could see all the evidence, considering it as if I had been in a court-room. Therefore, I got out of bed and in the early-morning light looked for a piece of paper to write down my ideas. I settled upon the flyleaf of *The Origin of Species*, one of the two books I had brought, and placed the title 'Arielle Marchal: Guilty of Murder' at the top of the page, which I neatly underlined, then drew a line down the middle, with one column headed 'FOR', the other 'AGAINST'.

Under 'FOR', I put the first reason to suggest her guilt: she had been publicly accused by Nancy Wilson, who was her friend and who was in the bedroom adjoining Samuel Wainwright's. Set against this was the magistrate's observation that Nancy was untrustworthy. I knew Arielle had refused to speak at her trial and that, too, must go against her – if she was innocent, surely she would have defended herself. Most damning of all was the bolt of silk cloth, cut from the section that was wrapped around the child's body, and which was found in her lodgings. I could not explain that.

But the arguments against her being the murderer were also strong. Everyone at the inquest had agreed that the killer must have been inside Teesbank Hall on the night of the murder. Arielle was not. She had been sent away from the house and this seemed to me the strongest argument against her guilt. As well, she had no reason to kill an innocent child – any hatred she might have felt about her dismissal would surely have been directed at Mr and Mrs Wainwright. Other people might have had a stronger motive and here my mind kept returning to Clara Wainwright, the jealous sibling whose name had been left off the family gravestone. She was in a temper on the night of the killing – I played around with the phrase 'Clara suffered from murderous jealousy', and wrote it down on the 'AGAINST' side, because it gave someone else a motive.

I wanted Arielle to be innocent, irrationally I knew. She felt like another desperate version of me, alone and an easy target for blame. Although I tried to be objective, I needed the evidence to fall on the side of 'AGAINST', but always there was the white silk, the final piece in the jigsaw that I couldn't resolve.

At the bottom of the page, I wrote down the mysteries around the living. The way Eleanor was monitored at all times. The unexplained entries in Mrs Jenson's ledgers, the coded letters C and D, and the monthly payments of twenty-five pounds to Gate Helmsley. I knew there had been a man in the attics that night, but Agnes and Mrs Jenson had denied his existence. All these things must have significance and I was sure they were somehow linked to the murder and whatever dark secrets lay at the heart of this family.

Nancy Wilson would know. Always it came back to Nancy Wilson.

CHAPTER TWENTY

Although it was only twenty-two years since the murder, it seemed like ancient history – as obsolete as candles are to us now in a world of gas and electric light – and Nancy Wilson was part of that world, a dead name written on the yellowing inquest papers. It was a surprise therefore when, a few weeks later, Mrs Hargreaves said in passing to Mrs Jenson, 'You'll not believe who I saw in Stockton, walking around with no sense of shame?'

Mrs Jenson looked up with interest, the small dark eyes calculating and alert. 'No, Mrs Hargreaves, who was that?'

'Why Nancy Wilson, Miss Eleanor's old nursemaid. She saw me, too, but walked away as if I wasn't there.'

'She is an ignorant girl.' Mrs Jenson shrugged but clearly Nancy's presence in the area was not news to her. 'I heard Nancy lost her place in Sunderland after she fell into drinking and bad company. She's working now as a laundress in Stockton. At Atkinson's Laundry, which she was lucky to get for she was given no character when she left.'

Mrs Hargreaves was about to comment upon this or perhaps ask a question but Mrs Jenson looked at me and seemed to indicate with a movement of her head that no more should be said. The cook nodded, and they returned to other matters. I suspected that Mrs Jenson might reveal more about Nancy Wilson but only once the two of them were alone. I had imagined her long dead and buried, along with the four oldest Wainwright children and Arielle Marchal, but that couldn't be the case. Eleanor had told me she was sixteen at the time of the killing and she must only be thirty-eight or so now. I was absolutely convinced the nursemaid was the key to finding out what had happened on that summer's night over two decades ago. If I could speak to her and ask what had happened, perhaps she would be prepared to reveal her secrets. At the very least, I could observe her and decide whether she was lying or not.

Stockton was six miles away as the crow flew, and it was impossible to walk there and back on one of my rare Sunday afternoons away from Eleanor. The only way I could get to the town would be by accompanying Mrs Jenson on her weekly visit to order provisions and see her sister. However, I had angered her when I thought I had caught sight of Uncle Thomas Stepford and refused to return there the following week. Certainly, she had never asked me again.

One evening, Mrs Hargreaves was grumbling to the housekeeper about the poor quality of the meat delivered to Teesbank Hall. Although the Wainwrights were very free with their money, they were always given the worst cuts.

In the end, Mrs Jenson declared, 'When I go next Wednesday, I shall speak directly to Mr Smyth, the master butcher, and tell him we must be treated more fairly.' She was a formidable woman, despite her diminutive size, and held some standing in the area.

I saw my chance and startled them both by speaking. 'Mrs Jenson, may I accompany you to Stockton? I have some personal business I must attend to.'

Mrs Jenson was taken aback by my request. What business could I have to attend to? She fell to her default position. 'Miss Eleanor cannot be left unattended. Surely any personal business can be conducted by correspondence.'

I held my main bargaining point. 'I've often covered for Mrs Anderson when it was not my time and never complained.' This was true, as the nurse was frequently inconvenienced through drink or sheer cussedness. 'Agnes can watch over Miss Eleanor for a few hours, and I will be no trouble to you at all. I need be with you only during the journey.'

That she would see so little of me seemed to convince her and it was agreed that I might accompany her.

And so it was that, in the dog days and heat of the August sun, I found myself in Stockton. Knowing no more of Nancy Wilson than that her place of employment was Atkinson's Laundry, I had only the conviction and confidence of youth to allow me to believe I would find her. Mrs Jenson quickly unburdened herself of me, and we agreed that we would meet by the Shambles at noon.

The town hummed with activity. It was market day and brightly coloured stalls were set out across the width of the high street. The air was filled with the piercing calls of the men and women who worked there, all competing for custom. I found an elderly stall-holder, whose face seemed kind, and asked her where I could find Atkinson's Laundry.

She was a little taken aback. 'Why, it's in the old part of the town, near Bishop Street but it's not the kind of place for a young lady like you. Why would you want to go there?'

'I have a parcel to deliver on behalf of an acquaintance,' I lied, then thanked her and set off in the direction she had indicated. I had no time to dawdle: Mrs Jenson was a stickler for time-keeping and I would have to present myself at twelve, whether or not I had found Nancy Wilson.

As I walked quickly through the narrow streets, I clung to the shade, the dark fabric of my gown a blot against the bright sunshine of the day. There was a church tower and clock at the centre of the town, so I could measure the time. Although I had worried Nancy Wilson might be difficult to find, it was easier than I had expected to locate the place where she worked: Atkinson's Laundry was part of a collection of ramshackle dwellings which clung to the back of the finer residences of Bishop Street. It had been the site of an outbreak of cholera five years previously and the buildings were cramped together and tumbledown; dank pools of water congregated at their foot and patches of moss covered the lower reaches of the walls. Even on this, the brightest of summer days, there remained a sense of darkness and pestilence about the place.

It was against such a backdrop that I met Nancy Wilson. A small, neatly written sign above a low door informed me that this was Atkinson's Laundry and I knocked, quietly at first, but then more loudly when there was no response. Aware of time passing, I turned the handle and found the door open. As I entered the gloom of the building, clouds of steam swirled around me and I suspected even on the coldest of days it was warm there – today the heat was unbearable.

'Is anyone here?' I shouted hesitantly.

I heard a voice from within the building, whether a cry of greeting or a shout of challenge I couldn't tell. The atmosphere was unwholesome – even the air itself was humid and oppressive. The powerful stench of coal tar soap could not mask what lay beneath. The stink and sweat of the poor.

'Who is it?' The woman's voice was harsh and suspicious. 'Is that you, Edith?'

'No, ma'am,' I replied. 'I am Harriet Caldwell and I wish to speak to Nancy Wilson.' A figure emerged from the adjoining room.

'You're speaking to 'er now. I'm Nancy.'

Astonished, I looked at her carefully to see if there was any trace of the young nursemaid, who had stared out from the sepia photograph of Teesbank Hall over twenty years ago. She seemed much older than a woman in her thirties. Her face was heavily lined and her teeth were stained brown from chewing tobacco. With a damp cloth, she wiped the sheen of sweat from her forehead.

'What can I do for you, miss? If it's Mrs Blatchford who's sent yer then tell 'er the sheets should be ready by end of day.' There was a definite smell of alcohol about her and a painted-on smile failed to mask the belligerent expression beneath.

'I've not been sent by Mrs Blatchford. I have come of my own accord. I'm the governess at Teesbank Hall.'

She stopped short at this and stood with her hands on her hips. 'Why are yer here?' she demanded suspiciously. 'I've nowt to say about that place.'

'Please, I beg only a few moments of your time. Can I ask you some questions about the murder of Samuel Wainwright?'

'If that's all you want, you'd best leave now for I've nowt to say. It was a long time ago and I did my duty then, said all that was to be said.'

'I believe there were more things that weren't said.'

She ran her fingers through her heat-dampened hair. 'Nowt to say, you heard me. Who's sent you here – poking around where no one should?'

I wondered how I could reassure her I had no intention of harming her. 'No one has sent me,' I said. 'I know about the case because I have been shown documents. By Miss Eleanor.'

'Miss Eleanor,' she sneered. 'Them papers are mine by rights. Have yer brought them back?'

I shook my head.

'Then tell 'er I don't forget. They belong to me and I will get them back. Anyway, why've you come, if no one's sent you?' Nancy demanded.

'I know about the murder but . . .' I paused a moment '. . . I don't think Arielle Marchal was responsible and I want to find out the truth.'

She folded her arms now and stared me full in the face, 'Arielle Marchal killed Samuel Wainwright. Why are you trying to claim otherwise? D'you think I did it?'

'No, no, it's just—'

'You're calling me a liar, are you?'

'Could you have been wrong?' Even as I said it, the words sounded inadequate – if she was lying, she would hardly admit the fact to me.

'I wasn't mistaken and she killed the poor bairn.' She turned to retreat into the steam of the washing room.

In my desperation to know more, I called, 'Then why has Clara Wainwright's name been left off the family tomb? I believe it's proof her family knew it was she who had killed her brother, out of a terrible jealousy.'

She turned around as if stung. 'You don't know anything for all your fine ways.'

'I know an injustice has been done,' I said. 'Surely it can't harm you to reveal the truth after so many years.'

'D'you want to know the truth?' she jeered. 'Clara Wainwright isn't dead. She's alive and as well as she can be.'

I gasped at this revelation. 'How can she be still living? Her own mother said she was dead.'

'Well, she lied.'

And Susan Wainwright's words came back to me now, spoken into the darkness of a June night, as she thought of her children: 'All the rest are gone.' She hadn't said they were all dead. Matthew, Samuel and Martha lay in the cold earth but not Clara. I knew then that Nancy spoke the truth. 'Where is she, if she's not at Teesbank Hall?'

'I can tell you for a price.'

'I have sixpence,' I replied.

She laughed. 'In that case, I've work to do. So, if you've nowt for me, you can get out.'

I was glad to leave that foetid place, my head spinning with the revelation that Clara wasn't dead. But this knowledge left me no nearer to understanding the full story. Why on earth would the Wainwrights deny the existence of their own daughter and where was she now living? It seemed to me that Nancy Wilson's words confirmed Clara's guilt. The Wainwrights would have hidden her crime – they couldn't bear the disgrace of public disclosure – but would know she was too violent to live with them. I wondered whether Eleanor and Henry realized they had a living sister. Certainly, they never spoke of her.

And Mr Hughes's account of the arrest had dutifully noted that Arielle Marchal was pregnant, so not one but two lives would have been taken wrongly when she was hanged outside Durham Prison. As Mrs Jenson and I travelled back to Teesbank Hall and chatted about inconsequential things, this chilling thought ran through my head.

When we arrived home, I was surprised to see Henry loitering outside the front of the house, nervously glancing at his watch and tugging his collar. Remembering Eleanor's words about how they had laughed together about me, I felt embarrassed in his company – not that it really mattered what he thought of me.

'Mr Henry, sir. What are you doing still here? Your train goes in less than an hour.' There was more than a hint of annoyance in Mrs Jenson's question.

In reply, he looked at me, not the housekeeper. 'I'm glad to catch you both. I went to find you in the schoolroom, but Agnes said you were out.'

'We've been to Stockton to buy provisions,' I replied.

'The date of my journey up to Scotland has been brought forward and is to start today, so I've had to pack more quickly than I expected. I'm afraid the lavender will have to wait.'

'Lavender?' Mrs Jenson said bemused. 'Why do you want lavender?'

'It keeps the midges away,' I told her, which seemed to confuse her even more. 'Despite the threat of insects, I think your visit to Scotland will be a good deal more interesting than our trip to town, sir.'

'I've been looking forward to going. I'll be away for several weeks and didn't want to leave without saying goodbye.'

Mrs Jenson looked at him suspiciously and I felt myself blush slightly. His intense blue eyes were fixed upon me.

But I couldn't forget how Eleanor had said he thought me plain and laughed about me. To break the awkward silence, I asked him, 'Will you travel with your friends?'

'Just Richard. Edward's gone ahead to oversee the lodgings in Inverness for his parents and sister. We'll meet them up there.'

'Ah, so Rosalind Merryweather is going too. Can we expect any good news?' Mrs Jenson wished to know.

For some reason, I didn't want to hear the answer, so asked, 'Do you plan to spend much time in Inverness?'

'Definitely. A week or so, at the very least, while we get together some climbing equipment and go on excursions. We're hoping to scale some of the peaks in the Black Cuillin.'

'Well, sir, you are in danger of going nowhere, if you stand around talking to us.' Mrs Jenson looked particularly sour. 'For you'll miss your train and there won't be another until tomorrow.'

Henry was in far too good a mood to be put out by her ill-humour. 'You are very wise, Mrs Jenson –' he bowed – 'but my luggage has gone ahead with Tom, the stable lad. I need only to walk to the station and that won't take long.' He smiled. 'Miss Caldwell, I hope you have an enjoyable few weeks. Mrs Jenson, goodbye and please commend me most especially to Albert.'

He caught my eye and with that he was gone, leaving me to remember the ridiculousness of the night when we had played whist together and Albert had made his pungent contribution to the evening. I was forced to suppress my laughter in Mrs Jenson's stern presence.

'Albert. Why on earth did he mention my Albert? Why the sudden concern? He has never shown the slightest interest in Albert before. Truly, young men are a closed book to me, Miss Caldwell.' She tutted. 'Now let us get ourselves inside and back to work.'

I sighed. Endless days stretched out in front of me and it was impossible not to feel envious of Henry travelling in the outside world. I walked slowly to the library, where I found no sign of Eleanor and went to the servants' hall to ask if anyone knew where she was. Eliza looked up crossly from a particularly filthy pot she was attacking with a scrubbing brush. 'Her and Agnes have gone for a walk in the grounds.'

It was a beautiful afternoon, but I was still surprised Eleanor had agreed to go outside – all her pent-up energy was usually spent pacing the floor of the schoolroom. It was only when she wished to visit the boathouse that I was able to persuade her to walk in the grounds. Otherwise, she took an obstinate pleasure in refusing to leave the confinement of the library. My surprise was even greater when they returned, because Eleanor was smiling and talking in the same animated manner she had when she was with Henry. I wondered why it was that Agnes, who was so quiet and meek, had managed to gain everyone's affections. Perhaps it was because she was kind, and kindness was in short supply at Teesbank Hall.

When Eleanor saw me, she asked, 'Did you see Henry as you returned? He was looking for you and Mrs Jenson to take his leave.'

'Yes, he was at the front of the house.'

'He's been in an irritatingly good mood all day. Mrs Jenson believes he is going to propose to the vacuous Rosalind while they are away together.' She turned to Agnes. 'You don't think he would be stupid enough to do that, do you? Grandmother would encourage the marriage just to spite me.'

'I don't rightly know, miss,' she replied. 'Miss Merryweather is very pretty and I'm sure your family would see it as a good match.'

I felt a pang of something like regret and turned away quickly. I didn't want either of them to see my face. But Agnes was sharp, and when Eleanor was out of earshot, she looked at me directly and said, 'No, miss, that way only heartbreak lies.'

'I don't know what you mean, Agnes,' I stammered, and hurried ahead to catch up with Eleanor.

Henry would be gone for several weeks. I reflected that whether he thought me pretty or plain, I would miss him. He was frequently absent from Teesbank Hall. When I first arrived, he had been studying at Durham and once his final examinations had finished, he was often away visiting friends. But he always seemed close at hand. When he was here, the mood was undoubtedly lighter and happier. Without him, the days would be flatter and darker.

CHAPTER TWENTY-ONE

Mrs Hargreaves had predicted several times that the situation with Eleanor would deteriorate without Henry's steadying presence at Teesbank Hall and, at first, she had seemed to be proved wrong. Eleanor and I had started to speak together with an increasing closeness, although we avoided any subjects of a personal or emotional nature. We were both lonely and our isolation from the wider world threw us into each other's company. All around us, great changes and innovations were taking place, but we were forced to live second-hand through newspapers and books. Henry had ordered a copy of the catalogue from the London International Exhibition for Eleanor, which she pored over for hours at a time, pointing out beautifully crafted jewellery from India or an innovation in corn threshing from America. In truth, we both knew it was no replacement for experiencing the world, but at least it gave us a glimpse of the events around us and was a safe subject for conversation. The dull days began to hold some value between us.

Towards the end of August, Mrs Jenson was called away to nurse her eighty-year-old mother in Middlesbrough. This disrupted the routine of the house and Eleanor became withdrawn and fretful. She declared that it was pointless to talk about the International Exhibition because it would just make her more miserable at not being allowed to go. Instead, she wanted to talk about Arielle Marchal. She said she could feel her presence much more strongly than usual and was sure there was something Arielle wanted to communicate. Once she tried to persuade Agnes and me to take part in another séance, but my terror was so obvious that she gave up on it.

Mrs Anderson now complained about her constantly and said it was impossible to force her to do anything. When I completed the ledger with details of what she had eaten, there were comments about bouts of crying and the more frequent appearance of the cryptic letters C or D and I wondered again what might be their meaning.

Mrs Jenson was to be away for five days, and by the third, Mrs Anderson was particularly flustered, when she handed Eleanor into my custody. 'I don't envy you,' she muttered, when my pupil was on the other side of the room. 'This has been the worst night. She was screaming blue murder. She don't sleep and that means I don't sleep. I can't take much more of this an' I don't care what they pay me.'

I looked across at Eleanor, who was sitting quietly, and it seemed hard to believe the nurse's words, but once Mrs Anderson had gone, Eleanor said, in a slow and reluctant voice, that she had a favour to ask of me. I was surprised because she hated to be indebted to anyone.

'What is the favour?' I wanted to know.

'Not here. We cannot discuss it here. We must go to the boathouse.'

When we had reached that place, she took out an envelope yellowed with age. 'I have never shown this to anyone before. You must promise me you will tell no one of its existence.'

'What is it?' I asked.

'You will see. You speak French, don't you? Are you also able to read it?'

'Yes,' I said. 'Why?'

'Arielle Marchal left behind a letter in the attic. In the room you sleep in. It was addressed to my father, but it was not delivered and remained unopened until I found it.'

'And the letter is in French?' I prompted.

'I cannot speak that language. It is forbidden in this house, but you can translate it for me.'

I will admit that my hand trembled as I opened the letter from Arielle. It was like touching the past.

Eleanor was very quiet. 'Perhaps it will explain what happened and why she still haunts us.'

Arielle's handwriting was surprisingly distinctive, with elaborate flourishes and in a lilac ink that had become faint over the last two decades, but I made out her words as best I could and translated it for Eleanor.

My very dearest Matthew,
You must now know without doubt that I love you dearly.
From the earliest time I was at Teesbank Hall, it was you
alone who showed me kindness. You cannot know how
much you have meant to me, when I was ignored by all, a
foreigner, an outsider in a hostile home. In dark January,
your gift of a bunch of snowdrops — so beautiful and pure —
told me that spring must come finally and that perhaps you
might care for me.

And when the lilacs bloomed, we first kissed and lay
together as man and wife, hidden in the shelter of the
boathouse. I knew it was wrong. Always, always I knew it
was wrong. There is Susan. Your cold wife, with her sickly
blue eyes and her protestations that our attachment will
bring disgrace upon the family name — as if that were the
most important thing! What do I care for disgrace? The
manservants whisper, 'Whore!' as I walk past and your
mother gives me the look of the Medusa, but I laugh inside
for I know our love will prove much stronger than their
disapproval.

Those days we went together to Harrogate, for me it was
the greatest happiness. That we might be openly seen and you
could take my arm in front of the world. The pearl ring you
have given me and the fine white silk, both of these are our
promises to the future — that we will be together one day. Yet
it hurts me that you cut our silk in two and presented one half
to your wife because you felt guilty about our time away. She
gave her part to Clara and Martha as a plaything. It has no

*value to her and she wishes to mock what I hold most precious.
You tell me I must try to understand and we will be with each
other in time, but how can I be patient when she has what
I desire most? To call you husband.*

*And now, the swelling of my stomach tells me I am to
have your child. I think I am happy for I know it will be
a boy, a fine son, who will make you proud. I long to tell
you but somehow the right time never comes and now you
are always busy with the estate and a hundred other
things.*

*Always now it seems so difficult for us to be alone but my
heart bursts to tell you my news. Instead of speaking, I must
write our secrets in my mother tongue. Pen and paper must
be my confidant, until I am finally able to tell you. Then I
hope that we may live freely as a family, with our dearest son
by our side.*

*With all my love always,
Arielle*

'He gave her the white silk,' I said.

'Yes, and gave Mother the other part of it.' Her voice was
quiet. 'I want to return to the house.'

She got up, left the boathouse without another word and
I followed her, several steps behind. Once we were in the
library, she sat at her desk but made no attempt to go on
with her work. Instead, she stared down at her hands, which
were opened wide in front of her. After a while, she said,
'Sometimes Arielle's spirit feels so close that her voice

whispers inside my head. But that letter, that voice, was not how I imagined her.'

I didn't like her talk of the dead and tried to change the direction of the conversation. 'Perhaps it's the way I translated what she said. It can be difficult to catch someone's true character.'

She now looked up and said in an oddly stiff manner, 'Do you believe in ghosts, Harriet Caldwell?'

'You know I don't,' I replied.

'Not even the ghost of Arielle Marchal? Although you know what you felt when we were in the boathouse. Think of what happened in that place. It's where she lay with Father and where Samuel was murdered.'

'No. I don't believe, I can't believe. Such things aren't possible.'

'Then you are a fool, you know,' she said angrily. With a sudden jolting movement, she swept the pile of leather-bound books from her table. 'None of these can explain how and why I feel as I do! I have been searching for an answer but there is nothing written here that tells me of the horrors that surround me, trapped in this place. Nobody knows the torment in my mind. It can only be the curse she placed upon us. I cannot understand it otherwise.'

Her distress was so absolute that I moved to reach out to her, to try to take her in an awkward embrace. She reacted furiously to my instinctive sympathy. 'Get away from me.

You fraud, you liar. If you try to touch me again, I will scream the house down.'

I stopped and felt myself turn white. Did she know that my existence at the Hall was based on deceit? How could she know that I was not Harriet Caldwell but in fact Harriet Fleet?

That wasn't what she meant. 'This place is haunted, but you will not admit that to me. You are trying to hide the house's secrets, along with the rest of them. You pretend to befriend me, but you're a liar!'

'I'm not a liar and I am doing no such thing,' I retorted. 'Why should I pretend? There are no ghosts, there is nothing but the material world.'

She faced me full on, her hands clasped rigid at either side, and opened her mouth wide in a terrible scream: 'You are a liar. You are a liar! I know that she haunts us and I will prove the dishonesty of your words. Other people agree with me.' Over and over again she repeated this. The sound of her screams chilled me and I didn't dare touch her or go near her. I stood helpless and impotent.

As was to be expected, the dreadful sound brought a flurry of activity from across the great hall. Mr Snowdon, the head gardener, came racing in, closely followed by Tom, one of the lads from the stables, then Diana Wainwright herself. 'What on earth is going on here? What is the matter with my granddaughter?' she demanded of me, as if it were somehow my fault.

'She insists on calling me a liar. I have done nothing. I swear I have done nothing.'

Eleanor wheeled round to face me. 'That girl is a liar! She is a fraud. I do not want to see her! She is trying to trick me.'

Diana Wainwright's face hardened. 'Stop this at once, Eleanor. You are making an exhibition of yourself. Miss Caldwell is merely a governess. Why should she want to trick you?'

'Sometimes I watch her when she least realizes and I see it in her face. She knows, you see, she knows. I took her to the boathouse.'

'What does she know?' the grandmother spat out. 'You promised there would be no more of this type of behaviour.'

'Miss Caldwell knows this house is evil and it is cursed. She is part of the conspiracy against me. You all want to deny the truth.'

'The truth?' the old woman said coldly. 'The truth is that you are embarrassing yourself and the family name in front of our inferiors.'

'Is that all that you care about? What people think of the Wainwright family?' Eleanor wanted to know.

'I will not pander to your delusions while you are in this hysterical state.'

And then, strangely, like a sudden shower that disrupts completely the calm of an April's day and is gone in an instant, Eleanor returned to her table and sat down. 'I have had quite enough of you all today,' she snapped, 'especially you, Miss Caldwell, and it is only ten o'clock.

How shall we make it to the end of the day in each other's company? You must disturb me no longer.' With that, she immersed herself in her work, ignoring the books lying on the floor around her and acting as if the outburst had never happened.

Diana Wainwright's eyes were cold as she looked at her granddaughter, but it was I she reprimanded. 'Miss Eleanor is calm now. You must try not to agitate her again. I shall ask Tom to stay close at hand, in case there is a further disturbance.'

I felt strongly the injustice that I was blamed for Eleanor's outburst, yet slowly, humiliatingly, I was forced to pick up the books and papers and place them neatly on her desk. Throughout all this, Eleanor remained silent. There was no talk of London and the new museums and galleries built there. Not even her desperate questions about the presence of Arielle Marchal's ghost in the house. In fact, she didn't acknowledge me at all. Her energy was focused solely on her studies.

In the hush of that great library, where the hands of the clock marched so slowly it seemed time itself had run down, I had leisure to reflect upon what she had said and to ask myself, honestly, whether she was right. Did I know in my heart the house was haunted? I had felt the thick sadness that hung around the boathouse and I had seen the face in my mirror. And there were other things too – the girl in the red cloak at the attic window, the sobs and footsteps – that I couldn't explain. The séance— Oh, God, I didn't want to think of the séance. Maybe the house was stained for ever by murder and the wrong done to Arielle Marchal.

Or perhaps it was my own demons that hung about me.

When the clock finally chimed seven, she turned to me and spoke for the first time since her outburst that morning. 'I would be a dangerous enemy. Don't ever betray me.' I felt like the prey of a dreadful, erratic predator, who might spring and attack me at any moment. I remembered how I had feared her as I entered the boathouse for the first time. I tried to hold her gaze to show I wasn't afraid, but it proved impossible. Her eyes were cold and unblinking. I turned away.

So far north, the light in June had lasted until eleven at night and the sun returned at four in the morning. Now a melancholy twilight came at a little after eight o'clock in the evening. I had already part decided that I would leave Teesbank Hall before the dark nights of December. By that time, I would have been paid half my salary in arrears and have some means of escape. It was grim enough in the height of summer, when the daylight stretched endlessly into night, but in the winter, when the days were a pinprick of light in gloom, then, I thought, it must be unbearable to be here.

And I longed to have a true friend. There were many evenings when I put pen to paper and began to write to Cousin Lucy, pouring out my loneliness and wishing we could be together somewhere safe and away from all harm. But I knew the risks were too great in sending the letter. It would be impossible to enclose a return address, for then my hiding-place would be discovered. I was forced to tear up the paper and hide the scraps in the bottom of my trunk.

On the evening of Eleanor's outburst, I was desperate to be outside and walked alone around the grounds until my feet ached and I was quite worn out. I was angry at the injustice that I had been blamed for her bad temper and my nerves needed calming. It was a full half an hour later than usual before I returned to the Hall. The shadows had already lengthened and it was more dark than light as I entered the desolate house. I collected a candle from the kitchen drawer and climbed the twisting stairs to my attic bedroom.

As was typical in country houses at that time, most occupants were early to bed, certainly the servants, who would rise again at five in the morning to begin the hundreds of daily tasks necessary to run such a great house. For myself, I was relieved that no one else was about, as I didn't wish to explain my lateness. There was not a sound in the house, but when I reached the top of the stairs and began to walk along the attic landing, I sensed that somebody else was up there. I couldn't have given a reason for my conviction – but, intuitively, I knew it. It was silent but it was the silence of someone holding their breath and waiting.

When I entered my bedroom, I sat before the cloaked mirror, too frightened to look around the room in its candle-lit darkness. I began to brush my hair and the flame flickered and burned, glowing orange and blue, as a current of air from an unseen source made it waver and dance. I turned to retrieve my white nightgown and stopped short. It seemed to be covered with the thickest of shadows. I reached down for it and my fingers felt something sticky and viscous. I held the candle high and saw in horror that blood was smeared across my gown – slashes of red ran across the virginal white material. I started in horror and recoiled, dropping the candle as I did so. The room was plunged into total darkness and a loud, piercing voice shouted over and over again, 'No, no, please, no!'

It was only later that I discovered the voice had been my own, loud and insistent enough to shatter the peace of the night and bring Mrs Hargreaves and the wide-eyed Agnes running to my room.

The next morning Agnes told me that they had found me slumped face forward across the bed. The candle had mercifully snuffed out as it fell, leaving only a scorch mark on the thin coverlet to suggest the damage the flame could have wreaked on me. Mrs Hargreaves had burst into the room ready to scold my outburst but had stopped on seeing the scene. They had somehow contrived to half walk, half carry me down the servants' staircase, so I had spent the night wrapped in a quilt and resting on the sofa in Mrs Jenson's sitting room.

They hoped my screams had passed unnoticed by the Wainwrights. However, as Agnes revealed to me later, that was not the case. While she served breakfast the next morning, Diana Wainwright called her over and demanded, 'What was that dreadful noise last night?'

'I don't rightly know, ma'am,' she replied, reluctant to say more.

But the old woman badgered her so much that the house-maid was forced to reveal the existence of the bloodied nightgown in my room.

'That will be Eleanor's doing. The girl is a danger to her-self and everyone around her. Things cannot continue as they are. Neither Matthew nor Susan can control her, and I will tell them so myself,' the matriarch pronounced, in response to this information.

CHAPTER TWENTY-TWO

When I came to, I had half-memories of Mrs Hargreaves bathing me in tepid water. As she washed me, she had hummed a sad and tuneless song, her hands gentle on my face and hair. I must have fallen asleep after that because I couldn't remember anything else. And now I was awake, I knew immediately this must be Eleanor's revenge for my refusal to believe in ghosts. I wouldn't let her defeat me. Pushing off the heavy quilt, I placed my feet carefully on the floor and called, 'Hello, hello.'

A few moments later I heard brisk footsteps outside and Mrs Hargreaves entered the room. There was no sign of the tenderness she had shown me the previous night. 'You're awake, then,' she said. 'It's after midday.'

I was surprised at how late it was, but responded, 'I need to be in the schoolroom.'

'Are you sure you're able? After last night, I mean.'

'Yes. Eleanor must know she hasn't beaten me.'

Mrs Hargreaves gave me a strange look, but replied, 'You'll need to be clothed, then. I'll ask Eliza to fetch your things so that you might change in here. Miss Eleanor's already studying and Agnes is sitting with her.'

'I won't be long in getting ready,' I promised, and dressed quickly.

When I entered the schoolroom, I thought that Eleanor's face registered a look of shock, but only for a moment, before a blank mask of indifference covered her emotions. 'I'm surprised to see you here today. I understood you were indisposed after the events of last night,' she sneered.

'It appears there has been some misunderstanding. I'm very well, Miss Eleanor, and ready to begin our work.' I faced my reluctant pupil defiantly and then, in a half-tone so Agnes wouldn't hear, 'Why did you do it?'

She smirked maliciously. 'I did nothing. It must have been her. The governess. Perhaps she is angry that you don't believe in her.'

'There are no ghosts in this house. This was only you and your actions.'

She stood up slowly, her right hand clutching at her left wrist, 'I was watched over by Mrs Anderson all night and she will vouch for that. It would have been impossible for me to enter your room.'

'I know it was you. The room could have been set alight when I dropped the candle. I could have died. How am I ever to trust you again?' My voice was rising with emotion and I saw Agnes looking over at us.

Eleanor had spotted it too and said curtly, 'You may leave now.' Agnes bobbed a curtsy and left quickly. Eleanor glared. 'You chose to come here. You must take responsibility for your choice.'

'You are responsible for it, only you.' I grasped her hands and saw there, beneath the fingernails, a line of red. 'Look, there is blood. I need no further proof.'

She pulled away her hands angrily, 'This is not proof. I did not leave Mrs Anderson's presence. Why would I want to go to your room?'

'You wanted to punish me because I refused to agree with you. Your bloodied nails tell the truth even if you won't.'

'I do not lie – don't you dare accuse me of that.' Her face was red with anger and she was so agitated that I almost began to believe her and decided I would ask Mrs Anderson at the first possible opportunity whether Eleanor had left her room the previous night.

But already her mind was on other things. She said, 'You have seen her, haven't you? In the mirror.'

Startled, I asked, 'Who do you mean? Why do you ask about the mirror?'

She half smiled now. 'When Mrs Hargreaves and Agnes found you slumped across the bed, you repeated over and over again, "The girl in the mirror. It is her doing. She will steal who I am."'

I couldn't remember saying those words, but this was my darkest fear, the one held in the hidden parts of my mind. It shook me that I had spoken my secret aloud. 'Who do you think I saw in the mirror?'

'Why, Arielle Marchal, of course. It was the mirror where

she prepared to meet her lover, my father. She was a whore but God knows she paid for it many times over.'

'She was not a murderess,' I countered. 'I know who the real killer is.'

'What do you know?' she demanded. 'Have you found Arielle's final testimony? The one she wrote before she died?'

I opened my mouth to answer her, but the door opened and Diana and Matthew Wainwright came into the room. I had never seen them in the library before and both Eleanor and I fell silent.

Her father spoke first. 'Eleanor, your grandmother informs me that there has been a recurrence of your affliction. She was forced to witness you shouting and throwing books.'

'Your behaviour was undignified, Eleanor, particularly in front of the servants,' Diana Wainwright added coldly. 'You have been warned many times, yet you seem to have little sense of the family's reputation.'

'Now there is this other incident where you have gone into the governess's room and bloodied her nightgown,' Matthew Wainwright continued.

Eleanor drew herself up to her full height and stood rigid, her arms held out stiffly at either side and her fists clenched. 'I wasn't responsible for what happened in the attic and I am not unwell, Father. If I suffer, then you know what ails me.'

His lips twitched with annoyance. He seemed about to signal me to leave the room, but his desire for discretion was too late because Eleanor began to speak, tonelessly and unrelentingly, 'You will not let me leave this place. You keep me trapped. It is nothing more than a prison.' Then she pointed at me. 'Why does she have to be here? I don't need a gaoler. Surely you can trust me.'

Even I could feel the distress in Eleanor's voice, but her father snapped back, 'You know what happened when you were allowed freedom, when we left you unguarded. There must be someone with you morning and night – it is what Dr Landown said.'

'Father, I promise you, I implore you. I will not repeat—'

Diana Wainwright cut her off mid-sentence: 'Not in front of her!'

Matthew said to me, 'You may leave the room. We have business that is only for the family. You'll be sent for when we have finished.'

I was glad to absent myself. But I was intrigued to know what action of Eleanor's was so terrible she must always be watched. When I had first arrived at the Hall and observed all three of them together at the dinner table, I had believed Eleanor had the upper hand. She had had the satisfaction of pushing her father to breaking point. But now I saw that her position was weakened and desperate.

Unsure where to go and not knowing how long their conversation would last, I sat uncertainly in the great entrance hall. I could hear occasional raised voices and what seemed to be Eleanor sobbing and pleading. Mr Wainwright emerged from the room first, his face flushed with anger, and was clearly surprised to see me there. He stood in the doorway, slightly out of breath, but gathered himself and instructed me to return to my post. 'Eleanor is fully aware of how she is expected to behave. There will be no further difficulties with her.'

Diana Wainwright was following him. Very slowly and deliberately, she looked back at her granddaughter and said, 'You disgust me.' She wanted me to hear those words.

I entered the library cautiously, worried as to how Eleanor would respond to me. She stood motionless by the window, staring at the world outside. She didn't acknowledge my presence. For the rest of the day, she stood there unmoving and I began to fear for her sanity. Even the piles of books, so neatly arranged on her desk, held no appeal. I knew the impossibility of expecting her to receive any kindness from me but I did ask whether she was quite comfortable and would she like me to ring for a glass of water. There was no response. Guiltily, I felt relieved. The emotional storm of her behaviour and its changeability had exhausted me.

My hours of waiting finally ended when Mrs Anderson arrived. Eleanor was still at the window, rigid and watching; she ignored the nurse too. Mrs Anderson took me aside and whispered, 'Mr Wainwright said we'd have no more trouble with her. Is that the case?'

'She has just stood there, silent,' I replied. 'What can Mr Wainwright have threatened that has affected her so much?'

She didn't quite catch my eye, but shrugged and said, 'Doctor comes tomorrow. Let's hope he puts her back on something to deaden her moods.'

That night I felt exhausted and too wrung out by the

day's events to make my usual trip to the boathouse. I ate quickly in the servants' hall, then planned to have an early night, until a red-faced Mrs Anderson came into the room and looked around. Seeing no one else there, she addressed me directly: 'Miss Eleanor refuses to get ready for bed. She's just stood there, stiff as a plank of wood.'

'What do you expect me to do?' I wanted no more dealings with Eleanor that evening.

'With Mrs Jenson away and Agnes who knows where, you'll have to help.' As she spoke, she slurred her words slightly and I remembered how Eleanor had been certain she wouldn't wake on the night of the séance because of the gin she'd drunk.

'I'm not having the Wainwrights blaming me for her turns. She shall be undressed and got ready for bed – that's what's expected. And if she won't do it by herself, then she must be made to.'

Reluctantly, I followed Mrs Anderson up to the main part of the building. Eleanor had a palatial room at the front of the house, which was expensively furnished. There was a large carved bed, a mahogany wardrobe and dressing-table, but it was stark in its emptiness – there were no books or ornaments or arrangements of flowers, which might have given the room a sense of personality. The walls were painted a dreary pea-soup green and were bare of pictures – Mrs Anderson saw me stare at the blankness and, as if guessing my thoughts, said, 'It's not safe to leave things out. She throws stuff around when she's in one of her tempers.'

Eleanor was at the far end of the room, standing by the window and staring at the darkness outside. 'Miss Eleanor, it's time you was ready for bed. I've brought Miss Caldwell up with me and she won't put up with none of your tricks either.' It was clear that she was on the verge of losing her temper and I wondered what had happened before she'd come to find me.

Eleanor made no response.

Mrs Anderson muttered, 'I've had enough of this.' She marched across the room and seized Eleanor's arm. 'Stop wasting my time. You should be dressed for bed. I'm not standing here for hours waiting until you decide you're ready. Mr Wainwright said I could do what's needed to make you behave, so I won't stand for no nonsense tonight.'

I was shocked at the violence of Mrs Anderson's words and how roughly she handled her, but Eleanor stood rigid and uncomprehending. I was frightened at what Mrs Anderson might do next and found myself saying, 'Perhaps you would like me to get Eleanor ready for bed.'

It seemed best that the older woman was out of the room, at least for a while. Earlier that day, I'd seen the cruel indifference of Diana and Matthew Wainwright towards Eleanor and now I saw how Mrs Anderson treated her. Despite what she had done to me, it was impossible not to sympathize with her desperate situation, imprisoned within the malevolent atmosphere of Teesbank Hall.

Mrs Anderson was only too happy to leave. 'I'll take thirty minutes or so in the servants' hall and then I'll be back. See what I mean, though? Nobody should have to cope with her.' She spoke as if Eleanor wasn't present and couldn't hear what was said.

Once left alone, I wasn't sure what to do. I closed the curtains and tried to speak in a soothing voice. 'Miss Eleanor, we must get you ready for bed. Please would you let me help you? It's better than Mrs Anderson.'

She stood mute and shook her head. Her face was white and she winced, as if in pain. Her arms were wrapped protectively around herself and her eyes gazed into the distance, her pupils enlarged and unfocused on her immediate surroundings.

'Miss Eleanor, Mrs Anderson will be back soon – why don't you get ready for bed and then she'll have no cause for complaint?'

Very slowly, very carefully, she began to unbutton her dress. I looked away and busied myself arranging her night-dress. When I turned to give it to her, I gasped in horror. She had a white chemise beneath her gown and fresh red blood seeped through the left-hand side. 'Miss Eleanor, you're bleeding!'

She stopped and looked wonderingly, touching the blood that was on her bodice. A flash of pain crossed her face. I went over to her and gently tugged at the fabric.

'Eleanor, what has happened? A doctor must look at this.' The sight that greeted me was horrific – her breasts had been scarred, with a series of cuts made across them. Most of the wounds were faded, crisscrossing her chest in a patchwork, but one cut was fresh, the cut that seeped through the white of her chemise. She stood before me, arms outstretched and I saw that her wrists, too, were covered with a lace of pink scars and scratches.

'Who has done this to you?' The cuts on her skin must have happened over many years because some injuries had healed, while others were more recent. 'Eleanor, who would hurt you like this?'

She had turned her face away from me. She was crying. She wiped the tears with her arm. 'Promise me you will tell no one what you have seen. Especially not this new cut.'

'How can you make me promise, when there is someone present who has harmed you?'

'The cuts aren't deep – they'll heal.' She turned towards me and implored, 'Tell no one. I will be in trouble if you do.'

'What trouble would be worse than this?' I exclaimed. I was appalled at the thought of someone in Teesbank Hall being capable of such violence towards Eleanor.

She shook her head. 'You don't understand. If you tell, then Father will do that thing he threatened.'

'Surely I can inform Henry when he returns. He always has your best interests at heart and would protect you.'

She shuddered. 'Henry, most of all you mustn't tell Henry. Please let me suffer alone and say nothing.'

She was so desperate that I was forced to promise not to reveal what I had seen, even though it went against all my natural instincts. In the minutes before Mrs Anderson returned, we cleaned the wound as best we could by dabbing cold water onto the freshest cut, so that the bleeding stopped. I wondered whether Mrs Anderson knew about the injuries or who might have inflicted them upon Eleanor.

That night, I couldn't sleep for terror. I had been certain Clara Wainwright was the murderess but what if that was wrong, and it wasn't Arielle Marchal either? Had someone mutilated Eleanor in the same way that her brother had been attacked? As rest escaped me, I counted through the people who had been present in the house when Samuel was killed and who were still here now: Diana, Matthew and Susan Wainwright, Mrs Jenson, Mrs Hargreaves and Mr Snowdon, now the head gardener. I thought also of the man who had lurked outside my bedroom and wondered if he might be connected in some way. Was the true killer still at the Hall and, if so, why wouldn't Eleanor reveal their name?

CHAPTER TWENTY-THREE

The Eleanor of the previous evening had been vulnerable and had begged me to hide her secret, but in the morning, she refused to speak to me. I tried to ask her if she was in pain and she turned away, as if I hadn't been there. She didn't attempt to read the books placed in front of her but instead tapped incessantly on the table with the fingers of her left hand. At first, I thought this was deliberate, to annoy me, but as the monotonous action continued throughout the morning, over and over again, I came to see that it was a signal of her total distress.

When Agnes brought up the meal tray and hesitatingly asked whether Miss Eleanor wished to eat, she indicated she had no desire for food. Usually I would have attempted to persuade her to try something but today I didn't have the heart and said nothing.

The day was endless and I sighed with relief when Mrs Anderson finally came to take Eleanor into her keeping. I had calculated that if I ate my meal quickly, there would still be half an hour or so of daylight left for me to walk along the river. After the drama of the last few days, I wanted to be outdoors and away from the house, seizing the final moments of summer before it froze into winter. During the day, the woods were still scattered with fat purple heather and the humming of lazy bees, but in the evenings, there was a cool breeze and the darkening skies confirmed the changing of the season. The melancholy sweetness in the air whispered the approach of autumn.

I walked briskly and it is likely the vigour and the bloom of youth traced some colour onto my face, which was usually pale from confinement in the classroom. I followed my usual route to the boathouse. Its position on the river was one of seclusion, facing away from the cruel shuttered windows of the house and looking out onto the water. There, I would be left alone with my thoughts. It had been designed so that the last gleams of the sun played upon it and the boathouse remained in light when all around was shrouded in shadow.

Although I knew of the horrors that had taken place, there was also a sense of underlying serenity and I wondered whether time had the ability to wash away all human wrong-doing, leaving only the peace of nature. I sat by the window, enjoying the final bars of evening light, when I was suddenly brought to reality by the voice I had least expected.

'Miss Caldwell?' It was Henry. He was supposed to be in Scotland, not at Teesbank Hall.

I worried that I might not be allowed in the boathouse

alone. I rose hurriedly and dropped into an awkward curtsy. 'I'm sorry, sir, I was about to leave,' I stuttered.

It was clear from his clothes and appearance that he had been riding for several hours – his boots were spattered with mud and his white shirt was open at the neck. His dark hair was tousled and he rubbed the sweat from his brow. He seemed to fill the enclosed space with his physical presence and I felt my heart thump within my chest. I was anxious that I had transgressed in some way, but I also felt an emotion that was new to me – an emotion both troubling and desirable.

'No, stay, stay. I didn't mean to disturb you. You were so deep in thought as I approached, I believed I had better give you warning, in case you were startled.'

He looked quite awkward, too. It was the first time we had been alone in a confined space and we seemed unsure of how we should behave. He stood several feet away, near the doorway of the boathouse, and I realized I would have to pass immediately in front of him to leave. I was in an agony of indecision about whether to stay or go – I was desperate to be out of his company, and the unsettling way I felt, but it was impolite to depart so quickly. Neither of us spoke for a good minute or so, and finally I was forced to break the heavy silence. 'I'm surprised to see you back from Scotland so quickly. Was your journey home a comfortable one?'

'What? Yes, yes, of course, thank you. I travelled to Darlington by train but there was no connection to Eaglescliffe. It was only the final section of the journey that I rode on horseback. I needed to be in the fresh air, anyway.'

I dared to ask, 'I thought your tour was to last much longer. Are your friends still up in Inverness?' For some reason, I didn't want to name Rosalind Merryweather.

'Yes, they are staying,' he said quietly. 'The Merryweathers have taken a house overlooking the loch and intend to be there for several weeks.'

'But why are you home so soon?'

'I have been sent for.' He added, 'I understand Eleanor's condition has deteriorated again.'

I tensed, as if this might somehow be due to a failing on my part and tried to defend myself. 'I . . . I find her difficult to deal with at times. She has been worse since you've been gone.'

'It's not you. It's . . .' His voice trailed away. 'She is very unhappy. She is so shut away from society and there are other things too.'

'It's such a big house and remote from the rest of the world. Hardly anyone has visited in the time I've been here,' I ventured.

A shadow crossed his face. 'People don't like to come to Teesbank Hall.'

'It could be Miss Eleanor needs to spend some time away. A change of scene, perhaps. She has talked of little apart from the London International Exhibition and the new museums in South Kensington ever since you mentioned—'

'My parents wouldn't allow it. Things have happened in the past that mean they won't let her leave Teesbank Hall.'

'As you say, sir.' I felt the distance between us increase. 'I must be getting back to the Hall. It is growing darker.'

I made to leave the boathouse, but he spoke to me again, as if he wished to keep me there a little longer. Perhaps he didn't want to be alone with his sombre thoughts. 'It's a very peaceful spot here by the water. My grandfather designed the boathouse as an anniversary gift for my grandmother, Diana. She was very beautiful and they were very much in love with each other. The story goes that he spent several weeks pacing the riverbank, trying to find the ideal place.'

'It was a perfect present,' I said.

'It was somewhere they could be alone together.'

It was hard to imagine Diana Wainwright as the object of romantic feeling – she seemed so shrivelled and ancient to me . . . so cruel and undeserving of love. 'That may explain why it feels such a special place,' I said, but still I could not forget completely the images planted by Eleanor of Samuel Wainwright's mutilated body hidden beneath the tarpaulin. I wondered whether Susan Wainwright had ever returned here after the murder of her son. There was no sign of remembrance of what had happened. The air of neglect that hung about the place suggested it was forgotten, that people stole there only when they wished to be alone.

He sighed, almost with despair. I wondered whether he was thinking about Rosalind Merryweather and their unexpected separation.

He and Agnes were the only people I trusted at Teesbank Hall, the only two people who had shown any kindness towards me, and this opportunity to speak to him alone made me bold enough to ask the question that had preyed on my mind. 'Sir, may I ask your view on something that has troubled me?'

He looked at me, surprised and expectant, but his tone was kind when he replied, 'Miss Caldwell, I'm honoured that you value my opinion. What is it you wish to say?' He came and sat beside me on the window seat, a few inches away. I was conscious of our closeness.

I paused. I knew the question I wanted to ask but not how to put it into words. Finally, I said, 'When Mrs Sterling, the vicar's wife, came to visit, she talked about her work with women, fallen women, at the St Mary Magdalene House of Charity in Highgate.'

He nodded, clearly unsure of what I would say next.

'Mrs Wainwright, your grandmother, said that those women were morally depraved and predisposed to sin, and all the more so because . . . because they were young.' I faltered here and saw that Henry was looking at me carefully, but I had to continue now. 'But Mrs Sterling said they were victims and most had been forced into a life of shame against their will, often by those who should have most care for them. I wanted to know what your opinion is. Do you think that in such a case the woman is to blame?'

'Miss Caldwell, we both know my grandmother has the harshest of opinions on many matters.' And I thought I heard a note of anger in his voice. 'It seems to me that

Mrs Sterling's view must be the right one. Surely anyone with an ounce of humanity or intelligence must lay the blame at the foot of the person responsible for the abuse. Certainly, never the victim. What do you think of the matter?'

'I hold the same opinion as you,' I replied quietly, and felt myself breathe more freely, but there was one more thing I had to tell him. I dared not break my promise to Eleanor by revealing the mutilation I had seen on her, but I could do the next best thing because I was sure the two were linked in some way. 'Henry – sir. There is another thing I would like to confide in you.'

He looked at me expectantly.

As the words came out of my mouth, they sounded foolish. 'A man came to the attic. I heard his footsteps in the middle of the night, right outside my bedroom door. And I saw him disappearing along the hallway, although I was too slow to catch him.'

He said carefully, 'Did anyone else see this man?'

'No,' I was forced to admit. 'Agnes was there but she saw nothing and Mrs Jenson said I must have been mistaken.'

Now he was silent.

'I know I saw someone.' My voice was too shrill.

Henry shook his head. 'Mrs Jenson is right. No man would dare to go up to the attics. It's forbidden. Try not to think about it – it must have been a dream or perhaps your imagination played tricks on you.'

But I knew he observed me strangely. I worried he might

think me foolish, so I said, 'You're probably right. My bedroom is out of the way and sometimes I find it difficult to sleep well.'

'How do you find life at the Hall?'

I realized this was the first personal question he had ever asked me. 'It is quiet here, sir,' I ventured, being unable to say what I truly felt.

'It's like a living grave,' he responded, with a strength of feeling that surprised me. 'If it was not for Mother and Eleanor, I would have no desire to return to this place.'

I noticed he didn't include his father.

'And you, Miss Caldwell? I know nothing of you – you are usually so quiet and reserved. Yet you do not seem to me to be a typical governess.'

I shrank a little in replying because I had no desire to reveal too much about myself, yet I must satisfy his curiosity to some extent. 'I didn't expect to become a governess but a change in my family's circumstances meant I had to find employment.'

He looked at me expectantly. 'And who are your family?' he asked.

'Oh, you'll not have heard of us!' I exclaimed. 'We are from Norfolk and Father and I lived in a flint and brick house near to Norwich.'

'And your mother?' he enquired.

'My mother died when I was seven.'

'I'm sorry to hear that,' he responded. 'It must have been a sad childhood.'

'Oh, no, no,' I assured him. 'Father and I were very close and we were happy. It was a quiet life because he was not a gregarious man and our social circle was small, but we were content until he died.'

'Do you have no other living relatives?' he asked.

I felt that cold dread rise within me. 'Only my uncle, sir, and his daughter. The estate was entailed and passed to him on my father's death. He was the nearest living male relative.'

And then the dark days began, the relentless voice inside my head told me.

'And your uncle didn't allow you to remain at your child-hood home?' I sensed a note of indignation in Henry's voice, at what he perceived as cruel treatment of an orphaned child.

'Yes, he would have allowed it, sir,' I stated mechanically.

Now it was my turn to be silent and I stared determinedly out at the river. I could not and would not answer him further.

A lone curlew called, looking for its mate. There were some things I would never speak of – to think of them was enough – and they reminded me that Teesbank Hall, living grave though it might be, at least was some point of refuge. I forced myself out of my recollection and asked Henry why he had come to the boathouse rather than going straight to the Hall after a journey of many hours.

He looked away from me, out onto the calm of the river and in the direction of the shuttered house. 'Because I hate that place and I must always prepare myself before entering it. After I'd stabled my horse, I came here to delay my return.'

'I'm sorry.' What else could I say? I had felt the antagonism of Teesbank Hall from the very first day.

For a moment we looked at each other. Then he broke the silence. 'There may be some truth that a change of scene would be beneficial to Eleanor. Is it true she wishes to go to the exhibitions in South Kensington?'

I think we were both glad to be able to return to less personal matters. 'She talks of little else. I suspect it would make her happy.'

'I'll speak to my parents. Perhaps they can be forced to listen this time. Father wants to shut Eleanor away from the world but it's destroying her.' He ran his fingers through his hair and, as if with a great act of will, stood up. 'Thank you for your advice, Miss Caldwell, but it's getting late. I think it's time we both went back.'

I nodded and he took my arm to help me stand. It was the lightest of touches, but the warmth of his hand burned through the soft cloth of my dress and an awareness of his presence filled my whole body. We stood facing each other for a moment too long, then pulled apart hastily.

'Miss Caldwell, I'm pleased to have met you this evening. It's good to see a friendly face at Teesbank Hall.'

I thought how strange it was that even Henry, the favoured son and grandson, the one who stood to inherit Teesbank Hall, should hate the place too. As we walked back, we spoke about Henry's trip to Scotland and what had happened at the house in his absence. He was full of enthusiasm for the Isle of Skye and planned to return there next summer. I wondered whether he would go with Rosalind Merryweather.

It was after eight o'clock and almost dark, yet the garden still held the scent of late summer roses and there was a dream-like quality about the scene.

'I remember your mother saying her childhood home was filled with roses, but the vases are always empty at Teesbank Hall. Why doesn't she have any flowers in the house?'

'Grandmother refuses to allow it. She claims the scent makes her retch.'

'What? Is that really the case?' I asked.

He laughed. 'No, it's just another tactic in the war she and Mother wage against each other. I don't think Grandmother would allow anything to make her ill.'

When we arrived at the Hall, Henry spotted a rose – a perfect pink rose in full bloom – in a flowerbed close to the house. He took a penknife from his pocket and plucked it. 'Why don't we risk her anger and smuggle it in? At least your room will smell of roses, even if nowhere else in the house does.'

I held it up to my face to breathe in its rich perfume. 'It's beautiful, thank you.' I was glad that the evening was wrapping itself in darkness because it masked the colour that flushed across my face.

He smiled and was about to say something when Diana Wainwright's voice rang out sharply: 'Is that you, Henry?

I've been watching for you from the door and thought I saw something.'

'Yes, Grandmother. I've just returned from Scotland.'

She came outside and held out her arms for him to embrace her. 'It's very good to see you, Henry. How is Rosalind?'

'She is thriving. The Highland air seems to agree with her very much and the Merryweathers have extended the lease on their house in Inverness.'

She smiled briefly. 'You must tell me all about her and the rest of the family later, but there is important business to attend to first.'

She looked at me with a cold, poisonous stare and I hid the flower behind my back, half hoping it would make her violently sick.

'Your return is not a moment too soon, Henry,' she said. 'Things have deteriorated and the family needs you. Come with me to the drawing room.'

He bowed to me, wished me a good night, then followed her into the main part of the house.

Once I was in my own room, I stood at the window for an hour or so, thinking about what had just happened. Henry must care for me at least a little, I reasoned, and that thought made my soul stir with joy. The room was flooded with moonlight, and the pink rose I held was a promise of new beginnings.

The mirror was still covered but I needed to confront the ghost girl. While the moon threw soft shadows around me, I put the pink rose into a jar beside the salvaged string of my mother's pearls. Next, and with trembling hands, I pulled back the thick woollen cloak from the looking-glass. She was there. She had always been there. But now I looked at her more dispassionately. I traced the curves of her face, my face. The passionate lips I had so long hated now seemed inviting, tender almost; the brown gold of my hair shimmered in the light. The secrets hidden in those dark eyes were less painful and I did not need to reject her. Who I had become was made up of all that I had experienced, good and bad. And I was stronger because I had escaped, and I had survived.

The face that looked back was beautiful – not the savage, wanton beauty my uncle wanted to impose upon me. The mirror reflected the choices I had made and how I had seized my destiny. The mirror glinted silver into the darkness. I would not need to cover it again.

CHAPTER TWENTY-FOUR

Even though Henry had returned to Teesbank Hall, it was still a tense and unhappy place. All the fight had gone out of Eleanor and she was nervous and fretful. I thought again of the livid scars across her wrists and body and wondered why she wouldn't reveal the name of her attacker.

Mr Wainwright could hardly contain his fury at his daughter and the incident with the bloodied nightgown had been the last straw. As part of her punishment, she was not allowed to enter the General Examination at London University, so all of the books on mathematics and natural sciences had been removed from the library. Other unspecified threats hung about the air, like a bad odour. Every day, she sat screwed as tightly as a coil, her arms rigid and her hands clenched, as if expecting to be attacked. She no longer studied, shoving away her remaining books and saying it was pointless. She would sit and stare into nothingness for hours on end.

For safety's sake, her nails had been cut short and the

knives were counted religiously after each meal – even Eliza took care none went missing. At first, Eleanor rebelled by refusing to eat but now Mrs Jenson stood over her at mealtimes, forcing her to take small spoonfuls of soup, which she swallowed, gagging. When she had tried to resist, the housekeeper said apologetically, 'Your father insists I'm to report immediately if you haven't eaten. You know what that will mean.' After this, Eleanor ate, but the flesh was melting away from her already slender body.

She was still adamant she had not smeared my nightgown, and Mrs Anderson backed her up in this, saying Eleanor hadn't left the room all night. However, it was in her interests to lie about any escape so no one really believed what she said. I was now a little frightened to be near Eleanor, having seen the horror of what she had done to my nightgown, and it put a distance between us that hadn't existed before. I was also worried she would blame me for the harshness of her punishment. But she seemed as indifferent to me as she was to everyone else.

The only person who could distract her was Henry and, occasionally, she would allow him to coax her for a walk in the grounds. Otherwise she sat listlessly indoors. He was often in the schoolroom – the Merryweathers were still away in Scotland and he had no university studies to fill his time. Sometimes he tried to include me in the conversation, but when he did, Eleanor would look at him with such distress that the words died on his lips and he stopped. I began to fear that he regretted the intimacy of our conversation in the boathouse.

One morning in the middle of September, Eleanor and Henry were sitting together talking. He had brought her an article about the Cardwell Reforms, a subject on which she had expressed passionate views in the past – but now she pushed it away. She sat sunken-eyed, worrying at the sleeve of her dress, until she had picked a thread loose.

'Ellie, you must take an interest in the world again. This won't be for ever.' He sounded like a parent with a small child.

'It is for ever. How can it be otherwise? You know the power they hold over me,' she said, then turned her head away and continued speaking to him in subdued tones. I couldn't hear her words, but her distress was obvious.

When she had finished, Henry exclaimed, 'Not Gate Helmsley? He wouldn't do that.'

I didn't catch her reply, but I was struck by Henry's words. I had heard of Gate Helmsley, but where? I remembered the list of mysteries I had drawn up on the night of the séance. Gate Helmsley had been on that list. It was the name against the payments in Mrs Jenson's ledger. The amount of twenty-five pounds – half my annual salary – paid out to Gate Helmsley each month. The housekeeper had been angry I had even been near the open cupboard, which contained the account book. And now the name seemed linked to Eleanor's extreme distress.

My thoughts were interrupted by the arrival of Mrs Jenson, who told me she wished to speak privately, and drew me aside to the window, although in the now silent room, her every word could be heard.

Her voice was cold with anger. 'Miss Caldwell, Eliza has come to me in tears. She was worried about breaking a confidence but felt she must when she saw the state of Miss Eleanor. I am most disappointed in you because I would have taken you for more sense.'

I was unsure what she meant.

'Eliza has told me all about the séance you and Agnes took part in with Miss Eleanor. Not long before the incident with the nightgown. It is very likely this playing around with dark forces is the reason for her latest breakdown and deranged actions. You can have very little idea of the consequences for her.'

I felt the blood drain from my face.

Taking my silence as acknowledgement of guilt, she continued, 'Your job was to protect Miss Eleanor. She is vulnerable and you have failed her. Eliza was horrified something so irreligious had happened under this roof.'

'Then she is a hypocrite,' I dared to say. 'It was she who first held a séance at Teesbank Hall and put the idea into anyone's head.'

'Eliza may be sharp-tongued at times, but she is a good God-fearing girl at heart – she wouldn't involve herself in such blasphemy.' She put up her hand to silence me, as I went to speak. 'Agnes will be dealt with too, even though she's just a silly little thing. I will have to inform Mr and Mrs Wainwright of what you have both done.'

It was unjust – I hadn't wanted to conjure up the dead and neither had Agnes, and we had been forced into taking part.

But now we were to be blamed. How Eliza must have relished the chance to get me into trouble.

Then Eleanor surprised us all: 'It was my idea. Agnes and Miss Caldwell are not at fault. I made them do it.'

'Is this the truth, Miss Eleanor?' Mrs Jenson asked.

'Yes. I would have no reason to lie.'

'Your father will have to know of it.'

Eleanor nodded bleakly.

When the housekeeper had left the room, I dared to speak directly to Eleanor. 'Thank you for telling the truth. You've saved me.'

For just a moment we looked each other in the eye before she turned away. 'I have condemned myself, though,' she said.

CHAPTER TWENTY-FIVE

That night, I was already exhausted by the events of the last few days and decided not to make my usual walk in the grounds. If I had seen Eliza, I would have confronted her over the trouble she had caused in speaking to Mrs Jenson about the séance but there was no sign of her anywhere. I had a solitary meal in the servants' hall, then went to my room, intending to have an early night. Indeed, I was so tired that I fell asleep almost straight away. I dreamed of Cromer, a seaside resort in Norfolk close to where Father and I had lived, which we had been to on holiday once.

The security of my dream was punctured by the sharp hiss of a match and in a moment I was fully alert. Someone was in the corridor. Just like the other time. The heavy footsteps, the harsh, ragged breathing and then the cigar's smell of spiced wood seeping into the air. He was back and directly outside my door. I held my breath. He mustn't know I was awake. A minute stretched into eternity before he began to walk rapidly away and I allowed myself to breathe freely again.

Climbing out of bed, I checked that the door was tightly locked, with the chair lodged against it. All around, there was a heavy silence. The candle had burned low and threw wavering shadows across the room. I pressed my hands together and prayed that he would stay away. And then, in the distance, I heard a young girl sobbing and shouting. Her cries were indistinct but by straining I could make out the words she repeated, 'Let me go, let me go, I beg you.'

She was desperate and I knew I had to help her. Trembling, I picked up the candle and left the safety of my room. It was the darkest and most deserted time of the night. I thought of waking one of the maids but a wall lay between us and I would have to reach the end of the corridor to fetch them. And there was not a moment to lose. I didn't know whether I should shout to reassure the girl that I knew she was there, or if that would just give warning to her attacker and put us both in danger.

The cries were becoming fainter and I feared I might already be too late. There were four doors along the corridor and I didn't know which room they were in. I remembered the night I had seen the outline of that man in the attics, how Agnes and I had searched but had still failed to find him. I couldn't fail this time.

The handle of the nearest door was stiff and wouldn't turn easily. The sound of my exertions must have carried for I heard a louder gasp of pain from further along the passage – it was the room of the séance. It was impossible to make out the words, but the victim was clearly still living. Then there was a crash and a fall and a terrible blood-freezing cry. I raced to that door, heart pounding, and, with a courage I didn't really possess, shouted, 'Let her go now. You must stop!'

At first the door wouldn't yield to my pushing. Although it wasn't locked, the wood had become swollen over time and didn't quite fit the frame, making it difficult to budge. In the fear of the moment, my fingers shook, making me clumsy. I put my candle down behind me so that I had both hands free and shoved hard against the door with my shoulder, which suddenly gave way and I half fell, half ran into the room. Darkness faced me and I could see nothing. I had ended up sprawled on the floor and now reached back to pick up the candle holder.

The tiny flame of my candle was the only light in that vast room, larger by far than my own bedroom, and my eyes had to adjust to the half-light. Piles of discarded furniture lurked menacingly around the sides of the room – darker shadows against the black night. And there, at the far end of the room, a man was facing towards the window, a cigar in one hand. At his feet lay a torn nightgown of white lace and cotton. As my eyes became accustomed to that fatal darkness, I saw who it was and cried out, 'Henry!'

To my horror, he walked towards me and looked down.

I was in a state of confusion, so much so that the face above me leered and merged, at one moment it was that of

Henry, but distorted, and the next became Eleanor, but somehow transformed. I whimpered with terror, desperate to escape from the room.

'Quiet. I won't hurt you.' The voice was harsh but unmistakably Eleanor's. 'It is myself I want to destroy.'

She pointed towards the large slanted window at the end of the room. In common with all of the windows in that part of the house, it was encased in the thick dark mesh that drove out light and trapped the occupants.

'My hands are bleeding from scraping away at the netting. See the blood beneath my fingernails.' She thrust her hands in front of me, 'I would throw myself from the top of the building but they have blocked that way out too.'

Mrs Jenson had told me the nets were to stop birds flying in and becoming trapped. She had lied. Now I saw they were to stop Eleanor escaping by the only means left to her. 'But what is so terrible you would want to die?' I asked, frightened.

'This,' she said, gesturing at her body with disgust. 'To be born a woman is to be restricted and constrained at every step.'

As my eyes adjusted to the dim light, I could see Eleanor was dressed in a gentleman's tweed suit, with her dark hair tied back, and heavy black shoes. That was why I had thought it was Henry. Yet it struck me that the angularity and oddness I had so often observed in her had disappeared. Even in this state of extreme distress, she was strangely more at ease in tailored trousers than in a silk dress and corset.

The discarded nightgown on the floor was her own, ripped into shreds and stained with the blood from her hands.

'Do you want to be a man?' I asked, confused.

'No,' she said resolutely. 'I don't want to *be* a man but I want to know what it feels like to have the power a man holds.'

'What do you mean?' I asked.

'I want to be free to think and act as I choose. To walk without being imprisoned in yards of silk and hoops of steel. When I dress in my brother's clothing, I practise having the same freedom that he does. A freedom that should be a woman's by right.'

'Yes,' I agreed. 'It is obvious that women have the same thoughts, needs and abilities as men, so why shouldn't we have the same independence?'

She was clearly amazed. 'You're not such a mouse, after all.' She continued: 'Two years ago, I was shown a brief glimpse of liberty.' She held out her hands to indicate the smallest of amounts. 'My governess, Miss Howard – Lilian – also believed that men and women should be on an equal footing. She saw that I was intelligent and frustrated – she opened my eyes to new ideas and ways of looking at the world.'

'Your parents couldn't object to that?'

Eleanor laughed bitterly. 'Surely you can imagine Grandmother's ideas about radicals and so-called freethinkers! And whatever she believes, Father will follow suit. When they found out the books we read and the ideas we discussed, Lilian was sent away, without even an opportunity to say goodbye, and I was confined at Teesbank Hall.'

'Just for thinking?' I asked, astonished.

'I did more than think,' she said, with a note of triumph in her voice. 'Following my sixteenth birthday, Lilian and I were allowed to stay with her aunt in Manchester. We were supposed to be studying sketching at Ashbourne's Academy for Young Ladies. Instead, we used to attend scientific lectures at Owen College – dressed as men, of course, for otherwise we wouldn't have been allowed admittance. As ladies, we were automatically barred from any knowledge that might be useful to us. And I wanted knowledge.' She laughed bitterly. 'Too much knowledge and that was my downfall. All the rest they might have forgiven but I wanted to know what it is to be physically intimate with a man.'

'You had a love affair?' I asked.

She snorted. 'Please don't imagine I am about to describe any great romance. After witnessing my parents' marriage, I have few illusions about love. No, I wanted to understand the desires of my body.' She paused a moment. 'And I needed to know if there was an experience – physical or intellectual – powerful enough to block out the dark thoughts that haunt me.'

'Was it strong enough?' I was genuinely intrigued.

'Definitely! I came to a mutually satisfactory arrangement with William, a self-educated labourer and Socialist – exactly the kind of man to terrify my parents.'

'And they found out?'

'Yes. Someone, I don't know who, sent them an anonymous letter about my ... my experiments. Father came to

Manchester and I was dragged home in disgrace.' She paused for a moment, and now her voice was torn between anger and despair: 'He told me I was morally depraved and had brought dishonour to the family. Him! How dare he of all people say that, when there isn't a servant safe from his wandering hands?'

I shook my head in sympathy. 'What about your mother, how did she respond?'

'Even she could see his hypocrisy. I think it gives her some quiet satisfaction to point out that I am truly his daughter in every way.'

'Is this why you're not allowed to leave Teesbank Hall?'

'Father tells me I can't be trusted and must be locked away. He wants me to be purged of my so-called unnatural desires and then they will try to marry me off to any fool who will take me. That is why I can't bear to go on living.' She sobbed. 'The only escape left to me is from myself.'

'What do you mean?'

'When Father brought me back here, I vowed to stop eating. At least I could have control over my body even if I had power over nothing else.'

She was always so very, very thin and now I knew the reason. 'And your parents know that you refuse to eat deliberately?'

'My loving parents. Oh, my parents know all about my aberration, as they call it. I disgust them. Father – no, Grandmother told you that, didn't she? After they had spoken to me in the schoolroom and threatened me with those terrible things.'

I remembered the deliberateness of Diana Wainwright's actions, as she had stood at the open door so I could hear her final insult to Eleanor. *You disgust me.*

'Now I must be watched over, in case there is a minute of the day when I might be what I am and think for myself.'

'Is that why Mrs Anderson has been hired?'

'Yes, also you and the other governesses who came after Lilian and who must suffocate my every waking moment. Mrs Anderson has the advantage of being a drunkard so sometimes I'm able to escape to the attic and pretend to be free.'

'It was you I saw then, when I opened my bedroom door, and thought there was a man outside. And it was your footsteps I heard pacing in the corridor,' I said.

'Yes. I was terrified you would unmask me and tell my parents – although they found out anyway from Mrs Jenson.'

'But how did you just disappear?' I had looked in all the rooms along the corridor and all had been empty.

'I ran down the servants' staircase.'

'But Agnes came up it and she saw nothing.'

'I passed Agnes on the steps – the servants have all been instructed never to speak of my deviance.' Her voice registered a note of contempt on the word 'deviance'. 'She could not acknowledge to you that she had seen me dressed as a man. Mrs Jenson also denied it to your face when you saw her, but I was called in for an interview with her and Father the next day.'

'Were you punished?'

'What would be the need? My parents know already that I starve my body and hack away at it with my fingernails. If I can find a knife, I use that too. That's why all knives are counted. I'm made to wear sleeves that are buttoned and long in case I try to write self-hatred onto my flesh. I want to destroy the female body that imprisons me. Here, in this dreadful, cursed place.'

Then I finally understood. There had been no mysterious attacker at Teesbank Hall. The scars on Eleanor had been carved there by herself. Her despair was so profound that I had no words to answer her.

'Mrs Jenson and Mrs Anderson write it down in the ledger. C for cutting, if I've slashed at my flesh and D for deviance when I try to dress as a man or express an opinion that isn't reactionary or ignorant.'

The letters, the letters in the account book – finally, I understood their significance. 'Why do they write it down?'

'Father insists upon it. It's so he can report to the doctor whether I am responding to treatment.'

'What kind of treatment?' I asked.

'They try to feed me medicines to stupefy my senses and prescribe long walks to keep my mind and body free from unnatural desires. Sometimes I refuse to leave the house just to spite them.'

I thought of all the long days we had been locked together in the library and I had been desperate to be outside.

Then she asked the strangest question, 'Do you think this

is Arielle Marchal's curse?' Her voice was sincere. 'I can't bear to go on living as I do. My family did a great wrong and now the dead suffocate the living.'

'It is human cruelty, not the supernatural.' I could give no other answer.

'You must think me a monster.'

'No!' I protested.

'I know I have been cruel to you. But everyone claimed I was a monster, said that I was unnatural and disgusting, and I suppose I became what they said. Yet inside I was so desperate.'

'How can it be monstrous to be yourself?' I asked. 'My uncle – my uncle was monstrous. He tried to make me do things.' I halted. I wanted to be honest, just as she had been, but I couldn't say the words. 'He was monstrous. I ran away from him. I know what it is to be desperate too.'

After a moment's reflection, Eleanor held out her hand to me and I took it. We sat together in silence. I thought of all the secrets we held between us.

The noise we had created had woken the household and in the distance I heard footsteps climbing the stairs.

She slumped forward. 'They have come now. Why did you stop me escaping?'

'You were crying out – I meant to call help.'

'Well, you failed in that,' she commented bitterly. She withdrew her hand from mine and covered her face with her arms. After the drama and tension, she was now exhausted. She sat against the wall, her knees bent, dressed in the stolen clothes of her brother. The jacket was too big for her and the sleeves fell away loose around her thin wrists, gathering at her elbows, so that the candlelight showed where the silver scars traced their way along her arms.

Soon the room was full of noise and people. Mrs Jenson was there, scolding, 'Miss Eleanor, you promised your father, and Henry too, that there would be no more of these escapades.'

Mrs Anderson lumbered behind her, out of breath, and already spewing forth a series of self-justifying excuses. 'She was gone in an instant. I had checked on her, made her answer her name and then she was gone. She won't take her draught. Is that my fault?'

Mrs Jenson didn't bother to reply but pulled Eleanor to her feet. 'Mr Wainwright will allow no more chances,' she said.

Eleanor said, 'Why do you think I tried to throw myself from the highest point I could find?'

CHAPTER TWENTY-SIX

The following day Mrs Anderson was dismissed from her post without a character letter. Mrs Jenson had long suspected that quantities of alcohol were being taken from the cellar and it now seemed certain that this was at the hand of Mrs Anderson, who was often incapacitated by the time she came to watch over her patient. Eleanor had escaped from her bedroom on several other occasions over the last year, although never with such potentially fatal consequences. It had been her sobs I had heard on that March night so many months previously, although that time Mrs Anderson had discovered her before she was able to do any harm.

A stout new lock was put on all the attic bedrooms, so Eleanor couldn't enter them. And this time, the Wainwrights did not seek a replacement nurse. There was an unusual closeness between Eleanor and Agnes, and it was decided that the housemaid should be promoted to the post, as a temporary solution. In any case, her parents had decided the situation was reaching a crisis point and Eleanor's needs could no longer be met at Teesbank Hall.

The next day, I was forced to present myself in the library at seven, although it was hard to stifle my yawns. Both Eleanor and I were tired and spoke little at first, but there was a sense of companionship between us that had not existed previously. In the glow of a warmer relationship, I pretended that some of the servants had talked about Gate Helmsley and asked, 'Do you know what it is?'

She snapped to attention as if struck and I worried I had said the wrong thing, but after a moment's consideration, she answered, 'It is a private lunatic asylum near the town of Helmsley in North Yorkshire. Somewhere the rich can pay to incarcerate any inconvenient family member whom they claim is mentally unfit or criminally insane.'

I digested these words carefully. 'Do patients go there to be cured?'

'It's a dreadful place. People do not leave it. Father threatens to have me secured in Gate Helmsley if I can't control my urges. He is rich enough to have me put there and no one will dare to question it.'

This was the threat, I thought, which had so oppressed her. But there were already regular payments being made. I decided to be bold and ask, 'Is that where your sister Clara is?'

Surprised, she looked at me. 'Yes, she has been there almost ever since . . .' Her voice trailed away. 'It is another of the things we don't talk about. How do you know about her?'

'Her name is in the documents from the inquest.'

'Of course.' Eleanor nodded. 'You have almost worked it out then.'

'You said, everyone said, the piece of evidence that condemned Arielle Marchal was the white silk cloth that was wrapped around Samuel's corpse. It matched the piece found by the coroner in her lodgings.'

'Yes?' she prompted me.

'Your father gave half of the white silk to Arielle and half to your mother. Arielle's portion was still in her possession when she was arrested. The part used in the murder was the other half. It was the cloth that became a plaything for Clara and Martha.'

Her voice dropped almost to a whisper. 'I always suspected that my sister Clara was the true murderess, but I couldn't understand how the white silk came to be wrapped around Samuel's body, if it hadn't been placed there by Arielle Marchal.'

'The letter?'

'When you translated it, I knew that Clara had the other piece of silk and the final piece of the puzzle solved it. What will you do with your knowledge about my family? My parents must have kept that secret for over twenty years.'

'I don't know. Perhaps Clara has already been punished enough,' I said.

'I hold one final document and I will show it to you now.' She opened the strongbox and took out an official piece of paper. 'Even Nancy Wilson has never seen this. I stole it from the bureau in Father's study.'

She placed it in my hands and I read the following:

GATE HELMSLEY PRIVATE
LUNATIC ASYLUM

NAME: *Wainwright, Clara* **AGE:** *14 years and 10 months*
ADMITTED: *10 January 1850* **ADMITTED BY:** *Mr Matthew Wainwright of Teesbank Hall (Father)*

REASON FOR ADMISSION: *Violent episodes and delusions*

MONTHLY FEE: *Eighteen pounds (said amount to be reviewed annually)*

FEES PAYABLE BY: *Mr Matthew Wainwright of Teesbank Hall (Father)*

EXPECTED DATE OF RELEASE: *Incurable*

DIAGNOSIS: *Delusional insanity and hysteria – marked delusion is present, which is destructive in nature, leading to acts of violence. This is linked to the patient making perverse and untrue revelations, which are often sexual or violent in nature.*

HISTORY: *Since earliest childhood, the patient has had a tendency to violent and disturbed episodes, which has intensified since the onset of menses. These episodes are accompanied by a profound hysteria, when she will lose control of her lower nature and lash out with the intention of inflicting harm on others.*

The patient displays little interest in her mother but talks obsessively about her father. This includes making false claims that she has witnessed him participating in sexual and degrading acts (see NOTE below). She has a close relationship with her sister MARTHA (who is two years younger) but is seen as a corrupting force on her more placid sibling. This was one of the factors that precipitated her incarceration. She has a pathological jealousy of her younger brother SAMUEL (now deceased), who she saw as replacing her in the father's affection. This is linked to her delusional belief that she is responsible for Samuel's death (see NOTE below).

NOTE – VERY IMPORTANT. MUST BE READ BY ALL PHYSICIANS AND ATTENDANTS WITH RESPONSIBILITY FOR CLARA WAINWRIGHT

The brother of the patient, SAMUEL WAINWRIGHT, was murdered by his governess in a case that became popularly known as the FRENCH MURDER (the murderess being of French origin). No mention of this must be made in front of the patient.

A primary manifestation of CLARA WAINWRIGHT'S delusional insanity is her belief that she was responsible for the death of her brother. She will claim she has a secret she must not tell anyone. Mr Wainwright has informed the Asylum that this is categorically not the case. Furthermore, the patient has been known to speak of perverse sexual relations between the governess and her father. This is most unnatural and distressing.

If the patient attempts to speak of any of the matters alluded to above, it is imperative that the Physician on duty is informed *immediately and that the patient is removed from the society of other patients. She must be placed in the restraining room; this is so as to avoid unnecessary agitation. The patient is untrustworthy and an hysteric.*

FAMILY HISTORY: *Mother was committed to York Asylum for post-partum lunacy in September 1840. Cured and released December 1840. No repeat occurrences.*

PATIENT'S CONDITION ON ADMISSION: *Due to her volatile and aggressive state, the patient had to be placed in restraints. She is physically robust, with no obvious external deformities.*

TREATMENT: *Mercury and calomel in the first instance to render acts of violence less likely. A full hysterectomy will be needed to remove the seat of her disease.*

I went to say something but at that moment the library door opened and Matthew Wainwright entered the room with his son. I shrank a little from the master of the house but Henry nodded at me reassuringly, as if to say there was good news. Eleanor, however, looked terrified. Clearly, she thought she was to be sent away to Gate Helmsley.

Without much preamble, her father announced Eleanor was to go to London.

'Why do you want me to go there?' A visit to the capital city was one of the things she most desired but she had such an absolute distrust of her father that her first assumption was it must be a punishment.

Henry stepped in. 'It's not what you fear, Ellie.'

He was stopped by a sharp glance from his father, who said, 'You will be taken to see a specialist doctor, a physician, who deals in the treatment of the brain. He has experience of dealing with degenerates and females with unnatural desires.'

'I am not a degenerate,' she said resolutely, 'and, Father, you of all people should know that my desires are natural. I won't allow myself to be undressed and poked and prodded again in a supposed attempt at a cure.'

'None of those things will happen, I promise you,' said Henry. 'He'll ask about what frightens you and find ways to help you recover.'

'You all know what frightens me.' Her face was set into a hard straight line of denial. Her strength of feeling was such that it even overrode her terror of her father. 'I cannot change who I am and I don't want to.'

'Things cannot continue as they are,' her father stated. 'There will be no further discussion. It is only thanks to Henry's intervention that I'm prepared to try this before seeking other, more permanent, remedies.'

I wondered then how much pleading Henry had done on Eleanor's behalf.

Henry produced the final bargaining position. 'If you see the doctor without a fuss and take whatever pills and tablets he recommends, then you can spend time in London and visit the museums of South Kensington and the London International Exhibition.'

Eleanor wavered. 'Is this true, Father? Will you allow me to have time in London?'

'If you'll see Dr Sedgewick in the first four days you're there, then you may visit where you wish for the rest of the week. It was Henry who suggested this would please you.'

'No, sir,' Henry said, 'it was the idea of Miss Caldwell. She says Eleanor talks of little else.'

'Miss Caldwell's idea?' Eleanor repeated, surprised.

I felt myself blush. 'I knew it would make you happy,' I said.

Henry added, 'Miss Caldwell has your best interests at heart.'

She thought for a moment, then smiled and said, 'Thank you. It's the thing I most desire in the world.' She came and sat next to me.

To my astonishment, I discovered I was to accompany the brother and sister to London, while Mrs Wainwright had finally been persuaded to visit her family in York. Mr Wainwright had his business to attend to in Newcastle. However, Diana Wainwright refused to leave Teesbank Hall, which would be largely closed for the period of one week, with only Mrs Jenson and a much reduced staff kept in residence.

The next few days were full of activity, as the accommodation and train tickets were booked, clothes washed and packed, and plans made. Eleanor, Henry and I sat together in the library, laughing and planning our itinerary, the concerts and exhibitions we hoped to visit. I finally felt that I was among friends. The only blot on my new-found happiness was the envelopes that were delivered every other day, addressed to Henry and bearing an Inverness postmark. Rosalind Merryweather's handwriting was as pretty as her smile and I couldn't explain why I had taken such a dislike to it.

CHAPTER TWENTY-SEVEN

We set off for London the following Monday, on the very first train of the day. We were travelling in first class and I reflected on how different this journey was from my desperate escape six months earlier, when I had crisscrossed the country by railway, changing lines and directions in an attempt to avoid capture.

Eleanor had been very quiet when we left Teesbank Hall, which I put down to the early hour and thought nothing more of it. Henry and I were excited and spoke about the places we would pass on the journey and the refreshments we intended to purchase on board the train. Eleanor, however, stared steadfastly out of the window and refused to join in our talk. She was picking away at the long sleeves of her dress and, with a jolt, I suddenly remembered the scars beneath.

By the time we arrived at York, she still hadn't said a word and her behaviour was so odd that Henry asked her directly, 'Are you all right, Ellie? You seem very quiet.'

'I am fine, Henry. I just didn't want to interrupt your

private conversation.' And with that, she shot me a poisonous look.

'Whatever do you mean, Ellie? You were very glad that Miss Caldwell was coming. She will be a companion for you.'

She replied, 'I don't need a governess spying on me, and if I were to choose a companion, it would not be someone as sly as Miss Caldwell.'

I felt cold inside. It was the old Eleanor speaking. 'Eleanor, why ever do you say that? I haven't meant to upset you. What is the matter?'

For the first time on the journey, she looked at me. 'Quite frankly, you don't need to have the intention to offend, your presence alone is enough.'

'Eleanor!' I stammered, shocked at the cruelty of her response.

Now her brother turned on her furiously. 'Eleanor, apologize at once. How can you speak to Miss Caldwell like that? She has never been anything but pleasant to you.'

'Miss Caldwell, I apologize most sincerely,' she said mechanically, her eyes cold as she scrutinized me.

The enjoyment of the journey was quite gone and none of us spoke much now. I had thought Eleanor and I were becoming friends, we had shared secrets, but in an instant it had gone. I had seen before how her fits of fury could arise from nowhere, then dissipate as quickly. I glanced across — she was still staring out of the window and I saw her furtively wipe away a tear. Her changeability frightened me. It was impossible to know how she would react. And it was equally impossible not to pity her.

We were staying close by King's Cross station, at the Great Northern Hotel, which was an elegant, sweeping building, with some one hundred bedrooms and every modern convenience. However, any excitement at being in the heart of London was wiped away by Eleanor's behaviour and the mood soured even more when Henry showed us to our lodgings and we found that Eleanor and I were to share a room. He mumbled that the hotel was very busy because of the International Exhibition and nothing else was available. My heart sank.

The violence of Eleanor's reaction shocked me. 'Do you still not trust me, Henry? I don't want *her* sleeping by my side. I don't want that woman anywhere near me.' Every shred of friendship between us had dissolved and the conversations of the last few months counted for nothing.

'Eleanor, there is . . .' Henry's words fell on deaf ears for she had marched from the room and slammed the door behind her. He turned to me. 'Miss Caldwell, I'm sorry for my sister's behaviour but I don't know what else to do. She must have someone with her. Her treatment will be an ordeal. I can't bear to think about how awful it will be . . .' He stopped to compose himself. '. . . and I'm terrified she will try to harm herself again if there is no one to watch over her.'

'If it's so terrible, why have you agreed to the treatment?' I asked, genuinely curious.

'The alternative would be worse.' He ran his fingers through his hair with despair.

'She would be sent to Gate Helmsley like Clara?'

If he was taken aback that I knew of his eldest sister's existence, he didn't show it. Instead, he walked over to the window and looked out at the golden autumn trees. 'Clara is fourteen years older than me and I have met her only once. When I was about eight, they took me to visit her. She had been cleaned up a little, because the asylum knew we were coming, but she was still dirty and unkempt. She had lost most of her teeth and there were red marks on her wrists from where she wore restraints at night.'

'Oh, God!' I put my hand to my mouth with horror.

'She reached out her hand and called me her dearest brother, but I shrank from her in terror and began crying. They had to take me out of the room and now she refuses to see me again. I'll never forgive myself for that.' He shook his head. 'Death would be better than Gate Helmsley. It was only by agreeing to the appointments with Dr Sedgewick that I could stop Father disposing of Eleanor in the same way.'

'Then you know that you have done the right thing,' I said.

Now he turned to me. 'But this? I don't understand why my parents won't leave her in peace. It will be too much of an ordeal for her and I'm terrified she will hurt herself.'

Without thinking, I placed my hand upon his arm. 'What else can you do? You're the only person who is trying to act in her best interests.'

'Thank you, Miss Caldwell. You cannot know how much

your words matter to me.' We looked at each other and instantly the intimacy of the boathouse was restored.

At that moment, Eleanor came back into the room and Henry and I moved awkwardly away from each other. She was as sharp as a whip and caught the glance between us. 'Henry, I wish to sleep. It has been a long day and I must be up early in the morning. Leave the room now.'

He half smiled at us both, shrugged and then left. Eleanor didn't speak again for the rest of the evening, but every so often I would catch her looking across at me, as if sizing me up in some way.

The next morning, the three of us took a closed carriage to Dr Sedgewick's consulting rooms, which were in Harley Street. For most of the journey, we sat in silence although Henry tried to break the gloom by pointing out sights from the window. Eleanor didn't respond and instead plucked at the sleeves of her dress, staring vacantly downwards. I thought of the scars that lay under the fabric and of how much unhappiness was written into them.

Once we arrived, Henry was forced to coax her inside the building. She would have trusted no one else. I waited outside and when he finally emerged, he was grim-faced.

'How was it?' I asked.

'Dreadful.' He shrugged. 'Dr Sedgewick is nothing more than a hard-faced businessman. I didn't want to leave her there alone, but he insisted I go. Apparently, there must be no interference in the special relationship between patient and physician,' he said wryly.

We were both silent.

'Let's walk somewhere, away from here,' he said. 'Poor Eleanor will be trapped there for several hours.'

We made our way to the nearby Regent's Park. It was a glorious late September day and we found ourselves by the lake, its surface blue and serene, the trees surrounding it taking on their autumn colours of orange and gold. I thought of Arielle Marchal, who had been wrongly executed on a beautiful day in autumn and didn't want to die but had cried out to the baying crowds that she would finally tell the truth. How terrible that no one would listen and her dying moments were drowned with shouts of 'Whore!'

'You seem miles away, Miss Caldwell. What are you thinking about?'

'Nothing, really.' I could hardly tell him that I was thinking of the French governess who had died in place of his sister Clara. I wondered whether it would be possible to make recompense to Arielle in some way.

We began to talk of other things and spent time listening to the military band playing at the centre of the park. Time disappeared and we found, to our astonishment, that it was almost three o'clock.

'We must return to meet Eleanor!' Henry exclaimed. We were forced to run the length of Harley Street and were still several minutes after the agreed time. We arrived out of breath and still smiling from the time we had spent together. Henry went into the building to meet her and she emerged slumped against his shoulder. She was pale and her eyes were glazed. Dr Sedgewick had given her a strong sedative to deaden her nerves and reduce what he described as her hysterical fits. I felt guilty that we had returned happy.

We went back to our hotel in the closed carriage, which was filled with a sickly stink of cherries.

'What on earth is that smell?' Henry asked.

Eleanor looked up at him. Her movements were clumsy and her speech a little slurred. 'Dr Sedgewick insists that I spray myself with a formula of chemicals, which he claims will encourage the gentler feminine fluids in my body to the surface and allow them to dominate over my mannish tendencies to rationality and physical pleasure.' Half laughing, half sobbing, she said, 'The man is a fraud. There is no scientific basis for what he says.'

She leaned her head against the carriage window and would say no more. When we arrived at the hotel, Eleanor insisted on going straight to our room and I was forced to follow her. I would have liked to help her in some way, but she was too proud to accept my sympathy. Her first action was to flush all the pills and liquids down the lavatory. I looked away. Having seen the effect they had, I didn't intend revealing her secret. However, she was forced to cover herself regularly with the foul-smelling spray. She insisted that I turned away as she coated her body in the cloying odour, then lay rigid upon her bed, complaining of a headache while silent tears streamed down her face.

There is a certain type of cherry bonbon, the smell of

which transports me to the horror of that time and brings back memories of her desperate humiliation.

I knew it wasn't easy for Henry to continue with the course of treatment, and he found her distress almost impossible to bear. Yet we both knew that if Eleanor didn't at least seem to comply with the doctor's instructions, Mr Wainwright would hold true to his threat to incarcerate her with Clara in Gate Helmsley.

The next morning, Eleanor refused to allow me to accompany them to Harley Street and I spent the day alone. I was quite content to wander around the nearby streets and await their return. By the fourth day, Eleanor absolutely refused to attend the doctor's consulting rooms and became hysterical at the suggestion she should do so.

'I won't get into that carriage to go there. I would rather die than go back to that place. He is trying to steal me from myself! I don't want to lose who I am.'

'Ellie, he is trying to help,' Henry pleaded, but his words sounded false to us all. 'You must go. Think of the consequences.'

When I looked at Henry, I saw how exhausted he was by the emotion of the situation – how crumpled and pale his face was, how torn he was between persuading her to go and letting her stay.

'Eleanor, please,' I said. 'It is only one more day. After that you'll be free to enjoy London. This time tomorrow, we'll be setting off for the exhibition.'

She didn't acknowledge my words and appeared not to be

listening, but she began to calm a little, finally getting into the carriage to take her to Harley Street.

As Henry went to follow her, he said quietly, 'Thank you, Miss Caldwell. It's not easy for any of us, least of all for Eleanor.'

'It's difficult,' I replied, 'but she has to go.'

There was that understanding between us again.

But Eleanor heard my words. 'You want to be rid of me,' she said, horrified. 'It's true that you would sacrifice me.'

'No, Eleanor, that isn't what I meant,' I said.

And Henry added, 'Ellie, you misunderstand. We just need you to go to Dr Sedgewick.'

'Miss Caldwell wants me gone. I know that for certain,' she replied.

I tried to reassure her, but she stared down at her hands, her skin blotched with anger. All that day, I thought about how I could make amends to her when she returned in the afternoon.

CHAPTER TWENTY-EIGHT

On the fifth day, Eleanor was finally able to claim her reward and we travelled to South Kensington station on the newly built extension to the Metropolitan Railway. Our plan was to visit the London International Exhibition over the next two days, then spend some time at the Royal Albert Hall. South Kensington was filled with excited crowds and the Museum rose like a vast palace of brick and cream among the surrounding trees. It seemed to me a fairyland, an impression further enhanced by the swelling organ music, which was playing continuously in the background. Inside it was possible to take a tour of the world and the exotic sights, colours and smells of distant lands, simply by walking the length of the museum's corridors.

For the briefest of moments, the three of us were united in our sense of wonder at the range of the exhibits, yet Eleanor's antagonism towards me was too strong for this to last. But I knew her moods were changeable and I hoped to make up with her, if I could only find the right time to speak to her in confidence. She stared eagerly about her as if trying to memorize every impression and sensation the exhibition offered, so she could imprint them on her mind and take them back to Teesbank Hall. We were at the very heart of the world – here were the most recent developments in the arts and industry. I watched Eleanor covertly. Her whole face was illuminated and her eyes shone with a childish wonder she could not conceal.

Suddenly she glanced at me and I saw her face harden. She believed I had been spying on her and hissed quietly, 'You shouldn't be here. Henry is my brother and you are not needed. Why can't you go?' The spell of unity was broken. She would gladly have left me behind at the hotel because I was an intruder on her precious time with him. Breaking the awkward silence, I asked Henry if I could return to the India court where I had been particularly taken with some of the intricate whitework embroidery from the city of Lucknow. I could see he was unhappy that I was by myself in the vast bustle of the building, but I promised to be no longer than thirty minutes. Eleanor smiled with cold relief.

The route I took from the Court of Agricultural Appliances led me through an assault on the senses. I was also walking in a direction that was against the flow of the general crowd so my head was slightly down as I moved determinedly forward. To my great surprise, in this city where I knew nobody, I heard a cry, a familiar squeal of joy: 'Harriet, dearest Harriet!' I turned and saw, to my amazement, my cousin, my dearest fair-haired cousin and partner in adversity.

'Lucy!' I cried, and we embraced. For a few moments we said nothing. Our mutual delight was beyond words.

And then a torrent of questions and admonishments: 'Harriet, where have you been? I have been so frightened for you. Why didn't you say a word before leaving?'

I had tears in my eyes, I was so happy to see my beloved Lucy again. 'I couldn't say anything. I was terrified of being discovered and I didn't want you to be blamed for my disappearance. I had to leave.'

Lucy nodded gravely. By this point, we had caused some degree of obstruction and several black-clad matrons tutted at us. She smiled at them, widening her clear green eyes, and apologized. 'I have unexpectedly met with my cousin. Please excuse us,' she explained. She giggled. 'Let's find somewhere quieter so we can talk properly.'

I felt a degree of reluctance. Henry was expecting me soon and the layout of the South Kensington Museum was confusing. I might not be able to find my way back to him if I went too far from the route we had taken. Yet how could I say no? It was beyond delightful to see Lucy, so coincidentally, and with no sign of Uncle Thomas Stepford. It was also clear we were in everyone's way. I nodded and followed Lucy, as she slipped behind one of the barriers cordoned off with a red silken rope. 'Where are we going? Are we meant to be here?' I asked, breathless at the subterfuge of stealing into this forbidden section.

Lucy placed a finger upon her lips and hushed me. 'Follow me,' she whispered. 'This is the route behind the stands.'

We wove between the billowing silk tents that separated the different sections of the exhibition. Lucy was sure-footed and knew exactly where she was going. I followed because I had no idea what else to do, caught up in the confusion and vastness of the great hall. I was becoming disoriented and clasped Lucy's hand more tightly to try to slow her down. I wanted to pause, at least for a few moments. Surely we had the privacy we craved, hidden as we were in the skirts of the silken tents. 'Lucy, Lucy, please stop,' I begged, 'or I'll be forced to return. People are waiting for me. I can't allow myself to become lost.'

'Oh, but, dearest Harriet, you have been found!' she exclaimed and now she held my hand ever more firmly. There was something about the determination of her grip that troubled me. 'Lucy, you're hurting me!' I tried to loosen her hold, but it was far too strong.

Although she glanced behind and exclaimed, 'This is such a marvellous game,' she seemed in deadly earnest and I knew I didn't understand the rules we were playing by. We skittered in and out of the billowing silk, breathless, gasping, apologizing to the knots of family groups we pushed aside in our haste to be – where I didn't know.

'We are almost there,' she reassured me, but her voice had an edge of steel to it that I had not heard before. 'I have the most incredible surprise planned for you!'

'Lucy – but, Lucy, what?' I was so innocent and so naïve. I prided myself on my rationality and ability to read any situation accurately, but I had been led straight into Lucy's trap.

Then I saw him. At the same moment he recognized me.

'We are here, Harriet,' she announced coldly and then, 'Look what I have brought you, Father. Are you pleased?'

The blinding light, frozen in time. I looked up at him and was trapped in darkness. There were people close at hand, a flimsy tent of silk separated me from the carnival mood of the exhibition, but all other sounds and sights had blurred and disappeared. I could see and sense only him. For a moment I feared my legs would give way beneath me, so strong was the effect that his presence had upon me.

Like a fool, I could only mutter, 'Uncle Thomas Stepford.' I didn't know if it was a question or a greeting, but they were the sole words my lips could form. He was a substantial man and his bulk made him more intimidating – people would instinctively step aside when they saw him. The features of his face were heavy and his greasy dark hair was plastered against his scalp. Worst of all, he wore the odour of unwashed bodies.

He would be angry. I knew that. Furious because I had escaped and outwitted him. I had been gone for six months and he was not a man who liked to be thwarted.

'I knew that you would find me in time.' His words were familiar. The recurring refrain that ran through my dreams. 'And you will not leave again. You are my ward and I'm your legal guardian. It is what your father desired.'

I opened my mouth to scream but the sounds of my distress were largely swallowed by the hullabaloo of the crowd.

He reached out to detain me and the horror of feeling his

hands on me again was so fierce I found the strength to shake free of Lucy's grasp and dart beneath the edge of the tent so that I was once more in the main part of the exhibition. My freedom was brief, as both Lucy and Uncle Thomas Stepford were wrong-footed for only a moment and quickly followed, both seizing hold of me. My distress was obvious and a number of the crowd turned to offer assistance and ask what the matter was. Smiling, Lucy thanked them for their concern and shooed them away. 'My dear cousin is often taken in this way. She suffers from hysteria when she is in public places and we must return her home before the seizure takes a grip of her.'

As I looked at her now – Lucy, sweet, green-eyed Lucy – I remembered Swaffham and how she had played the role of a demure young lady, when all the while mocking the adults who were duped by her charms. She had advised me never to trust anyone. I thought I was the only person in the world she was true to, but I saw that I, too, had been fooled.

The more I tried to break free from their clutches, the more my desperate actions seemed to confirm her words. Lucy thanked passers-by for their concern about my well-being and promised that I would be taken to a place of safety as soon as it was possible. All the while, Uncle Thomas Stepford gripped my arms tightly behind my back, as if supporting me, and hissed in my ear, 'You will make it worse for yourself if you speak out. And God knows you will suffer enough when we return to Swaffham. What good will protesting do and who will believe you?'

An intense terror gripped me so strongly that I fainted. When I came to, I had been moved away from the main part of the exhibition and into a small side room, furnished with a wooden table and chair. Only Lucy was with me, and she was forcing some tepid water into my dry mouth. I opened my eyes fully and looked appealingly at her.

As if in response to my unformed question, she said, 'Father has gone to hire a carriage to take us back to our lodgings in the Strand. Tomorrow morning, we shall return to Swaffham.'

'Lucy, you have betrayed me. You can't know what it is that I return to.'

I had half expected her to deny my statement, as I had never spoken to her about what had happened. I could barely frame the words in my own mind, let alone explain them to someone else, and had always believed Lucy's duty to her father must blind her to the kind of man he truly was.

She didn't deny my accusations. Instead, she answered matter-of-factly, 'If it wasn't you, it would have been me. I was glad to be done with it – the measuring, his supposed *research* into phrenology, the photographs. All of it.'

I gasped. 'You knew what he did?'

She laughed sadly, sardonically. 'Some of it. Do you think you were the only one singled out? I have suffered too, those long hours forced to stand motionless, waiting to be photographed. Please don't think you are unique. I was glad when he chose you for his project instead of me!'

'And you knew about the other things – the things he did to Gladys and would have done to me, if I hadn't escaped?'

She had the grace to look ashamed. 'He's a frightening man and I would never question him. There are some things it is better for me not to know.'

'You and I were the closest of friends.'

She shrugged. 'And he is my father. And you swore you'd never leave, but you did.'

'I was worried he might find out about my plans if I told you.'

'Yes, he would have,' she snapped. 'If only you had confided in me, I could have betrayed you straight away. Instead I had to take your place in the research, and I thought I was done with all of that.'

'Lucy,' I said sadly, 'you could come with me now. We could escape together . . .'

My words trailed away as she shook her head determinedly. 'You can't escape him, though you may think it's possible. I tried once but he will always find you.' She looked away now and her eyes darkened but then she continued, 'He was angry, you know, very angry. You had interfered with months and months of his research and now he will make you pay.'

I thought of the lines upon the canvas, meticulously tracking the rise of my height against the graph of Gladys's more inferior growth. I remembered the sly knock at the bedroom door.

Now I cast around desperately, looking for a way out. She was one step ahead, even in that. 'Don't think it's possible to escape. Father had the sense to lock us in together and you may knock and scream as much as you want, but everyone thinks you're a hysteric. The attendants have been told that you are secured for your own protection.'

I slumped against the stiff, hard-backed chair. I thought desperately of Henry and Eleanor. They were somewhere in the vastness of the exhibition courts. I was late and they were expecting me. Perhaps they had begun the search already. Time itself had taken on a dream-like quality and I didn't know how long I had been gone. My greatest hope of escape was when they tried to take me to the hansom cab. I would save my screams until then. Once buried in the depths of Swaffham, there would be no hope of fleeing Uncle a second time.

I heard the key rattle in the lock and Uncle Thomas Stepford stood before us. 'I have hired a cab,' he said to Lucy. 'It awaits us on the other side of the park.' He added, looking at me, 'I have told the driver that you're a lunatic and he should ignore any ridiculous accusations you might make. He had to be paid double to agree to take you.'

'You can't force me to go back there, Uncle, not back to that place. I would rather starve on the streets than be held prisoner in Swaffham.'

His face was immobile. Despite the courage and defiance of my words, I quaked inside with terror and attempted another tactic. 'Why are you so desperate for me to return?

I am only a burden to you. Surely it's better that I leave. I can make my own living.'

This time he deigned to give me an answer. 'Your fool of a father tied up all the free money of the estate in providing for you until you are twenty-five. If you're not in my possession, I can't get my hands on the income. Therefore, whether I want you or not, I must have you. What good is it to me living in that deadly dull house in Norfolk and no money to spend? It's a lucky chance that Lucy found you here, but we have been searching high and low and soon enough our contacts would have brought us to your hiding-place.'

Poor Father: he had meant to protect me from Uncle Thomas Stepford's cruelty and yet he had placed me in greater danger. Knowing his brother as he did, he must have realized that Thomas Stepford would make no kindly provision for me but must have his duty forced upon him through the binding conditions of the will. But he could hardly have expected that, such was the extent of my uncle's depravity, I would have been better off living and starving on the streets.

'Lucy, you're to go ahead and make a way through the crowd, while I support her,' he instructed his daughter. And then to me, 'Not a word from you or there will be consequences.'

He grabbed my arms from behind, so that I was unable to move freely and was half slumped against him. All the time he muttered at me, 'Not a word. It will make it worse.' My state of anxiety was such that I could hardly breathe and my whole body physically recoiled at the closeness to Uncle Thomas Stepford – the acrid smell of his unwashed suit and the strength of his grip against me. My mind was working feverishly, trying to decide how I could best make my escape.

We left the small side room and entered the throng of the exhibition. I felt nauseous, and the confusion of the sights and sounds merely added to my sense of disorientation. I saw faces move close towards me and concerned voices ask, 'Is the young lady unwell?' and 'Can we be of assistance?' I tried to open my mouth to beg for help, but Uncle Thomas Stepford dug his dirty nails into the exposed flesh of my wrist and Lucy said sweetly, 'She is overwrought. The excitement of the exhibition is too much for her. We must take her home as quickly as possible, so please let us through.'

I would have spoken, but I was in a state of shock and the words were difficult to form. In my newly assigned role of hysterical invalid, the crowds ignored me and nodded sympathetically at Uncle and Lucy. And then I saw salvation. As we hurried through the Manufacturing Court, Henry and Eleanor were standing at the far corner. Henry was turned away from me but his whole stance spoke of someone agitated and searching. I had failed to return in the thirty minutes we had agreed. My sense of relief at seeing them was overpowering, my desperation to be saved meant my whole body jerked in their direction, as if drawn by some invisible cord. Lucy felt me tense and looked where I was facing, 'So those are your friends,' she sneered, and pulled me tightly in the opposite direction.

As she did so, Eleanor turned and looked directly at me. I knew she had seen me because astonishment registered on her face. My distress was obvious and I silently pleaded with her. She stared at me, as if unsure of what to do next. I prayed she would remember how we had almost been close and how we had both been desperate and held that understanding between us.

The moment stretched to eternity as she weighed up my fate and then she turned away, tugging at Henry's coat and gesturing him to go along a different route. I was lost. My whole body sagged and I was limp with grief. We were nearing the doors of the exhibition and the prison gates of Swaffham beckoned.

Yet luck must have been on my side because, at the very last moment, there were loud shouts and agitation within the crowd: a gang of street urchins had broken into the exhibition, meaning to cause chaos and distraction and steal any well-fed purses they could find. The dirty and poorly clad children were enjoying leading some of the pompous officials on a merry chase and skittered and dodged among the crowds, while the attendants lumbered behind them. Everyone turned in their direction and Henry, Henry too, turned. He saw me then. His eyes widening when he recognized the shock and distress on my face, even from that distance. He forced his way through the crowd and strode across to my uncle.

'What are you doing, sir? Why do you detain my companion Miss Caldwell? Release her at once,' he demanded.

'Miss Caldwell?' Uncle stammered, surprised by the stolen name I had acquired and then he sneered, 'This is not Miss Caldwell. This is Miss Harriet Fleet of Swaffham Hall in Norfolk. Furthermore, I have every right to detain her. She is a runaway and a lunatic. I am her guardian. She is my niece and I will take control of her.'

Henry was shocked by this news and turned to me. 'Harriet. Is any of this true?'

In my drowning state, where words seemed to dance through my mind and be impossible to hold on to, I tried to explain to Henry. 'Henry, you know me well and I am no lunatic, but I had to run away from this wicked man. Please, I beg you for help,' I stuttered as the words finally came tumbling out.

Lucy reached across and touched Henry's arm lightly. Very earnestly she said, 'Father is not a wicked man. These are the ramblings of a lunatic and clearly she has deceived you as she deceived us all. She has been living under a false name. We must return her to a place of safety. It is for her own good.'

Dearest Henry, he did not hesitate to believe me even though all the evidence was stacked against. 'Miss Caldwell, or Miss Fleet, it doesn't matter which, has asked for my protection. I must therefore ask you to release her into my custody.'

Now Uncle showed his true colours, no longer hiding beneath his cloak of respectability, and he snarled, 'I am her guardian and have legal rights over her. She belongs to me until she is twenty-five. It is what her father's will stated and I must have her.'

By this time quite a crowd had gathered around us and Henry hesitated slightly. I feared that he would be intimidated but he responded, 'I am her employer, sir, and as such I demand that you hand her to me. You may, in due course, pursue your rights and furnish proof that what you say is true but, until then, I insist you let her go.'

'I will pursue my rights, make no mistake,' Uncle Thomas Stepford growled.

Henry ignored him. 'You will find us at the Great Northern Hotel. Ask for Henry Wainwright or send your legal representative to speak to me.'

In light of the reasonableness of Henry's words and the clear direction of the crowd's sympathies, it was impossible to continue his claim to me, but Uncle Thomas Stepford was not to be defeated. 'You shall see me again, sir. I shall personally attend first thing tomorrow, with my lawyer and the full force of the law.'

Reluctantly, my uncle and cousin released me from their grasp and I stumbled towards Henry. With his arm around me, he supported me through the curious crowd, which parted to let us pass. I was quite unwell and he was determined that I should be in the fresh air as quickly as possible and away from my uncle. His attentions were solely focused upon me but as we left the area, I turned and, to my surprise, saw Eleanor dash across to Lucy and speak to her. I didn't know what she said – it was hardly likely to be words in my defence.

The high emotion and drama of the scene meant my recollection of the immediate aftermath was somewhat hazy. I have flashes of memory, like vivid pictures in my mind. I recall leaning against Henry's shoulder as the carriage took us away from the scene and the comfort I felt in his protective presence. There was the attentiveness of his repeated questions as to my welfare and health, and his promises that he would allow no harm to come to me. Yet I knew that Uncle Thomas Stepford was devious – Lucy, too, as I'd discovered. They would not stop until they had me truly in their clutches, and I feared the law would support them in that.

It was also impossible to forget Eleanor's simmering resentment and how she had turned away when I was in danger. Although the immediate threat was averted, I knew it was not stopped.

CHAPTER TWENTY-NINE

I revealed to Henry a version of my personal history: my birth, my family, Father's death and the horror of falling into Uncle's clutches. There were some things it was difficult to speak of – it is only now in old age, when time has taken away some of their sting, that I can begin to describe something of the secrets shared by Lucy, Gladys and me, and whoever else Thomas Stepford had subjected to his clinical experiments. It is not something I choose to talk about at length for I fear that to speak of such matters has the power to evoke them once more and make them real.

The sad facts of the case were that, as I was only twenty-one and Uncle Thomas Stepford had been appointed my guardian and protector, I belonged to him, and initially it seemed I had little chance of escape. Henry had revealed to my uncle the true address of our hotel and his name – not realizing at that moment the severity of the situation I faced. I was terrified he might track me down and, according to the terms of my father's will, have me taken from the protection of an honourable man who cared for my welfare, and thrown instead into the full horror of his own desires. We decided I must leave London as quickly as possible and return to the safety of Teesbank Hall. Uncle Thomas Stepford didn't know where the Wainwrights lived and the position of the house in the north of England gave it a degree of safety.

Eleanor and I would return the very next morning, even though the Hall was partly closed and almost deserted, and our luggage would be sent on later. Henry had instructed the staff at the Great Northern Hotel that they must not reveal our planned destination to anyone. He hoped to send a telegraph via the General Post Office to prepare Mrs Jenson for our homecoming but it was likely we would arrive before his communication, so he had also written a letter for me to carry. In this way, I wouldn't have to recount the distressing circumstances of my flight.

In the meantime, he would engage the services of the best possible lawyers to fight Uncle's attempts to take me back to Swaffham. He felt confident that Thomas Stepford's cruel treatment of me and the appropriation of my income would be grounds enough to break any legal hold he might have over me. He would join us as soon as he had put in place all the legal necessities.

All the while, Eleanor's hatred of me burned.

Immediately after Henry had seen us off at King's Cross terminus, and we were settled in our railway compartment, Eleanor said, 'I knew from the very start that you were deceitful and now my suspicions have been proved true.'

'What suspicions?' I demanded.

'You are a liar, Harriet Fleet. You pretended to be some-one you are not.'

'I was desperate to escape and you of all people should understand that.'

'I understand only too well that you want to steal Henry from me. What was it you whispered to him? *She has to go?*'

'No. You know that's not what I intended. I meant only that you must go to Dr Sedgewick. You deliberately choose to misunderstand what I said.'

'Then how do you explain this?' she asked, taking a sheet of paper from her travelling bag, and handing it to me.

The writing was familiar and distinctive, with elaborate flourishes in lilac ink. I looked at her in surprise. 'Why, this is just like the letter from Arielle Marchal I translated.'

'It is exactly her hand. And it's the reason I know the truth about you.'

Dumbfounded, I stared at the letter. 'I don't understand what you mean.'

She snatched it back. 'Then I shall read it out loud for you and the meaning will become clear.' With the page held in front of her, she said, *'Dearest Eleanor, Beware Harriet. She is full of deceit and wants to destroy you. The English governess is in love with Henry and will sacrifice you to gain him.'* At this point, she paused and looked at me directly. She continued, *'She will have you sent to Gate Helmsley. Arielle Marchal.'*

My cheeks had flushed with colour at the mention of

Henry's name. 'The accusations are false. The dead cannot write letters,' I replied.

'Every word is true. Your face has already betrayed you. In any case, once my eyes had been opened to the truth, it was impossible to miss your simpering behaviour towards my brother in London.'

'I don't love Henry – Mr Wainwright, I mean—'

She laughed coldly. 'And if I needed further confirmation of the letter's truth, you're not Harriet Caldwell. Even your name is a lie.'

Feeling sick inside, I asked her how the letter had come into her possession.

'It was on my bed the night before we left for London.'

Now I understood her hatred on the train journey.

'Rosalind Merryweather is a fool but at least she's beautiful and well-born. What Grandmother would call *a good addition to the family*. But you? No, Henry wouldn't be interested in someone like you.'

Turning away, I said, 'This letter is nonsense. The dead don't communicate with the living. This is human trickery.'

'Human trickery? Look at the letter again. Isn't this Arielle's writing?'

I examined the letter reluctantly. 'It seems like her hand, but it could have been forged—'

'I've shown Arielle's letter to no one but you. We are the only people living who know her style. I presume you didn't write this letter.'

I shook my head, but as she said this, a kind of dread

seized me. I hadn't written the letter but what if Eleanor had? I'd read of such things in accounts of lunatics, where the deranged carried out terrible night-time actions which their rational daytime mind refused to remember. I had made myself forget the horror of the bloodied nightgown, but wasn't this a very similar thing? Eleanor found ways to attack me, then denied it to my face. All her hatred crystallized into lilac ink or spattered in blood across a nightgown. And her sister Clara, her murderous sister Clara. Both bound together by madness as well as blood.

'I had always dreamed of visiting London and your actions have quite destroyed that too,' she stated with cold fury. 'There is nothing more that I wish to say to you.'

Throughout the long hours of the journey Eleanor maintained a militant silence. I was exhausted and angry with her as well, so I had no real desire to speak. I already dreaded the Wainwrights' reaction to me, but I pushed such anxieties to one side.

In one respect, at least, Arielle's letter had spoken the truth. I could no longer deny my feelings for Henry. I knew he loved Rosalind Merryweather, but he was kind to me and treated me as an equal. He had protected me against Uncle Thomas Stepford and was sensitive enough not to enquire too deeply when I cried out at the thought of being returned to the place that should have been my home. He accepted me fully at my word that I could not and would not return to Swaffham. I knew an attachment between us was hopeless and impossible, but in these brief hours on the train, I could ignore reality and think about Henry.

When the train finally reached Eaglescliffe, Eleanor had enough money in her purse to bribe a man to take us the two miles in his cart – not for her the indignity of struggling through muddy woods to reach her destination. He refused to travel beyond the gates of the house and, as soon as he'd dropped us off, left quickly, without looking back.

It was twilight when we arrived and Teesbank Hall was darker and gloomier than I had expected, especially after the bustle and excitement of London. Most of the servants had been sent away, so it seemed even more desolate than usual. Mrs Jenson was a long time replying to our attempts to enter the house but finally opened the door.

When she saw Eleanor and me standing there, her face registered shock and not a little displeasure. It was clear Henry's telegraph had not yet reached Teesbank Hall. I wondered if she was glad of the times when Eleanor was away and her moods didn't rule the house. Mrs Jenson's response seemed at first quite strange. 'Teesbank has not been aired, young ladies. I don't know if this is the right time for you to be here.'

'We've had to leave London,' I said, and handed her the letter from Henry. 'This will explain the circumstances.'

She took the document from my hand and read it with disbelief. 'Is this true?' she asked me.

I hadn't seen the contents of the letter, but I could guess what his words were likely to be so I nodded. 'We've had a terrible time. Miss Eleanor and I are exhausted. Have you anything to hand that we may eat or drink?'

'Agnes will see what can be found in the kitchen,' she replied.

Eleanor hadn't acknowledged Mrs Jenson or our return to Teesbank Hall. She stood to one side, exuding anger and displeasure. Mrs Jenson turned to her now. 'Miss Eleanor, may I take your travelling cloak? You must be sorely tired after your long journey.'

Although she didn't reply directly to Mrs Jenson's words, she now spoke in a flat, unrelenting statement of complaint. 'She has destroyed everything. The trip to London, the time I might spend away from here – everything she has destroyed.'

She was white and clearly distressed. Her eyes were glittering and wild and she looked desperately around the hallway. I will confess I was frightened of her when she was like that.

'I knew in the end this would happen!' She pointed at me. 'She has always lied. She is not who she says she is. She has come into our home and tried to fool us with her meek mask!'

'It's not true, Mrs Jenson. It's not true!' I cried in my defence.

'She lied. She stole the name of Harriet Caldwell. It's not her own name. And now she wants to steal Henry too. I sensed from the first day I set eyes on her that she was false but no one listened to me, as always.'

Mrs Jenson moved towards Eleanor because she was fast becoming hysterical. Eleanor flinched at her touch and made her body rigid so that she was invulnerable.

'Miss Eleanor, you're tired after your long journey and that is why you speak as you do. You must calm yourself,' Mrs Jenson told her in a firm tone.

'No, I will not calm myself. Father and Mother are away, so I shall send her from the house myself. They would not allow her to stay here.'

I feared the truth of Eleanor's words. Mr and Mrs Wainwright would have no qualms about dismissing me because of my deceit. Mrs Jenson was irresolute. Only Henry's letter stood between me and immediate destitution.

Mrs Jenson now changed tactic. 'Miss Caldwell cannot leave this minute. It is already hurrying towards darkness. She must stay the night.'

'In the morning, she will go,' Eleanor commanded.

Mrs Jenson equivocated. 'Perhaps. We shall see in the morning.' She obviously hoped Eleanor's mood would have settled by then.

The agitation produced by our return and the heated conversation that took place between us had clearly disturbed Diana Wainwright, for she suddenly appeared, a furious collection of fur wraps, her aged face contorted with anger. Her icy blue eyes quickly surveyed the scene. She looked at me and declared, 'She is the sly one. She deceived us all. God protect Henry from her, with her false ways.'

Eleanor seized her hand. For once they had a common

purpose – united in their hatred of me. 'I know you saw it from the start, Grandmother.'

The last two days had been nightmarish. To see and confront Uncle Thomas Stepford once more and to realize Lucy had always been dishonest, had not been my true friend, that had been terrible. But gnawing at me was the terror that they might take me back with them, that I was their property and would have no say in what was to happen to me. And then the draining effect of the terrible flight from London and the hours of travelling in the cold hatred of Eleanor's company. It was more than I could bear.

I leaned against the hall table, dizzy and overcome. I must have looked ill because Mrs Jenson glanced across at me and then said, with a greater degree of determination, 'Miss Caldwell cannot leave the house at this hour. She must go to her room and remain there. Her fate will be decided in the morning. In the meantime, Agnes will sit with you, Miss Eleanor, until you are more settled.'

I knew my days were numbered and, in one final act of defiance, I climbed the beautiful, curving stairs at the centre of the house. Eleanor shouted after me, 'You'll be sent away as soon as my parents return. Unless your uncle comes to reclaim you first.'

'What do you mean?' I stopped short.

'I told your cousin we were returning to Teesbank Hall.'

I felt my legs almost give way beneath me, and I had to clutch the banisters to stay upright. 'You can't know what you've done and the danger you've placed me in,' I told her.

Briefly she had the decency to look shamefaced, but then said defiantly, 'You'd have had me sent away to Gate Helmsley and taken Henry from me.'

I shook my head, but already I was planning where I should go to next.

When I reached my attic room, I slumped upon the hard, unyielding bed, close to total despair. I had kept myself strong and resolute for so long, but it was not enough. I didn't know where to go. I wished desperately that Henry was there. But he was not. I had tried so hard, had not stopped since Father's death, and now I felt empty.

Although my mind was agitated, sheer exhaustion began to overwhelm me. In a state somewhere between waking and dreaming, I thought of Arielle, my predecessor, seduced and brutalized and destroyed. I thought of the dark secrets of the Wainwright family, of the madness that seemed to haunt them. I was convinced Clara had been cruel enough to kill her innocent brother out of jealousy. Matthew Wainwright had allowed his pregnant lover to die for the crime, and now Eleanor. I knew she was violently jealous and I feared her.

My terrors were real. Not the fantasies of an overheated imagination. I was deadly tired but must be watchful – here at the top of the house where the black wire meshes at the windows enclosed me. Eleanor had tried to throw herself to eternity and escape the torment of the present. Would I ever be desperate enough to seek the same route? I could offer myself only one crumb of comfort. If Henry were to return before Uncle Thomas Stepford arrived, then all would be well. I knew he would protect me and not allow me to be taken away. Yet if he were delayed for any reason, then I was lost. Mrs Jenson would be ruled by Eleanor and Diana Wainwright, and they would both willingly hand me over.

It was while I was in this state of feverish uncertainty that I heard soft, hesitant footsteps in the attic. I sat bolt upright from the bed and listened carefully. Another time, I might have hidden under the covers and pretended nobody was there – now I had nothing to lose and clambered out of bed, taking my candle with me. As I opened the door, I was surprised to see Agnes in front of me. She started as if guilty.

'Agnes, whatever are you doing up here?'

Her hand fluttered to her face and she opened her mouth to respond but at that moment there was a terrible commotion and hammering on the front door down below. My heart died within me. I knew with certainty it was my uncle come to claim me.

'It is Uncle Thomas Stepford,' I whispered to her in terror.

She looked at me, calculating the situation. 'Quickly, we must get you away from your bedroom. This will be the first place they'll look.'

I heard his voice in the hall, loudly demanding to have what was his by rights and to be told where I was. I could hear the muted sounds of Mrs Jenson's voice but not catch the words she said. I feared the noises would wake Eleanor. And then nothing would stop his claim on me. Eleanor would be happy to see me gone, and Mrs Jenson would be relieved her decision had been made for her.

Agnes grasped my hand. 'I've thought of somewhere.'

She led me along the dark corridor to the final door – the door of the room where Eleanor had tried to kill herself and where we had held the séance. She opened it with a key she produced from her pocket.

'This will be the best place. They've put a new lock on – it's too sturdy for your uncle to break.'

I followed her with relief into the gloomy room, which was lit by the silver light from my candle and the pale moon shining through the large window. It was only once we were safely inside that I thought to ask again why she was in this part of the attic. She looked at me carefully. 'I've brought something for you. Miss Eleanor told me you wanted to know the story of Arielle Marchal. This is the final part. Even she has not seen the last testimony.'

'You have it?' For a moment, the terror of discovery was forgotten in my curiosity at her reply. 'Why do you hold it?'

'You'll see when you read it.' From her pocket she produced a large envelope. 'This tells the truth about Samuel Wainwright's murder. You'll be safe to read it here – I have to take the key because Mrs Jenson will miss it but I'll lock the door so no one can reach you.'

'Thank you,' I said.

'I'll go downstairs to see what's happening.' She half smiled at me. In the flickering candlelight, I saw her large trusting brown eyes widen. 'I'll be as quick as I can.'

With that she was gone and I was left in semi-darkness. I opened the envelope and took out a yellowing document, but it was almost impossible to read, so I moved next to the window, where the moonlight helped me to make out the words more clearly. With a shock of recognition, I traced the elaborate flourishes of the handwriting in lilac ink.

The Posthumous Testimony of Arielle Marchal being written at Durham Prison the night before her execution.

4 October 1850

My darling child,
You will hear many terrible things about me and my existence will cast a shadow across your life; I cannot undo that. And I must pour the balm of a lifetime of love into the dry pages of this letter. You sleep so peacefully now, your breathing soft and regular, and I can hardly bear to turn away from you, even for a moment. But I must write the truth for you.

In the morning, I will walk out to the gallows, in full view of the world, and feel the hangman's cold hands place the noose around my neck. Already I can hear the crowds gathering outside, waiting to see me die. The warders tell me thousands have come and they make a holiday of it. Street-sellers shout out their wares of oysters and fried fish, people jostle for the best view and I hear my name chanted in obscene songs.

I am to die for killing Samuel Wainwright on 11 August last year – the so-called French Murder. I would have been

*put to death immediately except that I was carrying you.
As is the custom in this country, my execution was delayed
until you were born and had been weaned, so I have had the
bliss of knowing you, even though it has been for such a brief
time.*

*I was so sure I would have a boy – a healthy son for
Matthew Wainwright – but no, I have you, my beautiful,
lovely daughter, who I must leave alone and unprotected in
this world, just as I was left alone.*

*I was born in 1831 in Provence to Jean and Ines Marchal,
who had a farm near Sault. My mother died when I was only
five years old and I have named you in her memory. I hope
you will be a strong woman, just as she was. My father
replaced Maman far too quickly, with a cruel wife who
pretended to love me until she had children of her own and
then my place at the table became cold.*

*They sent me away to a convent when I was twelve years
old, where the nuns taught me all the accomplishments
necessary to make a satisfactory marriage. I was a good,
obedient girl, who was a favourite of the sisters. When I was
seventeen, Papa died in a farming accident. The second wife
sent a brief letter to the nuns. He had left little money and she
had no intention of paying for me to be maintained at the
convent.*

*After the nuns received the letter, their attitude changed
and I knew what that woman must have said. I would have
to leave but no one knew what to do with me. Finally, it was
decided that I should go as a governess to England – I had*

shown an aptitude for the language and would be able to make
a living there. My stepmother paid for my passage on the
understanding that I would not return.

First, I worked for the Baker family in Aldgate in London,
where always I must escape the improper attentions of
Mr Baker and of the sixteen-year-old son Hugh. But
when he tried to force himself upon me and his mother
learned of this, it was me she blamed. She found a distant
friend, who needed a governess, and I was sent away to
Teesbank Hall in the County of Durham.

It was a dark place. The husband and wife, they hated each
other, and my pupils Clara and Martha ran wild. The older
girl was bad and made my life a misery, but most of all she hated
her brother Samuel – I would find scrawled across her
schoolwork, 'I hate Samuel. Samuel must die.' My only friend
was Nancy Wilson, who was his nursemaid and a similar age
to me. We would talk together about how we longed to be away
from that place and how we dreamed of finding love.

And then Matthew Wainwright began to come to the
schoolroom. At first, he asked only about the girls and whether
they were working hard but then he started to stay longer.
I grew to cherish these visits and his interest in me.

In the darkest month of January, he brought me a bunch of
snowdrops and I dared to hope for a future. He had a wife and
I tried to refuse his advances, but he was so persistent and
promised me that one day we would be married. I lay with
him for the first time on the earthen floor of the boathouse,
while the rain beat hard outside. Later, we stayed together in

Harrogate for three days as man and wife. He gave me a pearl ring and bought me a beautiful bolt of white silk – it was to be the stuff of my wedding dress, the cloth of your christening gown.

Yet, I think he was already tiring of me and, when we returned, he gave half to his wife, Susan, saying he felt guilty. I knew I was carrying his child, but suddenly we were never alone and I could not tell him of my delight that we were to have a son. Then Susan Wainwright's sister wrote from London with lies about how I had tried to seduce the son of the house in Aldgate. When Matthew was gone on business for several weeks, she sent me from Teesbank, saying I was a moral poison, who was a danger to them all!

Nancy Wilson helped me pack and I begged her to let me into the house once Matthew had returned. On the evening of 10 August, once it was dark, she waited to open the servants' door for me. I believed that when he saw me, everything would be as it was before.

I was smiling when I entered his study and did not doubt his constancy for a second. Not even when his voice was cold with surprise and he told me I shouldn't be there.

I pleaded with him, telling him I was carrying his son, and there was a flash of tenderness in his eyes. I dared to believe that he still loved me. But Diana Wainwright – that evil, interfering woman – came into the room. When I looked her in the eye and told her Matthew and I were in love and we were to have a son together, she laughed at me. Told me that my child could be anybody's and her son would not provide for another's bastard.

When Matthew went to protest, she told him that his only true son was Samuel and that he must do what was right for him by turning me away. I begged Matthew not to listen to her lies, told him that forcing me from the house would mean almost certain death for me and our child. He chose to listen to his mother and let her call me impudent and a whore. She told me to leave by the servants' door, or I would be thrown out by the stable boys.

I crept down the stairs and sat in the empty kitchen — I clutched my stomach and felt you kicking, the child the Wainwrights had condemned to death. He had betrayed me and the shock took me back to the other time, when I was twelve, and the second wife had hit me across my face and Father had pretended not to see.

That was the first occasion I had heard the voices in my head. The voices that demanded revenge for the injustices I had suffered. My half-brother Alain was playing outside in the spring sunshine and I struck him hard, like my stepmother had hit me. I was sorry afterwards and tried to pet him better, but he told his mother anyway. That was when they sent me away to the convent — they paid the fees and I had a new uniform each year, but no letters or visits.

I must have sat in the kitchen for several hours. The thick darkness of night was beginning to lift and the first glimmers of dawn were painting streaks across the sky. The voices in my head had only whispered at first but now they became more insistent. They told me to kill Samuel because he was the reason my child must die. I knew the voices wouldn't go away unless I did what they demanded, so I found the sharpest knife I could and hid it in my pocket. I climbed the servants' stairs up to the nursery.

Nancy was awake because Samuel had roused from a bad dream and was nestled in bed against her. She wanted to know what Matthew had said. How could I tell her the truth? I mumbled that he loved me and all was well. If she doubted this, she didn't say so, and then I told her I would take Samuel to play outside and pick daisies in the early dawn. I promised her that I would return him to his crib before she awoke. Samuel was sleepy and sulky. He began crying because it was cold and he didn't want to go outside. Nancy and I argued, and this woke Clara, who came into the bedroom.

Grumbling, Nancy left to check whether Martha was still asleep and it was then I begged Clara to persuade Samuel to come away. I promised she need never see him again and I would take him with me from Teesbank. She hesitated only for a moment and then began to speak to him in a coaxing voice and indulged him until he stopped sobbing. When he again protested at the cold, she snatched up the white silk that was lying on the floor and gave it to him to wrap up against the early-morning chill. Before she waved goodbye, she kissed him on the cheek and said it was to be their special secret. I smiled at Clara and told her she was my accomplice.

As I had known they would, the voices dictated the boathouse would be the place of death. While Samuel played on the earthen floor, I raised the knife above him, cutting clumsily at first and trying to block out his desperate screams.

I was observing myself from the outside and my conscience tried to speak but the other voices were too strong. It was his life for my child's life. The Wainwright family would know the horror of feeling absolute despair – just as I did.

Afterwards I was ashamed and sobbed when I looked at the daisies mingled with his blood, so I tried to make amends by wrapping him in the shroud of white silk and then I hid the body under the tarpaulin in the boathouse. I washed myself in the river Tees and walked back to the farm in Appleton Whiske where I was working. The voices were much quieter now, but they said I wasn't really to blame. It was the fault of Diana Wainwright, who had turned her son against me.

I didn't speak in my own defence at the trial. What could I say? And, in any case, my silence had been bought, bargained for with the one thing I had left to sell. Three days after my arrest, Diana Wainwright visited me in prison. She wanted to make sure no scandal hung around the family name. She did not want me to speak of my relationship with Matthew and, in return, she promised she would find a respectable home for you after my execution.

It was all I could give you.

I asked her how I could trust her. She told me, 'Your child is my blood and I swear on the happiness of the Wainwrights that I will keep my word.' Hah! The minutes are already clambering towards my death and the warders laugh when I ask where the respectable family might be. She has broken her vow and I curse her and the family.

*There is nothing more to say, my dearest Ines. My heart is
broken that you will have no memories of me and that you
will never know how much I loved you. As I approach death,
I do not pray for myself but only for you, that you might find
the happiness and love I could not.*

My love always,

Arielle Marchal

Dazed I put the letter back into the envelope and, as I did
so, an official-looking form fluttered to the floor. I picked it
up. Stamped across the top in black ink was *Bishop Auckland
Workhouse* and beneath that were two dates, with handwrit-
ten comments added alongside them. On 5 October 1850,
the document had been received and signed for by the workhouse superintendent. Then on 9 October 1868, it had been
given to Agnes Smith. In brackets next to her name, it said
'Ines Marchal – the Posthumous Testimony is to be given
to her on her eighteenth birthday or departure, whichever
is earlier.'

CHAPTER THIRTY

I sat, feeling cold at heart. Arielle Marchal was the murderess. And Agnes, what of Agnes? I heard the key turn in the lock. 'You have read it?' she said. In her hand, she carried a blazing paraffin lamp.

My shocked face was all the response she needed.

'The workhouse superintendent decided I would be tainted if I kept my mother's name so he changed it to Smith, leaving no link to my past. And no one could be bothered with the French name Ines, so I quickly became Agnes.'

'You are Arielle Marchal's daughter.'

'She was the mother who should have loved me. She was cruelly used. Matthew Wainwright bears part of the blame for that but most of all it is Diana Wainwright and I'll take my revenge.'

'What do you mean?' I asked.

At that moment Eleanor appeared. Her expression was ice-cold and she glared at me. 'Agnes has always warned me how you wanted to take Henry away and leave me to rot in

Gate Helmsley. And her words were confirmed by the letter Arielle wrote from the grave. The one that she left for me before we went to London.'

'Eleanor, I would never condemn you to that place. That letter was not true. It must be a forgery.'

'She's warned me all along and told me about your sly ways and how you only pretended to befriend me to steal Henry and stop us carrying through our plan. You are like all the governesses after Lilian.'

'What plan? Agnes, why have you lied about me? I never intended to betray Eleanor. We had almost become friends. Eleanor, I swear to you, I wouldn't hurt you.'

There was such a note of sincerity and distress in my voice that Eleanor looked confused for a moment.

'Don't listen to her, Eleanor, she's speaking poison,' Agnes said. 'Miss Caldwell's trying to stop us doing what we must to clean the house. You know what needs to happen. Go ahead to get started and I'll follow you in a moment.' The Agnes who spoke now was not the timid little mouse with the trusting brown eyes, but someone altogether different, almost commanding. Eleanor turned away and I noticed she was carrying something heavy.

'Eleanor—' I started to say.

Agnes cut in quickly, 'There isn't much time. Quickly, Eleanor, we don't want to fail at the last moment.'

The two young women smiled at each other and Eleanor disappeared down the corridor.

Agnes looked at me defiantly. 'She always chooses to believe what I say over anyone else.'

'Does Eleanor know you're Arielle Marchal's daughter?' I asked, unsure how I might proceed now that all the landscape had changed.

'And Matthew Wainwright's. We're half-sisters.'

Of course, I thought.

'I told Eleanor about the relationship between us after Lilian Howard was sent away. It was impossible to get close to her while that woman was here. And Eleanor was much easier to influence once she'd gone.'

'What do you mean?' I reassessed everything I believed about Agnes.

'She wants to help make amends for what happened at Teesbank Hall. How can that be a bad thing?' she replied. 'It means my mother's soul can rest in peace.'

'Did you tell her Arielle was the murderess?'

'She doesn't need to know that. She believes Samuel was killed by his sister Clara and, ironically, the letter you translated seemed to prove it. No –' she shook her head – 'you're the only person I've shown the letter to. My mother doesn't carry the moral guilt for what happened.'

'But she killed an innocent child. What she did was evil.'

'Don't ever dare call my mother evil.' Agnes's eyes hardened. 'She was not at fault. I won't have her blamed.'

'And Eleanor is vulnerable. This house has damaged her and now you're using her.'

'She has allowed herself to be used – she was obsessed with the murder. It wasn't hard to feed her belief that Teesbank Hall is haunted.'

'You've done that deliberately?' I asked.

Agnes shrugged in response. 'I needed her to help me and she already half believed, anyway. The false séance was my idea – there was supposed to be a message from the dead governess telling Eleanor to take revenge but your hysterics stopped that.'

'So, Eliza didn't have a séance first?'

'No.' She laughed. 'She wouldn't dare – she's far too God-fearing. And I stole knives for Eleanor whenever I could.'

'But you knew she cut herself?'

Agnes didn't answer that question. Instead she said, 'I was worried that you and Eleanor were becoming too close and I didn't want her confiding what we planned. You might have stopped her. It was better to keep the two of you enemies.'

A bleak realization began to grow within me. I needed to get away from the window and towards the open door. It was dangerous to stay and I had to keep her talking. 'Stopped her doing what?'

'Oh, you'll know soon enough and it's only right that two of Matthew Wainwright's three living daughters destroy Teesbank Hall.'

'The false letter Eleanor received the night before we went to London. That was you! But it was in Arielle's handwriting?'

Agnes laughed. 'I simply copied my mother's style from her last testament – the document you hold in your hand. In any case, was the letter false, Harriet? Anyone with eyes in their head can see you love Henry. Surely you want Eleanor gone.'

I tried to contradict her, but she continued, 'It was me who bloodied your nightgown. I wanted to break the trust between you and Eleanor. I knew she would be blamed and nobody would believe her denials.'

As she was talking, I had gradually moved nearer to her. Suddenly she noticed. 'If you come any closer, I'll drop the lamp on the floor and the paraffin will set fire to the room.'

I stopped. 'Why did you come to Teesbank Hall?'

'I had thought it could be my home,' she said simply. 'When the workhouse superintendent gave me my mother's letter, I finally had a family – a father and others joined to me by blood.'

'The Wainwrights?'

'My poisonous broken family. When I saw their cruelty – particularly that of Matthew and Diana – I knew I had to take revenge for the death of the mother I never knew. I would fulfil her gallows curse.'

'What's going to happen?' I moved an inch closer to the door.

'It can't hurt to tell you now. Over the last few months, we've collected paraffin. When Eleanor bought time from you with the murder documents, she helped me hide it about the estate.'

'But why paraffin?'

'We're going to clean Teesbank Hall for ever and it must be tonight.'

'Why?'

'While you were away, Mrs Jenson confided in me that Matthew Wainwright was going to commit Eleanor to a private asylum, despite his promises. I had to act quickly. She needs to be part of this.'

I darted for the door but Agnes was too fast for me. She slammed it shut and turned the key in the lock. 'Everything is finally in place. I won't be stopped by you.'

'Agnes, please open the door,' I begged.

'No! You'll warn everyone what is about to happen and you've called my mother evil.' I heard her footsteps disappear down the corridor.

I was trapped – but how could I shout for help, when my only rescuer was likely to be Uncle Thomas Stepford? I slumped against the wall as the dismal irony of my situation hit me and the confusion of angry voices below formed a backdrop to my misery. There was the sound of doors opening and closing, and heavy footsteps on the stairs, coming ever closer to the top of the house, which seemed to signal discovery by my uncle. I tried to reassure myself that Agnes didn't mean me any personal harm and, at least, in this room it would be impossible for anyone to enter.

As I sat there, the room began to grow hot and airless.

Then I heard Mrs Jenson scream piercingly with shock and Eleanor's voice, terrified yet triumphant, shouting, 'It's done! It's all in place. We have done what we promised.'

And then a man's voice, deep and familiar, but shouting with horror, 'Good God, the house is ablaze. Eleanor, what's happened?'

'It's no more than I promised Arielle Marchal's wronged spirit. It will make us all clean, Henry. It is the right thing to do.'

'This is madness. You have put everyone in danger. Where's Harriet? You must tell me now.'

It was difficult to decipher her response above the sound of crashing wood and crackling flames, but she must have told him where I was hidden, because moments later I heard him running up the stairs and shouting my name. Terror had now replaced my previous inaction and I hammered desperately on the door, as acrid smoke seeped into the room and I tasted it against the back of my throat. 'Henry, I'm here. In the first attic bedroom but the door is locked!'

'Thank God I've found you, Harriet. Stand away from the door, while I attempt to force it.' I heard him coughing as the thick smoke invaded his lungs.

I moved to the side of the doorframe and heard his frantic attempts to batter down the sturdy door. But it would not budge. How terrible and ironic that I was within inches of being rescued and it should fail.

'Henry, you must save yourself. It's impossible to break this door. Go quickly before the flames cut off the top of the building,' I implored, but he didn't answer me and continued hitting the door with what sounded like a heavy object.

I looked around the room. The windows offered no

escape. I thought of Eleanor desperately clawing at the metal net, her fingernails bloodied and broken. How terrible to die consumed by flames. With a strange clarity, my mind wandered back to a history book I had found on the bookshelves of Father's library. It was a gruesome tale of martyrs, who had died several hundred years ago. The author claimed those sentenced to die by burning would pay the executioner to strangle them first so they were spared the agony of the fire. When I asked him about it, he had assured me that the fumes would render anyone unconscious, long before the flames reached them.

The noises outside had now stopped. The corridor was deserted. Almost overcome with heat and smoke, I prayed to my Maker that the end would come without pain.

Then I heard desperate footsteps and raised voices. Henry had had the presence of mind to run downstairs and fetch the master key from Mrs Jenson's cabinet. He had returned with Tom, the stable lad. Just as I was sinking into unconsciousness, the door was opened and they dragged me from the room and carried me down the servants' staircase, whose enclosed nature offered a protection against the fire that the sweeping central staircase did not.

I was laid on the damp grass outside and coughed myself back to consciousness, forcing cooling air into my lungs. Mrs Jenson and a group of other frightened servants clustered around me, keeping a respectful distance, dark shadows outlined against the orange flames of the burning building.

'How is she, Mrs Jenson?' Eliza asked the housekeeper.

'I don't know. It's impossible to tell now – we must wait until we have proper light.'

Another dark shape pushed through the knot of people. Uncle Thomas Stepford. He demanded, 'She is my niece. I must see her at once.'

Taking him for an affectionate uncle, they stepped aside and then he was there, hanging over me, his bitter breath warm against my face. 'Will she live? Will she live?' he wanted to know. They believed his agitation was the desperate concern of a loving relative and tried to reassure him I would survive. That wasn't the answer he wanted. I knew he calculated my death would release the income from Father's estate.

He reached down to touch me and I screamed hysterically. My throat was damaged, but I forced out the words, 'Get him away from me. Don't let him touch me.' My terror was such that he was forced to step back, embarrassed.

'I think you'd best leave her be for now,' one of the stable lads told him.

'She is my niece and I'll not leave until I have what is mine.'

'In time, in time,' said Mrs Jenson, attempting to soothe him. 'For now, she must be allowed to rest.'

Reluctantly, he stamped away, threatening all the time that he would return. I was too busy with the task of recovering. My lungs were still burning despite the cool air I was trying to draw into them. What my uncle intended to do to me was a horror to be dealt with in the future. I forced myself into a sitting position and Mrs Jenson came over to support me. 'Where is Henry?' I asked her.

'He's gone back into the house. Miss Eleanor is missing.'

'No!' I protested. 'It was she and Agnes who started the fire. Eleanor could be luring Henry to his death.'

She looked round quickly, checking whether the others had heard what I said. 'You are delirious, Miss Caldwell. Miss Eleanor would never harm her brother and you must never say she was responsible for the fire.'

I dragged myself to standing, desperate to find Henry, when suddenly I saw him illuminated against the flames, carrying Eleanor in his arms. He was staggering and his face was blackened by the smoke. Gasping for breath, he sank down in a gesture of despair, before gathering himself together again. Eleanor lay on the ground. Her dress was burned away and some curtains from one of the windows had been fashioned into a kind of cloak and bed for her. Henry began to oversee operations, fetching water from the river to quench her peeling skin and I went across to ask if I could help.

He looked at me, concern etched through his haggard face. 'She wanted to die,' he cried. 'Why wouldn't she leave?'

I couldn't answer him.

When Eleanor finally came to consciousness, she croaked into the darkness, 'We should all have died. All been gone. We are cursed. Why did you let me live?' Over and over again, so that her chilling words became part of the horror of the night and were for ever embedded in my memory.

The Hall was totally and irrevocably destroyed. The fire smouldered for several days and locals came to gawp at its ruin. Great pieces of masonry, blackened fragments of documents and furniture reduced to ash covered the area. All ruined. All gone. The aspirations of the Wainwright family were destroyed in one night of uncontrolled madness.

Eleanor's parents were spared from the fire, simply because they were away that night, and Agnes was determined that Eleanor should take part in the destruction. But Diana Wainwright did not survive. For some reason, her door had been locked from the outside and no one could find the key.

The fire was blamed solely upon Agnes, who was described as a disaffected servant, taking a terrible revenge because she was about to be dismissed. It was a lie, of course, but the Wainwright family were well used to lying. And Agnes's body was never found. The ferocity of the fire was such that everything above the ground floor was destroyed and there was no trace of her remaining. Some said she had deliberately walked into the heart of the fire, choosing to die, but others claimed they had seen a young woman, with trusting brown eyes, hurrying to Eaglescliffe station to catch the last connection to London. For all I know, she might still be out there, alive and well.

CHAPTER THIRTY-ONE

Eleanor and I were taken to the home of the Reverend Mr Sterling and his wife. The small box room at the front of the vicarage was made up for me but any rest was impossible. All night there was a constant traffic of people. I heard Uncle Thomas Stepford at the front door, loudly demanding to know where his niece was hidden and threatening to take me back to Swaffham that very night. Shrinking in terror, I hid beneath the covers of the bed. There were concerned discussions, too, about the state of Eleanor. I wanted to tell them all that she had started the fire and intended to destroy her home.

But I didn't, of course. I was sufficiently a part of the Wainwright family to understand secrets must be kept. And Eleanor really was very ill. In the first few days, her life hung in the balance. By dousing her in water, Henry had lessened the scarring to her skin, but he couldn't undo the damage from the smoke she had inhaled. Her hoarse, painful breathing filled the silence of the vicarage, as her body forced air into damaged lungs. Doctors were coming and going constantly from her room and it was clear from their serious, muttered conversations that her life was in danger.

Maisie, the young maid-of-all work, had been given the task of sponging Eleanor's damaged body with cold water. On the third day, she confided in me that she was terrified of Eleanor. 'I don't mean to be uncharitable about one that's afflicted, miss, but she do frighten me so.'

'But why?' I asked.

'Well, miss . . .' She paused a moment, and then the words came tumbling out. 'She sits there propped up on her pillows like and her face is all dead but her eyes, her eyes is so alive and watching.'

'What is she watching?'

'Everything but most especially when a doctor's there. Then she stares as if she would remember their every action. I wouldn't be a doctor in that room for all the tea in China.'

'Maisie, that's ridiculous. What else can she do but look at what's going on around her?'

'It seems to me she's giving us all the evil eye and I don't care who knows it! Everyone's always said them Wainwrights is cursed.'

In the end, the vicar's wife was forced to take over Maisie's duties in the sickroom because she refused point blank to go back in there when Eleanor was awake.

As for myself, although we were in the same house, I saw Eleanor rarely after the night of the fire because my presence agitated her so much. I suppose Agnes had poisoned her against me and she still believed the truth of the ghostly letter from Arielle. Indeed, it was easier for us to have as little as possible to do with each other. I had been more affected by the fire and the distressing events of the last few days than I cared to admit. Most of my time was spent sleeping, although I was haunted by the thought of Uncle Thomas Stepford. Each time I heard voices downstairs, I feared it was him come to claim me and, in the most terrifying of my nightmares, his face hung over me again – his breath warm and sour – as he demanded to know whether I would live or die, and prayed for my death. I was glad to learn he had returned to Norfolk two days after the fire, although Mr Sterling told me that he continued with his threats to take me back into his guardianship.

Mr and Mrs Wainwright had already decamped to her brother's house in York and never returned to Teesbank Hall, not even to survey its ruin or to bury his mother. The only family member who attended the funeral was Henry, who had stayed at the vicarage in the first few days, then left on urgent business. I saw very little of him, partly because I was too unwell and partly because Eleanor would scream in protest if he left her sight for a moment. When she was finally judged well enough to travel, the Wainwright carriage came to take her to her parents in York. She left without a word of farewell to me and only the most grudging of acknowledgements to the Sterlings.

The vicar and his wife allowed me to stay in the vicarage and showed great kindness, helping to nurse me back to health. Mrs Sterling – Elizabeth – became a true friend and insisted I stay as long as I needed to recover. I think she was happy to have a friend close at hand. It was a relief after the strain of life at Teesbank Hall to give myself over to the role of a convalescent and spend my time doing very little apart from reading. My injuries and illness – for I had fallen into a fever after the horrors of that night – were excuse enough to avoid thinking about what the future might bring.

I longed to hear from Henry, but it was four long weeks before I finally received a letter. He enquired after my health and hoped that I was well, but the tone was formal, one of a distant acquaintance, not an intimate friend. He said Elea-nor was still unwell but had started to make some small recovery from the fire and now spent her days reading med-ical textbooks so that she could understand her condition better. He hoped to visit the Sterlings soon but current cir-cumstances made that difficult. There was much to be resolved in relation to the finances of his family and the future of Teesbank Hall, which must occupy the majority of his attention.

He apologized for the sombre nature of his letter but could be the bearer of some portion of good news. Uncle Thomas Stepford had agreed to be bought off from any claim to me for the sum of £250, an amount I understood Henry had provided. Furthermore, he had renounced on my behalf any right to the income Father had put aside for me up to the age of twenty-five. It was expected. I knew Uncle would demand a high price and I was just relieved to be free of him. Henry's lawyers had unearthed a bequest to me of a thousand pounds from my mother's side of the family, which would be payable in four years' time. At least that would give me some degree of independence in the future.

I had settled myself to read his letter with such anticipation. Now, as I reflected on the coolness of his tone, tears pricked my eyes. I accepted he was in love with Rosalind Merryweather and knew that I could never compete with her beauty or her unsullied disposition, but still I had thought there was a warm friendship between us. I hadn't cried once in the weeks following the fire, but now I was in floods of tears, my face pressed against the sofa.

That was how Elizabeth found me and she looked at me with sympathy. 'What is the matter, Harriet? What has upset you so much?'

With a gesture I indicated the letter that now lay on the floor. She asked whether she might read it, which she did with a look of the utmost concentration upon her face. When she had finished, she stated with her characteristic honesty, 'You are in love with Henry.'

It was impossible to lie to Elizabeth. 'Yes,' I replied, 'and I know that love is not returned but his letter is so cold. I had thought we were friends.'

She sat on the sofa and, taking my hand, said, 'He was distracted in the days after the fire but was always determined that you should be looked after properly. His concern was most sincere.'

'But why hasn't he visited since?'

'He saved you from the fire, didn't he?' she said.

'Yes, he risked his life. He's a most noble and upright man.'

She paused, as if deciding whether she should continue. After a moment, she took my hands in hers. 'Dearest Harriet, just before Henry left, he had a long talk with my husband. I understand he has some attachment to Miss Merryweather.' She sighed. 'Her family had been away in Scotland, but once they returned, he intended travelling to Long Newton to propose to her.'

I gasped. Although this was not unexpected, I still felt it as a fresh pain.

'I'm very sorry, Harriet.'

'Surely that's no reason for Henry to behave coldly towards me.'

'It's possible that Miss Merryweather sees your friendship with him as a threat. Perhaps it's only right that he has distanced himself from you.'

'What threat could I pose to Rosalind Merryweather?' I said bitterly.

'You are beautiful and principled. That is a very great threat indeed.'

I shook my head. 'Thank you for your kind words, Elizabeth.' I crumpled up the letter. 'If you would excuse me, I'd like to go to my room for a while.'

Elizabeth and I didn't speak about Henry again. I know she worried about me and, a few times, she began to ask me about my feelings towards him, but I shook my head. It was easier not to dwell on the subject. I hardened myself against any thoughts about Henry and tried to heal my broken heart.

Although I had been affected by the fire, I was young and resilient. After a few weeks, good food and sleep had restored my health. I became increasingly restless staying indoors and Elizabeth suggested that I should go for a long walk each morning. In time, this became something of an obsession and I wouldn't miss a walk no matter how cold or wet the weather was. I would borrow sturdy boots from her and walk until my feet ached, but my heart did not. The banks of the Tees and its surrounding areas are picturesque and I was able to find new routes along the river and across the nearby meadows. Eventually I realized that the one route I had studiously ignored led to Teesbank Hall.

About six weeks after the night of the terrible blaze, I finally felt strong enough to return and I followed the path I had taken all those months earlier in March. It seemed a lifetime ago, so much had happened since. Then everything had been new and strange and now this landscape was familiar and had become a part of who I was.

I followed Jackson's Lane towards the river and turned the corner, foolishly expecting to see Teesbank Hall as it had been. The skeleton was clear and the vastness of its size meant no fire could totally obliterate it. The upper floors jutted precariously against the cold blue sky and the smell of fire and acrid smoke still hung about the place. I couldn't see it without thinking of that night. I stood for a moment and relived the chaos, the shouts of terror, the terrible crackling sound of the flames eating away at the house, and then of myself, gasping for breath on the damp grass, lying in darkness.

Now all was quiet. It was a place of death. The only signs of life were the curlews that wheeled and spun through the sky. I walked silently and in awe. It seemed a symbol of the destruction of the Wainwright family and I contemplated how, try as we might to achieve glory on this earth, it could all be taken in an instant. The house had been Joshua Wainwright's attempt to establish a dynasty. It now lay in ruins. I looked beyond to the beauty of the river and the meadows, and the stark splendour of the woodlands, still touched with the last remnants of autumn's gold and orange. These are the things that will endure, I thought.

It was while deep in such contemplation that I heard horses approaching and men's voices. I was partly hidden behind a corner of the house so that they couldn't see my presence until they were almost upon me. One of the voices was Henry's. How to describe my feelings? On the one hand, I couldn't stop the joy at the presence of one still so dear to me and, on the other, the sharp pain that he was in the area and had chosen not to visit me.

I, at least, had a few moments to prepare my emotions and my expression before we were inevitably brought face to face, as the line of his trajectory meant we must be. I saw his face flush with surprise and, I fear, embarrassment.

He dismounted from his horse and bowed towards me.

'Miss Caldwell, I mean Miss Fleet, I didn't expect to see you here.'

'Sir, I felt in need of some fresh air and have walked from Eaglescliffe to Teesbank Hall.'

'It's almost totally destroyed,' he said, gesturing towards the blackened shell of his former home. And then he added, 'Would you like to walk, Miss Fleet? There are some things I must discuss with you.'

He turned to his acquaintances, two gentlemen whom I had not seen before, but who had about them the appearance of a workman-like efficiency and organization. They were smartly dressed in the top hats and greatcoats popular at that time. 'Sirs, if you would excuse me for a short while. I have unexpectedly met with an old acquaintance and wish to speak privately to Miss Fleet.' They made their agreements and Henry offered me his arm.

When we had walked a little way from the others, he turned and studied me carefully. 'You seem to be quite recovered from the effects of the fire,' he said.

'Yes,' I replied. 'I was ill for a short time, but I feel much stronger and more like myself again.'

'I'm glad of that,' he said.

And with that, we fell into an uneasy silence. My heart was bursting with so many different things to say but my tongue could not form them. Of course, through it all burned the question of how he could be there, so close at hand, and not attempt to see me. I knew I owed him much. He had rescued me from Teesbank Hall and freed

me from Uncle Thomas Stepford. Even if I had been mistaken in believing his feelings for me were those of a close
friendship, I at least owed him a debt of gratitude and so it
was that I broke the awkwardness that lay heavy between
us. 'I must thank you, sir, for saving my life.'

He made a gesture as if to suggest it was nothing. I knew
this was not the case. He had risked his own life by staying
in the attic when he might have become trapped in the
burning building.

'And also, sir, I must thank you for interceding on my
behalf to Thomas Stepford and freeing me from the obliga-
tions he held me under.'

He seemed more comfortable, now that we were on the
safer ground of a neutral topic for discussion and fell into a
detailed explanation of how he had been lucky enough to
engage the services of one of the finest firms of solicitors in
London and how they had negotiated everything on his
behalf. How Thomas Stepford had seemed adamant that as
he and Lucy were my only living family, and being such
loving relatives, he could not relinquish his rights to me.
Henry said that the case had seemed hopeless, but his legal
friends had assured him that this was merely a ploy to push
my price higher. And so it proved. Once Henry's advisers –
Cragside, Johnson and Co. – had returned with a third offer,
Uncle Thomas Stepford had felt able to give up on his deeply
held affection for me as soon as the ink on the contract
papers was dry and the money in his account.

Then, forcing myself to keep my voice steady, I said, 'I

believe that congratulations are due on your betrothal to Miss Merryweather. Mrs Sterling told me the happy news.'

He shook his head. 'There is to be no betrothal. In the immediate aftermath of the fire, I did ask for Miss Merryweather's hand in marriage, but when I went to see her, I found that there had been a change of circumstance.'

'What change in circumstance?' I asked, filled with curiosity.

'Well, the reason the Merryweathers had extended their stay in Scotland was because of the growing attachment between Miss Merryweather and my university friend Richard, who was the other member of our party.'

'The one whose family own half of Northumberland?'

'The very one. I arrived at Long Newton to find that Rosalind and Richard were, in fact, engaged to each other.'

'I'm so sorry, Henry. You must be very unhappy.' I reflected that he would feel something of my heartache.

'Oh, no, no, not at all,' he replied.

Seeing my confusion, he continued, 'I felt that I was morally obliged to ask Rosalind to marry me, that my behaviour towards her must have made it seem that that had been my intention and it would be wrong of me not to do so. However . . .' He paused.

And I was forced to ask, 'However?'

'However, I felt immensely relieved that she had fallen in love with someone else.'

I was stunned.

'Of course, she was very apologetic and very sweet, but she said that in my absence, she had spent more and more time with Richard and found they were similar. Whereas when Rosalind and I had spent any length of time together, we discovered that we had very little to say to each other and were not similar at all. I found her —' he searched for his words — 'very pleasant, but nothing more.'

As we walked, I had kept my eyes firmly upon the ground, but now I dared to hope. At a turn in the path, we both stopped and looked at each other with an intensity that seemed to last a lifetime. I traced those beloved lineaments and features, longing for him to take me in his arms and say he would never leave me. Then I spoke haltingly because I knew the words I said next carried the greatest importance and could decide the direction of my life.

'Henry, I am grateful for everything that you have done for me and am for ever in your debt but . . . but . . .' Now I struggled for the words, until finally I must ask outright, 'How can you be here and not see me?'

His gaze broke and he looked away from me. I hoped that he would say he had only just arrived in the area, and that as soon as he had completed his urgent business, he would hurry to see me.

He did not. Instead it was his turn to hesitate. 'I've had much to do over the last few weeks. The house, as you can see, is in ruins and so are the fortunes of my family.'

I was later to discover the full truth of this statement. As soon as Joshua Wainwright was dead, Matthew Wainwright had set about selling off most of his father's assets in coalmining and instead made disastrous investments in land. He wanted to establish himself as part of the local gentry but had, in fact, almost entirely lost or squandered a fortune through extravagance, high-living and bad business decisions. It turned out that he had raised several mortgages against Teesbank Hall in order to secure more funds. When the building was destroyed, so too was the collateral. The two gentlemen with Henry were representatives of the indebted bank, seeking to find any value in the property that might partly cancel out the enormity of the debt.

Henry turned away from me and walked a little ahead. I walked faster to catch up with him. 'I'm sorry to hear that your family is so afflicted, Henry, but I'm sad you didn't wish to see me. I would have been able to offer you the comfort of a good and grateful friend. Even if you do not love me,' and here, I will confess, my voice had a catch in it, a half-suppressed sob, 'even if you do not love me, as I love you, still you have been my protector and friend when I had none and I would offer to you the dearest of friendship and support in gratitude.'

Now he stopped and turned to face me, seizing both my hands and gazing into my eyes – oh, that the moment could have been preserved for ever! 'My dearest Harriet, I do love you, completely, which is why what I must do is all the harder.'

'I don't understand, Henry. What do you intend?'

Still looking at me, still holding my hands in his, he said,

'Eleanor is ill. The fire has badly damaged her lungs, along with God only knows what afflictions of the mind. Father still wants to send her away to Gate Helmsley.'

'That would destroy her,' I said.

'Yes, and it's only because I've promised to be responsible for her that he hasn't carried out his threat. She's at my uncle's home in York and will accept no one's care but mine. I worry for the days when I must be away on business. It means I can't leave her company for any great period of time.'

'She holds you to ransom!' I couldn't help but exclaim.

He gazed at me quizzically and must have thought I lacked sympathy for it was clear that Agnes had manipulated her into taking part in the terrible revenge. She had cynically exploited Eleanor's desperation, nurtured in that house of secrets and murder. But how could I be expected to forgive her? And now it seemed the man I loved was about to sacrifice his life to her.

Ignoring what I said, Henry continued: 'Growing up, my parents were too wrapped in their own misery to have much affection for us. Therefore, we are closer than most siblings and I can't let Father dispose of her to Gate Helmsley.'

I nodded sympathetically, trying to subdue the words that leaped to my lips to plead against his choice.

'I didn't see you because I couldn't think how to explain my actions. Whenever I was in the district, I've longed to visit but have known what I must tell you and so delayed our meeting.'

My heart was fit to burst.

'I've no choice but to devote myself to nursing Eleanor until she recovers or dies. No one else can do it and her life is one of misery enough.'

But what of me? I longed to cry out. I stifled the words. What he said and intended to do was the honourable and right thing, I knew that. Eleanor was vulnerable. She couldn't survive without Henry. Yet it was my heart that was broken. I'm not one of those women given easily to weeping so I must sometimes seem unfeeling and lacking in feminine sensitivity. Yet within my heart, there raged a torrent of sorrow far greater than the floods of tears that some women seem so easily to muster at such times. I couldn't speak and needed a few moments to compose myself before I left my love, my one true love, for ever.

Henry was no longer looking at me. I felt he was giving me a few moments' grace to digest his words before we moved on to our separate lives. It was then he spoke. 'You must doubt the sincerity of my feelings for you because I say that we have to part yet there is nothing false about my love. If I could ask you to wait until Eleanor no longer needs me, then we could be married, but she may always be dependent on me and I can't expect such a huge sacrifice of you. It would be selfish of me to persuade you to throw away the days of your youth, your chance perhaps to have children.'

As he spoke, I felt my whole world revolve and right itself.

'I'm no longer a wealthy man. Once I realized the amount

of money my family owed, I knew it was impossible for me to propose marriage, in any case. I would bring nothing but debts and the bad blood of the Wainwrights.' And here he clenched his teeth with real anguish.

At this, I could be silent no more. How could he believe that I loved him for the extent of his fortune? And so I assured him with the most passionate of words that I would gladly wait for him for ever. That I could love no other man and that I would rather waste my life in waiting for him than live a life of indulgence with the richest man in the world. There were many vows and pledges. I think we both cried. And he held me so tenderly in his arms, as if I were the most beautiful and precious of women. And we kissed. My happiness was complete, even though our attachment was to be deferred until some unspecified point in the future, because at least I knew that he loved me absolutely.

THE AFTERMATH

Eleanor fought to recover from the effects of the fire with a determination that astounded the doctors who had written her off as a permanent invalid in those early days. And being released from the prison of Teesbank Hall and its horrors meant that her mind was gradually healed too. But, with the same tenacity that she clung to life, she held on to her suspicion that I had always planned to steal her brother. It meant we could not be in the same room and Henry was forced to divide his time between the two of us. Even in later years, there was still a frostiness.

One unexpected outcome of the fire was that Eleanor was determined to study medicine. She had observed at close hand the power doctors held over life and death and envied their knowledge. Predictably, her parents were appalled at the prospect but by the time she was twenty-one, she had reached the age of majority and was legally beyond their control. She had recovered almost fully from her injuries when she made her escape to London, aided by her friend and former governess, Lilian Howard. Lilian was teaching at a boarding school in Kentish Town and was able to provide financial support. Eleanor was among the first undergraduates to enrol at the London School of Medicine for Women and later gained one of the highest marks in her year.

When she graduated in 1881, Mr Wainwright declared his only consolation was that his mother was dead and hence spared the shame of having a woman physician in the family. Eleanor and Lilian moved to a three-storey house in Camden and took up bicycling and avant-garde literature. Lilian had long been at the forefront of the demand for women's suffrage and was imprisoned several times for this cause. For many years, Eleanor worked at the New Hospital for Women, where she specialized in the treatment of burns.

Her health had always been fragile because of the damage done to her lungs by the fire. She and Lilian had long planned their retirement and moved to a house in the Cotswolds, which came with vast gardens for them to tame. However, their dreams of a rural idyll were disrupted by the outbreak of the Great War. Eleanor was persuaded to return to medicine and practised at the military hospital in Kent, where she gained a reputation for her brusque manner and pioneering work with burns patients.

Sadly, she died last year, partly as a result of the long hours she had worked at Queen's Hospital. Eleanor and Lilian were only able to enjoy a short period of peaceful tranquillity at their home in Far Oakridge. Her lifelong friend gained some small consolation from the glowing tributes to Eleanor's contribution to medicine, which appeared in her obituaries published in *The Times* and the *Manchester Guardian*.

Henry has always remained steadfast and our love for each other has never diminished. The day when we were married at St John the Baptist Church was the happiest of my life. I was then nearer thirty than twenty, but I think my heart overflowed with love enough to out-dazzle the most fresh-faced of brides. It was a quiet wedding, with just a handful of close friends present. The Sterlings came, of course, and Elizabeth was my matron of honour. Richard and Rosalind Wardhaugh made the journey from their estate in Bamburgh and presented us with an expensive silver tea service, which we still bring out for visitors. Mrs Jenson was also there and had invested in an elaborately feathered hat for the occasion. Matthew and Susan Wainwright were living in York, but stubbornly refused to attend the ceremony. However, Eleanor came – persuaded, I think, by Lilian – and there was a reconciliation between us of sorts, although she declared that Henry and I had become very provincial and dull.

I wanted to have children, but we were not to be blessed in that way. Yet I know that the absence of offspring gladdened Henry's heart because he held the most absolute belief that his very veins carried contaminated blood and it was right that his family should die out with him, try as I might to convince him that he was a good and noble man.

In any case, having Henry was enough for me and we have passed our years together in the greatest of contentment. We live in a pretty cottage in Eaglescliffe, a landscape so different from the soft, golden-bathed sunlight of my childhood in Norfolk but to me it is now home. All the wealth and riches have gone. Although Teesbank Hall is only two miles away from us, we did not return there for many years. It passed into the hands of the bank, along with all the surrounding land. I think they had hoped to make a great profit on its sale and it was purchased in time by a family of newly rich ship-builders from Middlesbrough, but at a much lower price than the bank had wanted.

The people of Eaglescliffe were accepting of Henry and me, and we took our place in the village. We have a small circle of good friends and live off the modest income from the village school we run. No one ever openly mentions the Murder House to us or speaks of what took place in the past, but I know many wild rumours circulate. I like to think we are not associated with such Gothic horror but instead have been allowed to live out our lives quietly and peacefully.

The one time we returned to Teesbank Hall, it was only to the grounds. Henry and I don't move in the same social circles as its new owners but there was an opening of the gardens, to raise money for those women widowed in the Great War.

It was strange being somewhere so familiar and yet so different. The Hall had been razed to the ground and in its place a modern monstrosity of solid red brick had been built. The gardens were familiar and I could trace in them the ghosts of our younger selves from almost fifty years ago. We walked as part of a group from our church, but I lingered a little behind. Henry has some difficulty in walking and I used this as an excuse to fall out of the general hubbub and conversation. He and I said nothing to each other, but we walked a little more closely together, breathing in the bittersweet memories of the place.

When we came to the boathouse, the recollections of the past were at their sharpest. It was secluded, away from the Hall, and had not been touched by the fire. I think the owner's wife had been charmed by its quaintness and age. She wasn't from the immediate area and didn't know the bloody history, so she insisted it remain. It had been lovingly maintained and freshly painted.

Once there, I was transported back. Here was the place where the body of Samuel Wainwright had been found mutilated and desecrated all those years before, where Arielle Marchal and Matthew Wainwright had met secretly to pursue their destructive lust, which would bring so much horror. Yet it was also where Henry and I had begun to fall in love, away from the prying eyes of the household.

It was the most beautiful and sunny of days, but as I stood on the threshold, I remembered the sense of chill when Eleanor had first lured me into entering. I hesitated for a moment, frightened that I would feel again the cold fingers of the past, reaching out to the present. I entered and blinked, as my eyes adjusted to the darkness of the room after the blinding light of day.

I felt nothing. All memories had fled. And I wondered if the death of the principal players in the tragedy, all those old ghosts, Matthew and his cold wife Susan, Diana the controlling matriarch, and Arielle, damaged, murderous Arielle, meant that finally the ghosts of the past had disappeared for ever.

ACKNOWLEDGEMENTS

A big thank you to my excellent and lovely editor Jane Wood for always being so positive and perceptive, and to the team at Quercus, in particular Florence Hare, and Hazel Orme, whose feedback made me smile. Thank you as well to my fantastic agent Giles Milburn for his invaluable help and support, especially at the manuscript stage, and to all at the Madeleine Milburn Literary Agency, particularly Rachel Yeoh.

I am hugely grateful to Tammy Evans, Catrin Huws, Tony Widdrington, Kathryn Donnelly and Sue Gardner for their incredible enthusiasm, excellent advice and friendship. Without their encouragement, I'm not sure I would ever have finished drafting and redrafting *The Deception of Harriet Fleet*.

Finally, lots of love and thanks to Izzy and Maddie for not begrudging me the many hours spent writing (and also for being generally amazing), my parents for always supporting me, and lastly to my lovely husband Mark, who has always believed in me and in this novel.